HARD KILL

HARD KILL

J. B. TURNER
HARD KILL

THOMAS & MERCER

Text copyright © 2016 J. B. Turner
All rights reserved.

Published by Thomas & Mercer, Seattle

www.apub.com

Amazon, the Amazon logo, and Thomas & Mercer are trademarks of Amazon.com, Inc., or its affiliates.

ISBN-13: 9781503936614
ISBN-10: 1503936619

Cover design by Stuart Bache

Printed in the United States of America

For my mother

One

The headlights appeared out of the darkness on the dirt road that led to Jon Reznick's isolated home. He was sitting on his front porch with a mug of strong black coffee, trying to figure out whether he should reach for his Beretta. He didn't often get visitors to his ocean-front home on the outskirts of Rockland, Maine. And certainly not before dawn broke.

He gulped down the rest of his coffee as he was bathed in the harsh headlights of the oncoming cars. The tires crunched the bone-dry earth, rutted by the current heat wave. The birds in the trees took flight.

Three vehicles?

The lead car, a black Suburban, pulled up in a cloud of dust. A few moments later, the rear passenger door opened.

A man wearing a dark suit and tie emerged. He walked toward Reznick and flashed a badge. "Special Agent in Charge of Boston, Jimmy Richards," he said. Perspiration beaded his forehead. "Jon Reznick?"

Reznick remained seated. He stared up at the Fed but stayed silent.

"Sorry to drop in on you like this. But we need to talk."

Reznick shrugged. "So talk."

"I've been asked to speak to you in person by Assistant Director Martha Meyerstein."

"About what?"

"I think it's better if you come with me."

"Not possible."

"Excuse me?"

"I'm catching a flight down to New York later this morning to visit my daughter."

"That might be a problem. You're required to come with me, sir."

"*Required* to come with you? I'm not required to do shit."

"Jon . . ."

"You can call me Reznick or Mr. Reznick. Look, Mr. Special Agent in Charge, I don't know you and I've sure as hell never met you. You turn up on *my* property unannounced. So I'd appreciate it if you could leave me alone."

SAC Richards's gaze wandered over the salt-blasted wooden house Reznick's father had built many years ago. He sat down on the porch step beside Reznick and stared toward the three vehicles. "Here's the thing. You need to come with us, Reznick. She asked specifically for you."

Reznick said nothing.

"She couldn't make it herself. Back-to-back meetings with various intelligence analysts. But she thought it was appropriate for someone to talk to you in person."

Reznick closed his eyes for a moment. His gut reaction was to tell them to take a hike. His trip to New York was something he'd been looking forward to for weeks, not having seen his daughter, who was at boarding school, for nearly four months. He'd paid for the tickets, the fancy hotel room, not to mention Springsteen at Madison Square Garden. But he was in Meyerstein's debt. He owed her.

"You need to tell me more."

SAC Richards sighed. "I've only been told what I need to know."

"What exactly do you know?"

"We need to find someone."

"That's it?"

"More or less. It's on a need-to-know basis."

"I'm guessing the FBI doesn't send Special Agents in Charge of Boston all the way up here in a three-car convoy for the sheer hell of it."

Richards stared at Reznick.

"Who's gone missing?"

"You'll find out soon enough." The Fed looked at his watch. "You need to get your ass into gear. You got five minutes to pack a bag, Reznick. Let's get to it."

Two hours later, after a turbulent flight from Owls Head's small airport, they touched down at Dulles, where three Lincolns were waiting.

They drove east. The first tinges of a blood-red sky appeared as the sun peeked over the horizon, throwing long shadows. Reznick called his daughter and left a message apologizing for having to cancel at such short notice. Then he told her he loved her. And that he would make it up to her when he got back home.

Richards turned to Reznick. "I don't know many people that would drop plans to see their daughter at a moment's notice."

"The only person I'd do that for is Meyerstein."

"You mind me asking why that is?"

Reznick sighed. "The long and short of it is I was supposed to be carrying out a job . . . but it went wrong. And my daughter was kidnapped. Meyerstein tracked me down to Key West. But instead of hauling my ass in, she let me find my daughter . . . in exchange for information about a guy I was supposed to kill."

"Jesus H. Christ."

"So there you have it."

They sat in silence for the rest of the journey.

After about fifteen minutes, Reznick saw a sign for the town of McLean. Upscale and affluent. They headed down tree-lined streets and past huge mansions with manicured lawns and electronic steel gates.

He couldn't see any street signs, only trees. And, in the distance, men in black, standing guard outside a six-story concrete building. The car stopped at a set of hydraulic steel barriers. The window wound down.

"United States Police," a guy in black wearing shades said, emerging from a guardhouse, walkie-talkie crackling. "What's your business?"

The driver had his FBI lanyard scanned. "We good?"

The guard nodded as he handed out an individual access badge to each of them. "We were expecting you. Remember, you must wear these at all times."

Reznick and the Feds all clipped on their badges.

Then the guard handed over a pale-blue card to the driver. "This is to enter the facility gate."

The driver nodded and they were waved through, with the other two Lincolns following behind. They headed to a parking garage at the rear of the building, where a two-man team rechecked the individual access IDs—taking particular time over Reznick's—and escorted them into the lobby.

More security, and airport-style scanners. Two large welcome mats with the words *Liberty Crossing*.

Reznick knew exactly where they were. It was one of the most secure facilities in the United States and it housed both the Office of the Director of National Intelligence and the National

Counterterrorism Center, shielded behind steel barriers and armed guards. He'd once been told that at least 1,700 federal employees and 1,200 private contractors worked at Liberty Crossing, which was the nickname for the complex.

An NCC official escorted them to the elevator and they rode it to the fourth floor. He led them along a windowless corridor until they got to a glass door, two cameras scanning the entrance.

He punched a long numeric code into the keypad. The doors clicked open and he ushered Reznick inside.

"Take a seat, Mr. Reznick," the official said.

Reznick did as he was told and he was left alone. He looked around. White walls, modern prints. The *Washington Post* on a small table. He looked at the clock and sighed. He hated waiting.

Time dragged. More than twenty minutes later, the official returned.

"They'll see you now."

Reznick got up and followed the man through to an open-plan office. Wooden desks, geometric-patterned carpets. Then it was down a long corridor to a conference room with plasma screens on the walls. Gathered around a large oak table were six men and one woman.

Meyerstein looked up, as did her right-hand man, Roy Stamper, who Reznick already knew. Meyerstein stood and shook his hand.

"Glad you agreed to join us," she said.

Reznick was introduced to those around the table: all members of the intelligence community with high-level security clearance, including the head of the FBI Hostage Rescue Team and a "special advisor" to the Department of Homeland Security.

He shook their hands. He knew all about strategic analysts and rated their skills highly. They were the ones who sifted raw data and tried to figure out the big picture, providing people like Meyerstein with an understanding of what was known about a threat and what wasn't. But they were also concerned with trying to determine what threats lay over the horizon.

"Take a seat, Jon," Meyerstein said after the formalities were over. The only person who hadn't been identified was the man sitting to her left.

Reznick sat down and looked up at the clock on the wall. 7:03 a.m.

"You mind telling me why we're here at this ungodly hour?"

The man to the left of Meyerstein cleared his throat. "My name is Lieutenant General Robert J. Black. I am employed by the Defense Intelligence Agency, although for the last year I've worked out of an office at the Pentagon. Now that we're all acquainted, let me lay down some ground rules."

Black's gaze lingered for a moment on each and every person in the room.

"What I'm about to tell you is not to be discussed and, secondly, is not to be acknowledged. Only the team working on this, plus the President, know the details. And that's the way it's going to stay." A few nods. "A senior diplomat—a military attaché, Major General Dennis O'Grady, who also worked as a national security advisor in a previous administration—didn't show up for a scheduled appointment with me, after supposedly meeting with a trusted source of his in Bethesda forty-eight hours ago."

Reznick shifted in his seat. A few people in the room scribbled down notes.

"Now, I want to make it clear that this is very, very out of character. Seems to have just vanished. O'Grady worked in the Middle East for the best part of twenty years and was a special advisor on the Persian Gulf and Southwest Asia for the State Department."

Meyerstein nodded before she interjected. "While General Black will be providing oversight, I will be taking the lead. We've got a fifteen-strong team working solely on this special access program. This means only those around this table—and some hand-picked intelligence specialists and NSC officials—have access to this most sensitive of classified information."

Lieutenant General Black leaned forward and allowed his gaze to wander around the assembled faces. "Assistant Director Meyerstein's word is law. She will report back to me as and when she decides. We want to keep this tight. In-house. But for now, your primary responsibility is to find O'Grady before it's too late."

Two

Once Black had gathered up his briefing papers and left the room, Meyerstein cleared her throat and looked at the stern faces around the table.

"At this stage, it's not possible to rule out that this is a terrorist-related incident with an international connection, so let's bear that in mind." She flipped through some papers in front of her. "First things first—I want O'Grady back safe. That is my top priority. The basic investigative legwork has already been started. We're piecing together his movements in the last week, we're speaking to his wife and children, and I've ordered bank records and cell phone records to be subpoenaed. I've also ordered a track-and-trace on the cell phone. But so far, nothing."

Larry Verona, a CIA senior intelligence analyst, said, "Can I play devil's advocate for a moment?" A few puzzled looks. "Is it possible, just possible, that he's simply run off with his mistress? Can we rule that out?"

Meyerstein nodded. "O'Grady is a devoted family man. It's a fair point you're raising, Larry, but that angle is not on our radar."

"What's the DC police saying?" Reznick asked.

"As it stands, we're bypassing the DC police on this."

Clearly this was no run-of-the-mill disappearance.

"Ordinarily, we would have issued an all-points bulletin within the first four hours. But that wasn't appropriate in this case. The media would have gotten a hold of it and that's the last thing we need." She turned to Stamper. "OK, Roy, I know it's early days, but what's the latest?"

Stamper picked up a remote control and flicked a switch. A huge color photo appeared on the plasma screens. It showed a fifty-something man wearing a beige linen suit—his face flushed crimson, possibly with the heat, a glass of wine in hand. "This was taken only last week. It shows O'Grady at a reception being held by the US embassy in Qatar. The next day he flew back to Washington. Two days ago, O'Grady left the house he shares with his wife and three kids in Chevy Chase and drove to a meeting. Never seen again." He looked across at Lieutenant Colonel Ed Froch, a State Department official. "Can you update us on who he was supposed to be meeting with?"

"I believe O'Grady was meeting with a high-placed source, the name or identity of whom only O'Grady knew."

Stamper sighed. "We need that. Can you look into it?"

"I'll get on it. But it may take time."

Meyerstein bit her lower lip. "Christ. So we don't have any footage? What about the GPS?"

"He vanished off the grid at 10:37 a.m. Eastern Time nearly forty-eight hours ago. And that was that."

Meyerstein leaned forward, hands clasped. "I need more details about O'Grady's work. Your area of expertise within the State Department is the Persian Gulf?"

Froch nodded.

"By that you mean Iran?"

"There are other countries we cover but, yes, our main focus is Iran."

"Now, you say you don't know anything about O'Grady's meeting. But I don't buy the fact that the State Department has no clue about this whatsoever."

Froch gave a thin smile. "I said that we don't know the identity of *who* he was meeting. But we have some intel."

Meyerstein stared at him, long and hard. "Colonel Froch, are you being deliberately obstructive?"

Reznick had been wondering the same thing. He didn't like the man's smartass attitude.

Froch remained cool. "I can assure you that's not the case. In my line of work, we must be very careful what can and can't be shared with the wider intelligence community."

"Let's cut to the chase. Tell me everything you know."

"Well, as far as we can tell, O'Grady was liaising with a Bosnian émigré originally from Sarajevo."

"And that's it?"

Froch said nothing.

"Tell me more about this meeting."

"I've put in a few calls to those who knew O'Grady better than I did. Nothing. The trail goes cold."

Meyerstein arched her eyebrows as she leaned back in her seat. "What do you take that to mean?"

"Maybe O'Grady got careless. Maybe he was being followed. We just don't know, as O'Grady had autonomy, more or less, in what he did."

"Sounds to me like a lack of oversight."

Froch looked around, making eye contact with everyone, as if trying to gauge their mood. Then he fixed on Meyerstein. "I don't accept that. I think an experienced diplomat who had moved in such circles for so long needed leeway."

"So much so that we don't know who he was seeing and where the hell he was?"

"Like I said, he needed leeway."

"You mind trying to explain the connection between Bosnia and O'Grady's area of expertise?"

"The Iranian sphere of influence is always there. Bosnia was the fallout from the fragmentation of the former Yugoslavia. The Serbs were allies of the Russians, so we were sympathetic to the new Bosnian state. The Bosnian Muslims amount to less than half of the population and are deemed among the most secular and liberal in the world. However, they are, by and large, not Shia, like Iran, but Sunni."

"So where does Iran fit into this?"

"The Shias constitute around seven percent of the Muslim population in Bosnia—about a hundred and sixty-five thousand people. So, while they're the minority, that's a lot of people who could be linked to Iran in some capacity, to a greater or lesser degree, and perhaps come under their influence."

Meyerstein pondered on that for a few moments. "So there may be an Iranian link to this?"

Froch shrugged.

"Take a guess?"

"They can't be ruled out, that's for sure."

Meyerstein looked across at her right-hand man. "Roy, your thoughts?"

"For me, there are echoes of the disappearance and death of military attaché Thomas Mooney in Cyprus, in 2007. If I remember correctly, his body was found a few days after he disappeared."

Froch stared down at the papers in front of him. "But that was deemed to be suicide, wasn't it?"

Meyerstein rubbed her eyes as if seriously sleep-deprived. "That was the official line." Her tone was harsh with Froch, almost dismissive. Reznick could feel the tension in the room.

She looked across the table at him. "Jon, I'll be looking for insights from you, too."

Reznick nodded and felt all eyes on him.

Froch shook his head. "No disrespect, but how can he know anything? This isn't his area of expertise."

Reznick stared at Froch. He'd met the type before. Arrogant. Full of themselves. He couldn't abide inflated egos.

Meyerstein leaned forward and fixed her gaze on Froch. "Colonel Froch, this is a joint task force and I'm taking the lead. We work together on this. Understood?"

Froch raised his eyebrows but said nothing.

"The question is: where do we go from here? Let's open this up." She looked at the NSA specialist at the table, who was taking notes on an iPad. "What do you think?"

The NSA guy stopped tapping on his tablet and looked up. "We're trawling through millions of calls, emails, and instant messages as we speak, looking to get a heads-up. I'm talking real time, message boards, the lot. We're on it. That's what I've been doing, in case you're wondering."

"Here's where I'm coming from," Meyerstein said. "I think there's a very real possibility that O'Grady has been kidnapped, or worse."

Reznick said, "The Iranians, as most of you know, work out of the Pakistan embassy, as they don't have their own now. That's where I'd start looking."

Meyerstein nodded. "Ed, you want to expand?"

"Currently, seventy-four Iranian nationals are accredited to the Interests Section of the Islamic Republic of Iran in Washington, DC. However, because the United States and Iran don't have diplomatic relations, none of the Iranians have official diplomatic status."

"So, their names would not be published on the State Department's Diplomatic List?" Meyerstein asked.

"That's right. They are, in effect, employees of the Iranian Interests Section. While they come under the umbrella of the Pakistan embassy, they maintain separate offices. The Iranians working there have permanent resident status in the US or are dual nationals, making it difficult to take any action against them. They attend cultural and social events within the Iranian community and maintain close ties to an Islamic Center in Potomac that is financed by a New York-based foundation. They also have an information section used for intelligence work. In addition, all staff members of the Interests Section hold green cards or US passports, meaning they are free to travel in the United States."

Meyerstein stretched, stifling a yawn. The red light on her BlackBerry began to flash—perhaps an urgent email or message—and she took a few moments to check it.

"Jon, your thoughts?"

"Yeah." Reznick looked across at the NSA specialist. "What's electronic monitoring telling us?"

The NSA guy sighed. "I only have a team of three, right in this building, doing the traffic analysis. Basically, trawling everything that's sent and received by—or phoned to and from—the Iranians, night and day. Encrypted, non-encrypted, language specialists, you name it. Anything flags up and we're on it straight away. We're tracing all the numbers called in the last forty-eight hours, but it's wrapped up in layers of advanced encryption. It's gonna take time."

"Something we don't have," said Meyerstein.

"This might have nothing to do with the Iranians," Reznick said. "I think we've got to be clear on that, too. But we can't rule them out. Perhaps we need to think about getting a team in close, keep tabs on these Iranians. Their houses, hangouts . . ."

"Reznick, we've got to remember that they're operating under the auspices of the Pakistan embassy and have surveillance detection units just as we do," interjected Froch. "They're not dumb. They know what to look for when it comes to observing those who're watching them."

"So we stay in this room and sit on our hands? Look, we've got to move on this. Around-the-clock surveillance is needed, and not relying solely on electronic monitoring."

Froch shook his head. "That's not practical."

Stamper said, "It's a good point Jon's making. The political attachés and military attachés can be a priority."

Froch cleared his throat. "We have no evidence, as it stands, that Iran is behind this. None at all."

Reznick stared at him. "I've already said that."

"We go with surveillance of the Iranians." Meyerstein looked around. "This is going to be a twenty-four seven operation until we find O'Grady. We meet up again in less than twelve hours' time, in this room. And I want to reiterate once again, this is strictly within the team. This investigation doesn't exist to anyone else."

When the meeting ended and everyone had filed out, Meyerstein pulled Reznick and Stamper aside. "Follow me."

She led them down a long corridor. Hanging on the wall were black-and-white prints of DC monuments at night, and framed extracts from George Washington's speeches. They took the elevator up to the top floor, then went through a series of keypad entries and along a carpeted corridor toward more doors. Meyerstein swiped a card and led them into a secure area, and to the office last on the right.

"This is where I'm based during this investigation," she said as Reznick and Stamper followed her inside.

It was all muted beige, with a dark teak desk and a couple of brown leather sofas, and four seats lined up against the wall. A huge TV on the wall showed a live CNN broadcast of the President speaking in Detroit.

"Take a seat, guys," she said.

Reznick and Stamper complied and sat down.

Meyerstein sat on the edge of her desk. "Firstly, Jon, very good to see you, I appreciated your input. Sorry I wasn't able to call you directly."

"I assume you didn't invite me here to make up the numbers."

Meyerstein shook her head. "Not quite. During our meeting I got an instant message from the FBI encryption guy, Special Agent Scott Liddell. His people have been looking over O'Grady's phone records. And they think they've finally pulled up the last number he called before he disappeared."

Stamper shifted in his seat. "Whose is it?"

"The phone is blocked. Now, I don't really know any of the guys around that table. And I don't know who I can trust. So I want the two of you to run a parallel investigation. You report only to me."

Stamper ran his hand through his hair and sighed. "I don't like this, Martha. The whole feel of this. Something's wrong."

Meyerstein nodded.

"But I also don't feel good with the secrecy."

"It's just the way I want it to run. The cell phone number that O'Grady called is owned by a twenty-two-year-old resident of Georgetown, Caroline Lieber. Does the name mean anything to you?"

Stamper shook his head.

"Ms. Lieber is the youngest daughter of Jack Lieber, real estate tycoon. You know anything about Jack Lieber?"

Reznick and Stamper both shrugged.

"Jack Lieber is the President's single biggest donor in New York City. And his daughter is a former intern at the White House."

Reznick felt his heart rate hike up a notch. "OK, we've now got something to work with. We need to get into her life, big time."

Three

The morning sun was throwing long shadows across the road as the SUV with Reznick, Stamper and the Feds inside edged along a leafy street in the Georgetown area of Washington, DC. The temperature on the dashboard showed it was 95 degrees. Smart houses and upscale cars lined either side, the sidewalks bustling with life.

They took a right onto Volta Place Northwest and pulled up outside an elegant townhouse. An American flag flew from the second floor, and fluttered in the light breeze.

Reznick got out first and Stamper followed. Reznick felt the sweat running down his back within seconds of stepping out of the air-conditioned vehicle and into the stifling heat.

"Damn, it's hot," Stamper said. He wiped his brow with the back of his hand and straightened his tie. "OK, let me do the talking."

"Fine with me," Reznick said as they climbed the outside steps.

Stamper gave three hard knocks on the door and cleared his throat, looking around as he waited for an answer. "Apparently she lives here with three other female students from Georgetown."

Reznick nodded but said nothing. He already felt frustrated at the by-the-book approach.

Stamper knocked again, this time five times, and rang the bell repeatedly.

"Who is it?" a tentative female voice said from behind the locked door.

"FBI, ma'am. Open up."

"What's it about?"

"Can you let us in, ma'am? We need to speak to Caroline Lieber."

"She's not here."

Stamper rolled his eyes. "Ma'am, can you please open up? We need to speak to you then, if she's not here."

"Look, I don't know who you guys are. I'd prefer not to open up the door to strangers."

"We're the FBI, ma'am." He held up his ID to the peephole. "See for yourself."

"Mr. Stamper, how can I be sure it's genuine?"

Stamper held up the court papers. "These state that we have the authority to gain entry to this property and interview Ms. Lieber or the occupants. This is a court order, ma'am. If you continue to obstruct us, we'll be forced to break down the door to gain entry. So, can you please open up so we can speak to you inside?"

A long delay, then the chain could be heard sliding across, the locks turned, and the door cracked open. A girl with sunken eyes and messy blonde hair pulled the cord of her pink dressing gown tight around her waist. It looked like last night's makeup was still on her face, dark shadows under her eyes.

Stamper showed his badge again. "Are you satisfied we're FBI, ma'am?"

The girl studied the badge for a few moments before running a hand through her disheveled hair. "I'm sorry, I didn't want to take any chances. Please come in." She opened the door wide, and Stamper and Reznick followed her down the hall to a brightly lit kitchen.

"I'm sorry to bother you," Stamper said. "Are you alone here?"

"Yes."

"Do you know where Ms. Lieber is?"

The girl shrugged. "I don't know. She might be staying with a friend from class."

"So you don't know for sure?"

The girl shrugged. "Look, I don't know much about Caroline. What's this about?"

"Tell me, when's the last time you spoke to Caroline?"

"Is she OK?"

"Please answer the question."

"Caroline? I spoke to her yesterday morning."

"Is there anyone she's close to or confides in?"

"She's from New York City, so her real close friends are all based there. She keeps to herself, really."

Stamper smiled. "You mind if we take a look around?"

"Actually, I do."

"Oh, why's that?"

"It's just that . . . well, the lease is in Caroline's name. I just feel it would be better if she was here before you go through the house."

"We have a warrant to search the house, if necessary."

The girl flushed crimson and closed her eyes. "It's just that . . ."

"Are you all right, ma'am?" Stamper asked. "Do you feel uncomfortable because we're going to do the search and you're all alone in the house, is that it?"

The girl grimaced. "It's just that . . . I'd rather you didn't."

The sound of a floorboard creaking above them.

Reznick was up the stairs before Stamper could speak. A skinny guy was heading across the landing toward the bathroom. "Don't move, son!"

The kid froze.

Reznick grabbed him by the collar and pulled him downstairs. The kid was trembling.

"Thought you were alone?" Reznick asked, staring at the girl.

She bit her lower lip. "He's not supposed to be staying over."

Reznick turned to him. "Empty your pockets."

The kid had tears in his eyes as he handed over a cube of hashish from his back pocket.

"Gonna flush it away, were you?"

"Man, it's not mine."

Reznick stepped forward. "I'm going to pat you down. You don't have any sharp objects in your pockets, do you?"

"Absolutely not."

"Because if you do, and I get cut, you're gonna be in a shitload of trouble. No syringes or knives?"

"Absolutely not."

"I hope not, for your sake." Reznick patted him down and emptied out the kid's other pockets. "He's clean."

Stamper pointed to the living room. "Let's take a seat in there." The girl and the kid both nodded and they went through, sitting down on a large, black leather sofa. Stamper sat down opposite them, but Reznick stayed standing, arms folded, by the door.

"OK, here's how it's going to work," Stamper said, leaning forward, hands clasped. "You cooperate with us, and we're all gonna get along just fine. Now, first things first, where's Caroline's room?"

The girl said, "First floor on the right."

Reznick headed up there and did a cursory search. The bedroom was tidy and smelled fresh, with white roses in a vase by the window. Two small pink teddies sat atop the white comforter on the queen-sized bed. The large desk had yellow sticky notes plastered all over it, probably for essays she had to write. A floor-to-ceiling bookcase with hundreds of books: Jane Austen, Henry James, Plato, biographies of Churchill, George W. Bush, and Condoleezza Rice, and some P.J. O'Rourke. He opened up the closet and saw her clothes were neatly hung up and her shoes laid out on the floor. He rifled through a bed-side cabinet. Silk panties, bras, and God knows what.

He headed downstairs. "She's a student, right?"

The girl nodded. "Politics, yeah."

"So where's the laptop, iPad, all that jazz?"

The girl bit her lower lip. "Her iPhone is on her day and night, and I know she also has a MacBook Pro up in her room. Did you miss it?"

Reznick shook his head. "It's not there."

"That's weird. It was there yesterday morning when she left, because she asked me to switch it off. She left in a hurry. She said she'd be back sometime this afternoon."

The young man cleared his throat. "Do you mind me asking what this is about?"

Reznick pointed at him. "Speak when you are spoken to."

Stamper looked at the girl. "What time did she leave?"

"Around nine. I think she was running late. It was just before I left for class."

"When did you return here?"

"I returned alone just after five yesterday."

"Was the computer still there?"

"I don't know—I didn't check."

"So what did you do when you got home?"

"Made some dinner for us, and Matt came around just after nine with a bottle of wine."

Stamper blew out his cheeks and shifted in his seat. "Tell me everything I need to know about Caroline Lieber. Is it normal for her to stay over somewhere with a friend?"

"Now and again, sure."

"Who does she stay with?"

The girl frowned and shrugged. "I don't know. Like I said, I don't think we're that close."

"Now, this is very important. Is there anything over the last week or so that's happened which you thought was strange or Caroline thought was odd? Anything unusual. What about any guy she's seeing? A guy from her class, maybe?"

The young man ran his hands through his hair. "Look, I don't see what this has got to do with me."

Stamper stared down the kid. "Here's a bit of advice. When the Feds turn up and you get caught with some hash in your possession, you have some explaining to do. Simple possession of a controlled substance comes with a maximum penalty for a first conviction of a hundred and eighty days in jail, not to mention a thousand-dollar fine. However, you shut up and I could forget I saw your little stash. You understand what I'm saying?"

The girl took the boy's hand, tears in her eyes. "We hear what you're saying." She closed her eyes as if racking her brain. "There was a guy."

Stamper nodded.

"Yeah, couple nights ago, a guy called asking for Caroline. An older-sounding guy."

"A guy called? Did he have a name?"

"I answered the phone. He didn't give a name. He said he wanted to speak to Caroline urgently."

"OK . . ."

"Caroline said that he was an old creep and was pestering her. She told me to tell him she wasn't home. He hung up."

Reznick wondered if this was O'Grady making contact with Caroline Lieber. He exchanged a quick glance with Stamper, who nodded, obviously getting the link.

"Did the guy say anything else?" Stamper asked.

"He just said it was urgent that Caroline speak to him . . . he had some information for her."

"What kind of information?"

"He didn't say."

"And the guy didn't give his name?"

"No. I've told you everything." The girl began to sob.

"Can you describe his voice?"

She dabbed her eyes. "It was slow, very deliberate, as if he was being careful what he was saying."

Stamper smiled, as if trying to reassure her. "You're really helping us. Just a couple more questions."

The girl sighed.

"Did Caroline ever talk to you about her internship last summer?"

"She did."

"And what did she say?"

"She said it was fourteen-hour days, but it was a fascinating glimpse into that world. Diplomats, politicians, Capitol Hill, all that. She loved it, but she didn't go on about it. She asked me not to talk about it with anyone. She's pretty discreet."

"I see. Did her parents ever visit her here?"

"Never. She went back to New York regularly, usually on a Friday at the end of each month."

"Going back to that laptop—do you have any idea what happened to it?"

"I have no idea, unless Caroline came back for it during the day. I guess she must have."

The young man said, "You mentioned something earlier about anything unusual in the last week or so."

Stamper nodded. "You remember something?"

"I don't know if it means anything, but I remember Caroline was howling and crying a week ago. Some guy had just dumped her."

"Some guy . . . What guy?"

The kid screwed up his face and looked at his girlfriend. "What did she say his name was?"

"Adam."

The kid nodded. "Yeah, that's the one. Adam had broken up with her."

Stamper cleared his throat. "So this Adam was a boyfriend of hers. You met him?"

The guy shook his head.

"None of us have," the girl said. "Caroline told us she'd started seeing this guy sometime in the summer. She was happy. But then he dumped her."

Stamper stood up. "Now listen, it's very important that you tell us everything you know. We need you to really focus on this and remember anything you can about this guy Adam."

The kid began to snap his fingers. "She said he wasn't answering her calls at the hospital when she called him."

"Hospital? A hospital here in DC?"

The kid grimaced. "Honestly? I really don't know. That's all I remember."

Stamper nodded. "I'm going to get some of my team in and have a better look around Caroline's room and the rest of the house, if that's all right with you."

The girl shrugged. "OK, of course."

Stamper handed her a card and thanked them for their help, then followed Reznick out of the house and into the searing heat.

⌣

After Stamper called out a three-man FBI team to conduct a thorough search of the townhouse, Reznick got back into the SUV's passenger seat as Stamper slid into the driver's seat, buckled up, and put in a call to the senior NSA computer expert assigned to the special access program. He requested all recurring calls from the landline and Caroline's cell phone to anywhere in the DC area to be flagged and analyzed. Within ten minutes, the NSA guy was back on the phone, and it was clear that Caroline Lieber had been making multiple calls to Georgetown University Hospital.

"That's got to be our next stop," Reznick said.

Stamper was frowning, deep in thought. He made another call. "Hi, Lenny. It's Roy Stamper. The human resources department of Georgetown University Hospital—I need to know where it's located." A long pause. "Arlington? OK, got that." He ended the call and turned to Reznick. "Fifteenth Street North, Arlington."

Reznick nodded.

Stamper turned the ignition key and they pulled away.

Ten minutes later, the SUV's GPS guided them into the parking garage of a large glass building.

Reznick and Stamper took the elevator to the third floor and headed along a corridor to a reception area.

Stamper flashed his badge and gave his best FBI smile.

"Good morning, ma'am. I'm sorry to bother you, but we have urgent business. I'd like to see the vice president of human resources, Ms. Wendy Greninger."

"Have you got an appointment?"

Stamper looked at her name tag. "Sadly no, Christine. But that's not usually a problem for us."

"Hold on." She buzzed her boss and picked up the phone. "Yes, two gentlemen from the FBI to see you, Ms. Greninger." A few nods, then she hung up and pointed to a door opposite. "You're in luck. She's in the training room."

Stamper smiled. "Much obliged, thank you."

The receptionist smiled back, and flushed as Reznick gave a polite nod. As they walked toward the training room door, Reznick put his hand on Stamper's shoulder. "Didn't know you could be such a smooth talker, Roy."

Stamper groaned. "Gimme a break, Reznick." He cleared his throat, and knocked on the door twice.

A voice from inside shouted, "Come in!"

Working on a laptop was a woman wearing a smart, dark-olive suit. She stood up and shook their hands.

"FBI, ma'am. I appreciate you seeing us without any notice."

The woman nodded. "No problem at all. How can I help you gentlemen?"

Stamper outlined that they were looking for a man called Adam who may or may not work at the hospital, and they would like access to the hospital records.

"I see," she said. "Can you tell me what this is in connection to?"

"I'm not at liberty to disclose that, Ms. Greninger. We hope, with the hospital's cooperation and consent, we can establish a few facts, and we'll be on our way."

"I'll have to run it past our CEO first."

"Excellent, thank you."

Greninger picked up the phone and dialed a number. The call dragged on for a couple of minutes as she explained the situation to the CEO. Eventually, she said, "Appreciate that," and ended the call.

She smiled at Stamper. "Presumably you want a list of only those named Adam who work at the hospital? In any capacity?"

"Whether it's full-time, part-time, medical, janitor, office worker, nurse . . . and their addresses and contact numbers, too."

Greninger got to her feet. "Just wait here."

Less than a quarter of an hour later, she returned with a printout.

"There are five Adams employed by us," she said. "All their details are here." She looked at Reznick. "You ex-military?"

Reznick said nothing.

"I can tell. I served, many years back. Military intelligence."

Stamper took the list. "Thank you, Ms. Greninger. We appreciate your cooperation."

"If there's anything else you guys need, don't hesitate to contact me."

Stamper said, "One final thing. We'd appreciate it if this conversation stayed within these four walls."

Greninger nodded. "That's a given, and won't be a problem."

They headed down to the parking garage and got into the car. Stamper quickly scanned the names and dialed the number of one of his team. "Josie—Roy here. I've got five names. I want you to run them through the system as soon as possible. Basically, I need the Adam who works at the hospital to be boyfriend material for a rich New York girl studying in DC." He nodded. "Exactly. Trawl the cell phone records of all of them. Keep me informed."

Stamper ended the call and they headed back into DC, stopping off at Martin's Tavern in Georgetown for a brunch of scrambled eggs, hash browns, toast, and coffee. After they'd eaten, Stamper emailed Meyerstein with an update.

A few minutes later, his cell rang. "Yup." He listened intently for a couple of minutes. Eventually, he spoke: "One long-term sick, one on sabbatical to India and one . . . doing what?" He nodded. "One retires next year, aged seventy-five . . . OK, that leaves . . . ?" He nodded again. "Forget the janitor. I'm interested in the doctor. There are logs of her speaking to his department on multiple occasions, is that right?" A pause. "That's the one. Pull up everything we have on him. Speak soon." He put his cell phone in his pocket. "Interesting."

"You got someone?"

"We think so. Lives no more than two minutes from here."

Four

The road through the woods was deserted as the headlights of Adam Ford's car strafed the single lane ahead. Lightning bugs glanced off his windshield. He looked in his rearview mirror and saw the silhouettes of the men shadowing him, in the car behind. He was miles from civilization, somewhere off Route 40, in the foothills of the Blue Ridge Mountains in Southwest Virginia.

As the miles wore on, he wondered what test they had in store for him.

The headlights behind him flashed. It was the signal that he was to turn right up ahead.

Ford spotted a homemade wooden sign with an arrow, and he headed down a dirt road for just over three miles until he came to a clearing. A man with fluorescent nightsticks guided him over to the left beside a clump of trees. He glanced in the rearview and noticed his shadows were no longer there.

His stomach knotted as he parked the SUV. Two masked men, dressed in black and sporting submachine guns, approached.

"Out of the car," one drawled.

Ford switched off his engine and got out of the vehicle. The same man stepped forward and frisked him. Then an electronic wand was run over his body.

"He's clean." The man cocked his head in the direction of a rutted dirt road. "Follow me."

Ford did as he was told, flashlights leading the way. Sweat ran down his back, insects buzzing all around. The air was thick, like glue. He could smell the forest. Dead leaves. Bark. Earth. Behind him, the sound of heavy footsteps.

They walked on for perhaps half a mile until they got to what looked like a heavily camouflaged wooden shed, most likely a bird blind.

The man opened the door. "After you."

Ford did as he was told and stepped inside. It smelled musty. A blue light was switched on. At the far end was a sniper rifle with a night-vision scope, resting on a tripod.

The masked man said, "This is your final test."

"I've already aced the long-range sniper tests."

"We know you have. But that was to test accuracy."

Ford said nothing, wondering what the man meant.

The man cocked his head in the direction of the rifle and tripod. "It's all set up for you. The weighting, the sights—it's perfect. I double-checked it myself."

Ford nodded.

"OK, let's do this. Assume position."

Ford complied, and laid himself flat on the floor behind the tripod. He used his left hand to support the butt of the rifle.

"We've checked wind speed and we've adjusted the scopes. It's all in place."

Ford placed the butt of the stock firmly in the pocket of his right shoulder. Then, with his right hand, he gripped the small of the stock. He placed his index finger on the trigger and planted his elbows on the wooden floor.

He closed his eyes and took a couple of breaths, enabling him to relax as much as possible. Upon opening his eyes, he saw through the pale green of the night vision what the scope's crosshairs were aligned with—and his blood ran cold.

A hooded man, with his back to Ford, was tied by ropes to a tree. The range finder showed he was 1097 yards away. Ford watched the man writhe as he tried to escape. But it was to no avail.

Ford's stomach knotted. "What's this?"

Behind him, the masked man said, "This is your test. Do nothing until I give the order. Do you understand?"

"Understood."

"OK, zero your weapon."

Ford said nothing. He adjusted the scope so that the back of the writhing man's head was in the center of the crosshairs. He zoned out as his training kicked in. A sniper had to take into account the myriad factors that could influence a bullet's trajectory: distance to the target, wind direction, wind speed, the angle of the sniper to the target, not to mention the temperature.

He felt calm. Assured.

He focused on his breathing. He felt detached.

"Do you know who this man is?"

"Nope."

"His name's O'Grady. Do you want to know why he's the target?"

"No."

"Well, I'm gonna tell you. This man has compromised the operation. That can't be allowed. Do you understand?"

"Absolutely. I understand."

"When you're ready. It must be a head shot."

The man's head was now hung low, as if he knew what awaited him. For a split second, Ford stared through the night-vision scope and tried to imagine the terror the man was feeling underneath the hood. He felt the cold metal on his trigger finger. He paused for a few moments.

He knew that military snipers who shoot over three hundred yards invariably aim for the chest. The loss of blood and the trauma will inevitably kill the target. But this was to be a head shot, usually used at close range.

He breathed in slowly, his yoga and meditation techniques kicking in. He peered through the scope and got the hooded head perfectly within the crosshairs. He was aiming for the "apricot," or the medulla oblongata, the part of the brain that controls involuntary movement at the base of the skull.

He felt the cold steel again on the ball of his finger and squeezed the trigger. The recoil was surprisingly slight. The noise blasted around the hide.

Through the scope, he saw the hooded man's head slump forward. Then two masked men emerged from the wooded area to the side.

Ford watched, fascinated, as one took a hunting knife from his belt and cut the rope that held the man to the tree. The body fell forward and the other man unrolled a body bag on the ground. They lifted the body into the bag.

"Move away from the rifle," the masked man said.

Ford got to his feet.

The masked man got out a cell phone and made a call. "Yeah, it's done." He handed the phone to Ford. "They want to talk to you."

Ford held the phone up to his ear. "Yeah."

"You passed."

Ford sighed. "What now?"

"The big one."

"You got a timescale?"

"When we know, you'll know."

"When will I hear from you again?"

"Soon."

He was about to respond, but the line was already dead.

Five

Reznick had been in the back of the stifling surveillance van for almost a day, its air conditioner broken, when Adam Ford pulled up outside his Georgetown home in a smart Mercedes convertible.

"Think I got something," he whispered into his lapel microphone.

Ford got out of the car, bag slung over his shoulder. He was lean and tall, with a strong jawline. Cropped blond hair, tanned complexion. He wore cargo pants, Topsiders, and a navy polo shirt. An all-American guy. But he also seemed to exude a superior air as he sauntered toward his house.

Reznick picked up the camera and zoomed in on Ford, taking some shots through the glass of the window. He watched as Ford walked up the stone stoop and pulled out his keys. Before opening the door, the doctor checked his watch and looked around. His gaze fell on the van.

Reznick froze, the only sound his heart beating. It seemed as though Ford was staring straight into the lens of the camera. Reznick swallowed hard. He'd been holding his breath for what seemed like an eternity. Eventually, Ford turned around and opened his front door, shutting it behind him with his foot.

Reznick exhaled. "Target inside house." He sent the photos via instant message to Meyerstein. Three minutes later, she called back.

"Our computer analysis shows that this is a perfect match for Adam Ford."

"Where do we go from here?"

"Look, I'm going to get Stamper down there now. He can talk to this doctor, find out what he knows. I want you to just stay in the van and see if he heads off anywhere. We'll check his cell traffic. You OK with that?"

"Fine by me."

She hung up.

Half an hour later, Stamper and his team pulled up in an SUV outside Ford's house. Reznick watched as Ford answered the door in his bathrobe, still toweling his wet hair, and ushered the Feds inside. A mere fifteen minutes later, Stamper and his men drove off.

His phone rang. It was Stamper.

"Hey, Jon."

"How did you get on?"

"He seemed very relaxed when I was asking questions. Very smart, very cool. And he didn't seem unduly flustered, even when I asked if he knew the whereabouts of Caroline Lieber."

"Where had he been?"

"Visiting an old friend in Southwest Virginia, apparently. We'll check it out."

"So you asked about Caroline Lieber?"

Stamper sighed down the line. "According to him, she occasionally helped out with his homeless outreach program. He said they were never an item, and that was that. No spark there for him. But she had thought there was something serious between them, and he had to get the Director of Medicine to speak to her directly about calling him at the hospital."

"So she was just spinning a line to her friends?"

"That's what he's saying."

"Do you believe him?"

"It's hard to say. He said she had once stayed overnight, and he slept on the sofa."

"Why did she stay over?"

"Well, according to him, she'd been locked out of her home after an argument with her roommates."

"So he doesn't know where she is?"

"No. We've checked the calls to his registered cell. Nothing. Says he never gave her his cell number. That's why she called the hospital."

Reznick groaned. "Backing up his story."

"I think we're wasting our time with this guy. I've got a couple things to check out, but the main thrust of the investigation is the Iranians."

"What else do we know about this Lieber girl's movements?"

"The GPS on her phone had her on the Georgetown campus. But after that, she just seems to have vanished. Turned up for her classes a couple days ago, and then gone. Nothing."

"What about a forensic search of his home?"

"I just spoke to Meyerstein. She wants you to stay where you are. Just in case."

Reznick sighed. "And all the time, O'Grady's off the grid. The same as Caroline Lieber. What the fuck is going on?"

"Sit tight, Jon, and let's see how this goes. Chances are, though, Ford has nothing to do with any of this."

The rest of the morning dragged, as the comings and goings of 38th Street NW were laid bare for Reznick. He managed to get the air conditioner working, the blast of cold a welcome relief. Outside, in the heat, he saw dog walkers, joggers, deliverymen, and the mail-man. Ford hadn't made a move in hours.

Reznick knocked back a bottle of water and popped a couple of Dexedrine to keep him going. He felt the amphetamines rouse his system, sharpening his mental antennae. He stared through the one-way window and continued to watch the world go by. The morning gave way to a blazing afternoon, as the heat seemed to warp the asphalt and bricks. All the time, he kept his eyes peeled on the townhouse.

He wondered if Ford was putting his feet up for a few hours. But the man could just as likely head out of the house at any moment. Reznick had to stay alert.

He wolfed down a cream cheese bagel, and peed in an empty plastic water bottle.

The afternoon gave way to early evening, the light fading. Still no sign of life from Ford. Jaded men and women, jackets slung over their shoulders, ambled down the street after a day's work, no doubt looking forward to a cold drink and a refreshing shower.

Reznick smelled his armpits and knew he could do with the same. The hours without air had stunk up the van with his body odor. His cell rang a couple of times—Meyerstein asking for updates and Stamper trying to raise his spirits with guy-talk about beers when it was all over.

A lot of people hated the soul-destroying, mind-numbing boredom of surveillance work. Reznick wasn't one of them. He understood that needs must, and someone had to stand watch. It would have been the easiest thing in the world just to tag along back to base with Stamper. To switch off, knowing the core investiga-tion was on terrorist groups, not some doctor who was unwittingly under surveillance.

But he knew that leads had to be earned. They didn't just land in your lap.

It was all about putting in the time, and sometimes—maybe—you got a break. But by God, you had to earn it.

The hours, sometimes days, of waiting, hunkered down in thick mud or deep snow up in the mountains of Afghanistan, or in fly-infested ditches smelling of shit in Iraq . . . now that was tough. By comparison, this was a breeze.

Reznick stretched out: a ten-minute routine he often used. He felt his calf muscles stretch. Darkness fell slowly.

Was this guy even working tonight?

He swigged some more water, pissed some more, and ate a stale donut. As a rule, in his experience, healthy eating was not compatible with surveillance work. Reznick focused on the door, green-tinged through the night-vision binoculars.

Just before 9 p.m., Dr. Adam Ford emerged from his home. He was talking into his cell phone, a jacket slung over his shoulder. Reznick quickly alerted Meyerstein.

"He's on the move. Heading south on foot."

The radio crackled to life—it was Stamper. "Got him."

A few minutes later, Stamper's voice came back on. "The subject has entered the hospital. Alone."

Then radio silence.

Reznick remained in the van, still observing the front of the house. His cell phone rang.

"Jon, how's the lonely vigil?" Meyerstein's voice was soft and warm.

Reznick snorted. "You know me, I'm a glutton for punishment."

"Jon, bad news. We've failed to gain a court order granting access to Ford's house."

"What?"

"Look, our counsel is appealing the decision, but it doesn't look good. There was a discrepancy in the papers being submitted, and the judge refused to sign."

"You serious?"

"It happens. We've filed new papers, but we won't be able to gain access until the morning at the earliest." Meyerstein sighed. "And we think Ford is telling the truth. We've checked him out. A more solid citizen you'll not find. Churchgoing, helps out at soup kitchens, set up his own medical charity for veterans, a top Washington surgeon, avoids parties, teetotal. Clean-living. Don't see how he fits into this at all."

Reznick was silent. He wondered if he should broach the subject or if he should let her do it.

"You still there?"

"You think there's a chance she's in the house?"

"No, I don't."

"What's stopping me getting inside and having a look around?"

"Jon, I couldn't condone that. Besides, what if he returned unannounced?"

"He won't."

"Look, this guy is not a suspect."

"You want to know where I'm at?"

"Sure."

"I think you've got to close this circle. He's a link back to Caroline Lieber. Until we're a hundred percent on this guy, I say I go in and have a look around."

Meyerstein said nothing.

"Get Stamper and his guys to cover my back."

Meyerstein was quiet. Eventually, she spoke. "What if I said we wouldn't stand in your way—how would that make you feel?"

Meyerstein's decision to allow him to gain entry had been unexpected, and Reznick wondered if she knew more than she was letting on. It felt good to be doing something, and he wanted to find out more about Ford.

His thoughts turned to the task at hand. He took a couple of minutes to change out of his sweaty clothes and into black jeans, T-shirt, and baseball cap. He checked his earpiece was still in place, then lifted up the small metal toolbox, checked the coast was clear, and pulled back the sliding door. He strode across the street and headed down the path at the side of the house.

Pushing open the gate, he saw a side door to the property. After switching on a tiny jamming device to disable any alarms or electronic sensors, he pulled some plastic shoe covers over his sneakers, so as not to leave any dirt or mess from footprints, and snapped on his gloves.

The distant sound of sirens filled the night air. He glanced around. Lights on across the street, but all quiet. He pressed his ear against the door and closed his eyes. He was listening for the merest sound inside. Perhaps a TV playing low.

But there was nothing. Satisfied it was all clear, he reached into the toolbox and pulled out a lock-picking set. A minute later, he was in the house.

Reznick's eyes slowly adjusted to the dark as he headed through a hallway into the kitchen, where he could see the glint from a metallic range. He pulled out a penlight from his pocket. The thin beam of light danced across black marble floors and a granite work surface. Sitting on a dining table were two large glass bowls of fruit, overflowing with bananas, apples, oranges, and pears.

He opened the fridge, and the light came on. Dozens of bottles of water, carefully aligned. Low-fat milk in three containers. Low-fat spread. The freezer contained packets of free-range chicken breast.

He opened a cupboard. Rows and rows of neatly arranged protein shake mixes, alongside several bags of basmati rice. The guy was something else. *Talk about a health freak*, Reznick thought.

He padded through to the living room. It smelled of beeswax polish—perhaps a hint of sandalwood. He pointed the penlight around the room. Large TV screen on the wall. Photos of the doctor at his graduation; with friends and family, eating out; wearing blue scrubs, face behind a mask. The sofas were caramel-colored, matching the walls.

He headed upstairs, the penlight showing the way. Two bedrooms. He quickly scanned the guest room. It was clear. Then he went into the master bedroom, which had expensive-looking hardwood flooring. He checked out the contents of the room. Gilt-edged photos of Ford in dark-blue rowing colors, his lean torso honed to perfection, muscle definition on his triceps. A framed Yale degree. A bookcase packed tight with medical tomes and political biographies.

Reznick went over to a huge closet and pulled back the doors. A small light came on, illuminating a line of sharp suits and crisp dress shirts. He checked a few of the labels: Hugo Boss, Ralph Lauren, Armani, Versace. Expensive. On the closet floor, arranged in neat rows, were polished shoes.

It was like something out of *GQ* magazine.

Reznick was a jeans-and-T-shirt sort of guy. Worrying about the cut of a suit always seemed to be the height of pointlessness.

He pressed on across the master bedroom and into an en-suite bathroom containing expensive shaving gels, aftershaves and moisturizers, carefully arranged razors, and soft white towels monogrammed with the initials *A.F.* in gold thread.

Reznick went back into the bedroom and pointed the light at the ceiling, where he saw a hatch for the attic. He reached up and turned a brass handle. The hatch opened and a ladder descended.

Penlight between his teeth, he climbed up into the attic. As the light bathed the darkness, he saw around a dozen hand-labeled wooden crates.

His earpiece crackled into life. The voice of Stamper.

"How long you gonna be, Jon?"

"Not long."

"You found anything so far?"

"Nothing to write home about."

Stamper said nothing.

"I'll be out of here in a few minutes. I just want to check downstairs to make sure I didn't miss anything."

Reznick climbed down from the attic and headed downstairs, back into the living room. A final look around. Nothing.

Outside on the street, he heard voices raised. A couple having an argument.

Reznick went through to the kitchen. The calendar on the wall listed various charity lunches, meetings with hospital benefactors, and other such stuff. At the far end of the kitchen was a door that led through to a utility room. A washing machine, and a huge refrigerator humming away, its blue light on. On the floor, a small Persian rug.

He bent down and lifted the rug.

A hatch.

He opened it and shone the tiny light down into the dark space. The guy had a fully equipped gym in his basement.

Reznick climbed down the stairs. Descending carefully, step by step. The smell of stale sweat and leather. On the walls were fitness charts showing impressive amounts of weight lifted, at what time and on what day. Time spent on the rowing machine. Strokes per minute. Beats per minute.

This was the gym of a fitness fanatic. Push-ups, pull-ups, squat thrusts; time spent punching the bags; circuit training.

The light shone on a ledge with a framed document. Reznick edged closer.

It was a letter from a mother in the Anacostia neighborhood of DC, whose son had been run over by a hit-and-run driver and had sustained multiple internal injuries. He'd been fighting for his life, but following extensive surgery had made a full recovery. She expressed herself *profoundly grateful for your lifesaving work, Dr. Ford.*

Reznick stared at the letter. He wondered if Ford used it to remind himself why he had got into medicine in the first place.

The earpiece crackled into life. "Jon, get the hell out of there."

"What? I haven't finished yet."

"You have now. Ford has just left the hospital on foot."

Reznick climbed the stairs and out of the basement, shutting the hatch. He arranged the carpet exactly how it had been, picked up his toolkit, and headed out the side door. He shut the door to the lock position, pulled out his trusty pick, and locked it again from the outside. Finally, he switched off the jamming device, reactivating the electronics and alarms.

Reznick's heart was beating fast as he headed down the path and across the street, baseball cap pulled low. He climbed back into the van and locked the door.

Stamper's voice came through the earpiece. "He's walking down the street now."

Reznick peered through the window as Ford approached the townhouse.

"Jon, you there?"

"Yeah, I'm out of there, don't worry."

A long sigh.

"Why the hell's he back so soon?"

"No idea. Just glad you made it out in time."

Reznick wiped the sweat from his brow as Ford entered his home. "On the surface, there's nothing untoward in the house I could see. Guy likes to keep fit. I didn't get time to check out the garage."

"No sign of Caroline Lieber, O'Grady, or anything to incriminate Ford in their disappearances?"

"Absolutely not." A light went on in Ford's living room. "But something doesn't feel quite right."

"What do you mean?"

"My gut feeling? I think there's a lot more to this guy than meets the eye."

Six

It was just after 2 a.m.—and Reznick was gulping yet another strong coffee inside the van—when he spotted Ford emerging from his home. He watched as the doctor, now wearing dark jeans, a white polo shirt, and loafers, climbed into his silver Mercedes, which was parked outside.

"He's on the move, folks!" he whispered, afraid of making too much noise.

Stamper's voice came over the radio. "Yeah, copy that. We're gonna swing by and you can jump in with us. We'll get one of my guys to take away the van."

Reznick sighed. "Hurry the fuck up," he said, as Ford drove away.

A few moments later, a Suburban pulled up. Reznick climbed out of the van and got in the back seat beside Stamper.

"You smell like shit," the Fed said.

Reznick grinned. "Bet you say that to all the boys, huh?"

Stamper shook his head, chewing his gum. "Gimme a break, will you?"

The Suburban sped off through the near-deserted streets of downtown DC in pursuit of Ford.

"You any idea where he's going?" Reznick asked.

"He's not on the hospital rotation for a couple weeks. Last-minute vacation, apparently."

"He's headed northeast," said the driver. "There he is!"

Reznick craned his neck and saw the Mercedes up ahead. "Yeah, I see him."

Stamper took out his radio. "Looks like our guy is getting on I-95 North."

"We're getting too close," Reznick said. "Back off."

Stamper turned and looked at him. "We've been doing this for a long time, Jon."

Reznick said nothing, and a silence opened up as they followed Ford, about a hundred yards back. Ten minutes into the journey, Stamper said, "I don't understand how he fits into this. I don't get it."

"Well, what do we know about him?"

"Privileged background. Private school, then Yale. Star student. All that. I don't think he fits anything we're interested in."

"He has a link to Caroline Lieber—and she's dropped off the radar. I don't believe in coincidences. There's a connection." Reznick looked ahead and saw they were now three cars behind Ford's car. "What else do we know about Dr. Adam Ford?"

"Like I said, not a lot. He looks pretty solid. Brilliant surgeon, incredibly bright, top of his class at medical school, does humanitarian work. Hospital chief executive told us, strictly confidentially, that he's a dedicated surgeon and loved by his patients. Although he did say he was a bit aloof at times, and didn't seem to forge close relationships with other staff."

"What else do we know?"

"Well, we've been trawling his bank accounts, and it's healthy, as you can imagine. He's got one point eight million dollars in stocks. Apple, Intel, Google . . . blue-chip technology stocks, mostly."

"What else?"

"He pays his taxes."

"Relationships?"

"Not a great mixer. A colleague said he was scrupulously polite, never flirtatious with female staff. And she never heard him talking about women or girlfriends."

"What about his parents?"

"Dead, but they were wealthy—solid suburbanites. Father was a lawyer."

"What about donations? Political leanings?"

"None. Worked around the world for the Red Cross after he graduated. Active humanitarian, I guess. But all in all, a very private man." Stamper leaned toward the driver. "Where's he going?"

"GPS on his cell phone shows he's still headed northeast. Baltimore, perhaps."

On the outskirts of Baltimore, they hung back as Ford pulled up at an all-night gas station. A visit to the bathroom, and then back in his car, still headed northeast. They passed the city, its lights in the distance.

Long silences punctuated the journey. Past Wilmington and into New Jersey. Then Cherry Hill and Trenton. Soon they saw signs for New York.

Stamper got out his cell phone. "Martha, we're about forty minutes out of Manhattan." He sighed. "OK. So what do you reckon? We just watch and wait?" He nodded. "Got it."

Union City, and then down to a crawl before the tollbooths at the Lincoln Tunnel. The first tinges of dawn lightened the sky as they emerged from the tunnel and headed through the snarling, early-morning traffic of Midtown Manhattan. The driver yawned, as did Stamper. They headed uptown.

Twenty minutes later, the driver slowed down. "Lenox Hill. Prime Manhattan." More than a hundred yards ahead, Ford pulled into a space outside a fancy townhouse. He then used a fob to lock his car and walked up to the front door, pressing the apartment buzzer. He waited for a few moments. A balding, middle-aged man opened the door, two young kids next to him. Ford flung his arms out wide, picked up the kids, and gave them a big hug.

Stamper was peering through powerful binoculars. "He pressed Apartment Two. Who lives there?"

A short while later, a text came through on his phone.

"William T. Rhodes, medical director of Lenox Hill Hospital." He sighed. "Rhodes has two kids—Amy and Alexander. They're the godchildren of Dr. Adam Ford."

The driver groaned.

Stamper fed the information back to Meyerstein. "Goddamn family friend, that's what he is. Visiting them on the first day of his vacation. Just great."

Seven

The Lowell Hotel on Manhattan's East 63rd Street was where Reznick, Stamper, and the driver decamped to freshen up in an eighth-floor suite. The hotel was about seventy yards away from the house Ford was visiting, on the opposite side of the street. An FBI surveillance unit was keeping watch.

It had felt good to take a long hot shower and put on fresh clothes, sourced by the hotel management.

"You feel better?" Stamper said, pointing to a room-service burger and fries.

Reznick nodded and began to wolf down the food. "I could get used to this life. Is this how the Feds slum it?"

Stamper rolled his eyes.

"So, what's the latest?" Reznick said, wiping ketchup off his chin with a napkin.

"We've activated the microphone on his BlackBerry. His whole conversation is being recorded."

"What's he said so far?"

"Talked about his work, his love of rowing, asked about his godchildren, said nice things to them."

"Nothing bad?"

"Absolutely not. The only thing of note is that Ford was told about an opening at Lenox Hill Hospital and asked if he was interested."

"What did he say?"

"Said he'd think about it, but he thought it was too early in his career. He wants to gain another couple years' experience with his trauma team in DC."

"Answer me this. Don't you think it's strange there was no laptop or anything like that in his home? I would've thought a highly educated, professional guy would need a computer to write up notes, email friends . . . you know what I'm talking about."

Stamper raised his eyebrows. "Maybe."

"Do you have a laptop at home?"

"Sure."

Reznick nodded. "So do I. So does every goddamn person I know. So where the hell is his?"

"Well, he can email from his BlackBerry. Perhaps he's got an iPad, I don't know."

"Well, if he has, where the hell is it?"

Stamper stayed quiet.

"Look, I don't mean to bust your balls over this, but it is an anomaly."

Stamper ran a hand through his hair. "Look—"

The radio crackled, cutting Stamper short. It was the FBI surveillance team, parked in a car outside the townhouse.

"Our boy's on the move," a female voice said.

A few minutes later, Reznick and Stamper were inside a new SUV, being driven uptown.

Stamper said into his cell phone, "He's heading north through Manhattan. We're heading across the Harlem River to the Bronx. We've got three cars on it. I'll keep you posted."

Reznick craned his neck and looked at the traffic bunching up ahead. He caught sight of Ford's convertible doing a steady fifty-five. "A drive in the sun after driving all night. This guy sleeps less than me."

"Bruckner Expressway, heading north. Where's he taking us?"

It wasn't long before the landscape turned industrial. Then it was down to a crawl through a low-income neighborhood. Abandoned cars, boarded-up shops and houses. Graffiti scrawled on tenements.

"Where the hell is this?" Reznick asked.

The driver turned around. "Hunts Point. I used to work in New York—I know the area. It's wall-to-wall garbage. Better than it used to be, but the place is diseased."

Reznick stared out at the urban decay. Living, existing, and dying in a few dilapidated square miles. He remembered it was the same area an old Delta buddy had been brought up in— Charles "Tiny" Burns. Tiny had vowed he'd never return.

They headed past the few commercial and industrial areas that were still intact.

Stamper stared out of the window. "It's a place Adam Ford isn't likely to be stopping, that's for sure."

They drove along the expressway through the Bronx, the views still brutal. A hopeless wasteland. Eventually, they found themselves heading into working-class Baychester, in the northeast section of the borough.

Then they crossed the Hutchinson River parallel to the railroad tracks, and it all changed. The gray and concrete gave way to the lush greenery of the suburbs. A golf course on the left, water on the right.

The driver said, "He's taken Exit Fifteen. He's now making a right onto Boston Post Road."

The car slowed down as they reached a stoplight. A few moments later, the light turned green, and they followed Ford when he turned right onto Pelhamdale Avenue.

"Seems to be heading for Pelham."

"What's in Pelham worth talking about?" Reznick said.

"Commuterville. First stop in Westchester—really nice place. Great schools. Guy that wrote *Primary Colors* lives here. Read that one time."

Stamper was snapping his fingers, as if to help remember. "What's his name . . . Joe Klein?"

The driver nodded. "Yeah, Joe Klein. Worked for Clinton."

Reznick peered up ahead. "So, where exactly is Ford headed?"

The driver kept up his running commentary. "OK, he's made a right onto Shore Road . . . Now a left onto Travers Island."

Up ahead, a huge whitewashed building with a terracotta roof. Beyond that, Long Island Sound, water glistening in the summer sun.

Stamper checked the coordinates on his cell phone. "New York Athletic Club. Very ritzy."

"Who's monitoring his cell phone to pick up any conversations?" Reznick asked.

A navy Suburban pulled up in the club's parking lot. "They are. If there was anything, they'd let us know. We've got a feed coming back to us. Actually, switch it on, Josh. We can monitor it ourselves."

The driver leaned over and flicked a switch on the dashboard. Stamper spoke into his radio. "Jerry, can you get two of your guys to do a recon? Find out where he is, eyeball and report."

"Yeah, got that, Roy."

Reznick said nothing. He would have preferred four guys down at the river for the recon. But Stamper had operational control of the surveillance operation. Reznick figured the last thing Stamper or any of the Feds needed was him griping about what they should or shouldn't be doing. Instead, he just sat in the back seat, eyes on the entrance to the upscale building.

A few moments later, they heard Jerry's voice again. "Roy, he's headed to the nearby boathouse."

"Jerry, is he with anyone?" Stamper said.

A crackly voice. "Negative, Roy."

"Your guys able to get into position to get a picture? I don't want us all to be milling around."

"I'll get on it."

Fifteen minutes later, a video message came through on Stamper's iPhone. Shaky but HD-quality footage of a tall man wearing a Lycra rowing outfit, Yale baseball cap, and wraparound shades. His white teeth clenched as he pulled hard in the sleek single scull.

Stamper shook his head. "What a waste of time. He's out there enjoying a beautiful day, and we're fucking around."

It was nearing the end of the day—the sky burnt orange and the shadows long—when Ford emerged from the clubhouse after an early dinner. He wore sunglasses, his hair neatly combed and gelled, and sported knee-length shorts, a navy polo shirt, and loafers. He climbed back into his car and sped off, unaware he was being watched.

Stamper called Meyerstein and gave her the update. He listened and nodded, and ended the call. He didn't say a word for a few moments, then let out a long sigh. "Goddamn."

"What is it?" Reznick asked.

"Fuck."

"What?"

"They've just fished the partial remains of a body out of the Everglades."

"And?"

"They got a head. That's all. But they're sure it's O'Grady. Bullet through the back of the head."

"Oh shit," Reznick said.

"Forensics is speculating that the body was thrown in. A gator ripped it to pieces, only the head remaining. Then, when it became swollen with water, it floated to the surface."

"Motherfucker. Who found him?"

"Airboat captain."

Reznick closed his eyes.

"Meyerstein is ordering us all back down to DC."

"And what about Ford? We just forget about him?"

"He's clean. He's a preppy surgeon. He's never even had a traffic ticket in his life."

Reznick stared out of the window as the deathly pallor of the Bronx sped by. He turned to Stamper. "Can I speak to Meyerstein, please?"

"Look, Jon, the decision's been made. Now is not the right time to speak to her, trust me."

"Can I speak to her?"

"It's not a good idea."

"Can I speak to her?"

Stamper sighed, and eventually relented. "Reznick wants a word." A brief pause. "I'll pass him over." He handed the cell to Reznick.

Reznick got right to the point: "I think it's too early to cut and run on this guy."

"There's nothing on him, Jon. I want everyone back to DC. I've pulled the plug on Ford."

"I think you're being hasty."

"Why are you getting so worked up about this guy?"

"My gut instinct."

"That's not a rationale for keeping the focus on Ford."

"Meyerstein, there's something setting alarm bells ringing in my head. I don't think we should let him out of our sight. And I don't think electronic surveillance can cover all the bases."

"I've made my position clear, Jon."

"If you want your team back, then great, get them back. But I want to stay. I'll do it on my own."

A long silence opened up between them. Eventually, Meyerstein spoke.

"Jon, I don't need this just now." Her tone was icy.

"No one needs to know. Just leave me behind—what do you say?"

A long silence. "Put Stamper on."

Reznick handed the phone back to Stamper.

"Yeah, Stamper here." He nodded a few times as the glass towers of Manhattan appeared up ahead. "OK, you got it." He ended the call and turned to face Reznick. "We're gonna follow him into town. And we'll drop you off at The Lowell. We've paid for the room up until noon tomorrow. I'll speak to the manager and let him know that you'll be staying until then."

"And after that?"

"After that? Who the hell knows?"

Eight

The afternoon's rowing under a blazing sun on Long Island Sound had left Adam Ford in a good place. He felt exhilarated, and even more focused. A calmness washed over him as he ate a delicious dinner with his friends and his godchildren, Amy and Alexander. Steaks, lobster, a glass or two of French wine—which he politely declined—and Chopin music in the background.

As he listened to the gentle murmur of polite conversation, his thoughts turned to his trip to the woods. He figured they'd been testing him, to see if he could carry out the cold-blooded killing of a complete stranger. He thought it had all been rather easy.

The men in the masks hadn't fazed him. The technical skill to carry out the thousand-yard head shot was beyond most mortals, but not him. He could see that they indeed had it all figured out. And he liked the fact they'd made him prove how committed he was to the task at hand. How single-minded. How unyielding under psychological pressure.

The sound of his friend yawning snapped him out of his reverie.

Ford smiled. "Long day?"

William Rhodes rolled his panda-like eyes, patted his small belly, and gave a weary shrug.

"Same old, Adam. You know how it is."

"Indeed. I'll be turning in early tonight, I'm afraid. I'm beat."

A short while later, he retired to the guestroom. He switched off the lamps and lay back on the bed, as warm air wafted in through the curtains. He'd learned to like William and Sandra and their two children. William had taken him under his wing, back when he was a resident, and had taught him how to be a great doctor. And William remained a useful contact. He was the embodiment of the New York medical establishment. He had influential friends. But Ford could only tolerate three, maybe four visits per year with the family.

His thoughts shifted to what lay ahead.

The more he thought about it, the more he wanted the day to arrive. He knew, however, that patience and the predetermined routine that had been laid out in meticulous detail by his handler were vital to ensure he got to his final destination. The whole operation had been concealed beneath layers of protection. It was quite brilliant.

The priority was the mission.

He would not fail.

Ford thought of his father on his deathbed, eyes shining as he awaited his fate. He remembered feeling nothing, but feigning grief. *Dad, I love you. I'll always love you. And I will never fail you. Never.* He'd felt it was the right thing to say.

He remembered his Yale graduation as if it were yesterday: his father's starched white shirt, and impeccable navy suit and matching tie, his inscrutable demeanor visible from the stage.

The sound of a blaring horn outside interrupted his thoughts. He got up and—as he had done for the last eighteen months at this time of night—did sit-ups, push-ups, and squat thrusts, before showering in the en-suite bathroom. After brushing his teeth, he drank a glass of cool water.

Wrapped in a huge fluffy towel, he lay down on the bed, carefully put in the earbuds of his iPod, and switched on his meditation exercises. As he listened to the soothing sounds of the sea, he let his mind wander. The events of the day flashed by.

He felt himself begin to disassociate.

Cleansing. Soothing. Cooling. Every ripple of water. Every wave crashing onto the shore.

Then a voice, a reassuring voice in the background, calm and clear.

When he woke, he sat bolt upright, struggling to remember where he was, iPod still playing. His iPhone was vibrating on the nightstand. It was 7:08am.

Ford rubbed the sleep out of his eyes and picked up the phone. "Yeah."

"Morning. How are you today? Did you sleep well?"

"Indeed. Very well."

"Remember, you're playing a part. Never let your mask slip."

"I hear you."

"We're getting close now. Real close to the day."

"The day can't come soon enough."

"All in good time, my friend. Stay safe."

Nine

Reznick yawned as the first pink glints of the new day reflected off the windows of the Upper East Side townhouse diagonally opposite, but there was still no sign of Ford.

Reznick was hunkered down on the second floor of The Lowell. Stamper had arranged a change of room, so that Reznick could continue the surveillance operation on his own. But he was beginning to wonder if he shouldn't have taken up Meyerstein's offer to be assigned to watch over the Iranians instead.

He went through to the bathroom, splashed some cold water on his face, and popped a Dexedrine.

He was alert. Ready for a new day.

A knock at the door, and room service arrived with his order of strong black coffee, freshly squeezed orange juice, scrambled eggs, and rye toast. The sight and smells of the food made Reznick feel famished, and he ate it in what seemed like seconds.

Just after 9 a.m., the black townhouse door opened and Ford stepped out with two smiling kids, presumably his surgeon friend's children. The children carried soccer balls under their arms. Reznick watched as Ford bent down to tie the laces of his sneakers and did some stretching, before heading west, laughing and joking with the kids.

"OK, doc, where we going today?" he said to himself.

Was this going to be another runaround?

Reznick headed downstairs to The Lowell's lobby, and was greeted by a cheery "Morning, sir" from the day-shift concierge, who opened the door for him and then pulled him aside. "Sir, I need to inform you that your room is available to you for another forty-eight hours, if you wish."

"It is? Who told you that?"

"I was told to pass on that message to you by the general manager. I believe that everything has been taken care of."

Reznick smiled. "Who took care of it?"

"All I know is that it's taken care of, sir."

It had to be Meyerstein. She was giving him more time—playing it cute. He admired the way she worked. He could only imagine the pressure she'd been under to find O'Grady.

He donned his shades, not wishing to dwell on that thought for too long. He headed west along East 63rd Street, crossing Madison, until he reached Fifth Avenue. Turning to look across the street, he saw Ford and the kids a couple of blocks ahead. Reznick jay-walked across Fifth Avenue, and watched Ford escorting the kids into Central Park at East 60th Street. Then they disappeared into the crowds. Quickening his pace, he eventually caught sight of Ford once more. The doctor was walking with the kids by the pond—goofing around with them, occasionally picking them up and high-fiving them.

Reznick slowed down as they headed along the path. Ford was clearly enjoying the kids' company, as well as the morning sun, fresh air, and exercise. They crossed the stone Gapstow Bridge, which arched over the northernmost part of the pond, and stopped for a few seconds. Reznick kept his distance, though Ford was clearly lost in the moment, pointing out to the children the huge skyscrapers dominating the vista.

Ford then led the kids to a wide grassy area and set them up for a game of soccer. Reznick sat down on a park bench that was out of their direct line of sight. For the next hour, he surreptitiously watched Ford kicking a ball about with the kids. Then he got up and walked toward an ice-cream vendor, and bought a cone. He stared across at the buildings towering over Fifth Avenue. His mind flashed to the Towers falling. He imagined his wife's last moments. The images were seared into him.

The sound of raucous laughter from a crowd of frat boys brought him back to the present. He glanced back at Ford, who was signaling to the kids to wind up the game. They quickly gathered everything up and headed off. He walked slowly in their direction, mindful to keep out of their front and peripheral vision. He followed them over 65th Street Transverse, past some huge trees, and across Sheep Meadow. Scores of people were on the lush grass—playing catch, lying in the sun, doing yoga.

Reznick watched as Ford hugged the kids and hauled them toward the Loeb Boathouse. He stopped around a hundred yards or so away from the lake, sitting down on a bench, shielded from the sun by some huge oaks. They boated for an hour, Ford showing off his rowing skills as the sun sparkled on the water, then retreated inside the boathouse restaurant for lunch. Reznick began to realize he really was wasting his time. The guy was clearly very fond of his godchildren.

At 2 p.m., after lunch and hours of playing in the park, Ford and the kids walked all the way home. They looked utterly exhausted, the girl on his back, the boy walking hand in hand with him.

Reznick watched them head into the townhouse and then returned to the hotel, feeling this was going to be another wasted day. He took the opportunity to have a shower and drink a couple of bottles of still Voss from the minibar. Then he ordered room service: a club sandwich, fries, and a Coke.

Feeling refreshed and rejuvenated, he took up his position by the window.

The rest of the afternoon dragged as the traffic crawled along East 63rd Street. Limos, yellow cabs, Bentleys, garbage trucks. On the sidewalks, nannies and mothers and frazzled young fathers pushed their kids and babies around in strollers, headed toward the park, while liveried doormen stood under apartment awnings, shielding themselves from the fierce afternoon heat.

At 5:55 p.m., with the far side of the street in shade, Ford appeared, carrying a small backpack.

"OK, where you taking me now, doc?"

Reznick took the stairs, and was heading out through the lobby in less than a minute. On Fifth Avenue, he stopped at a vendor cart and bought a hot dog, as Ford headed toward the park. Eating as he walked, Reznick entered the park and skirted the pond again, as he had done in the morning. Taking the exact same route, this time he observed Ford from more than two hundred yards back, as the park was quieter than earlier.

Ford sat down on a park bench, backpack at his side, and watched model boats being raced by two kids. The sky was on fire, the tops of the trees tinged with gold and reds. The doctor stared as if transfixed. Maybe he was enjoying the tranquility of the scene. Then he glanced at his watch.

Reznick took a seat on a fence, shielded by the leaves of the huge beech trees.

Ford glanced at his watch again and opened up his bag. He pulled out a large camera, and in a very deliberate and professional manner, began to take pictures of the pond and Gapstow Bridge. Then he wrapped the camera strap around his wrist and walked a few yards, before snapping pictures again.

Reznick had a good line of sight on Ford, but the doctor would find it nearly impossible to spot him, concealed as he was by the lush foliage and overhanging branches around the path.

The minutes ticked by.

Couples stood, arm in arm, on the bridge. Ford ambled onto it and leaned his camera on the stone side, facing due south, to take pictures of the Manhattan skyline. Then he shielded his eyes from the sun and pointed his camera due west.

Ford looked at his watch again, and then toward the iconic skyline. Then he took out his cell phone and stared at it for a few moments.

Was he picking up a message?

He checked his watch yet again. Reznick also looked at his watch. Precisely 18:22. Ford lifted his camera as the sun glanced off the lens, and pointed it due south toward the Plaza. He lowered the camera before repeating the motion two more times in quick succession.

On the surface, it looked like a keen photographer taking shots of Manhattan.

Look deeper.

Reznick was beginning to perceive Ford's movements in a different light. Was it possible that this was a signal?

Out of the corner of his eye, Reznick saw Ford head over the bridge. He hung back for a minute, checking for any sign of accomplices, shadows, or countersurveillance heading in Ford's direction.

Nothing.

Reznick followed Ford deeper into the park. The doctor skirted Sheep Meadow, then exited at West 65th Street and flagged down a cab.

Reznick did the same. "Stay with the cab four cars ahead," he said as they headed downtown.

The driver shrugged and glanced in the rearview mirror. "Who you following, man?"

"Keep your eyes on the road."

The taxi in front crawled through the early-evening Manhattan traffic until it pulled up at Grand Central Station, Reznick's cab drawing up slowly, a hundred yards back.

Reznick paid the fare as Ford headed into the cavernous rail terminal. Thousands of commuters jostled as they headed for their trains, while hundreds more caught a bite to eat in the numerous restaurants or coffee shops. The place was heaving. Seething. Security blared over the speaker system, alerting commuters not to leave their bags unattended.

Reznick lost sight of Ford for a few moments. He scanned his surroundings, and eventually caught sight of him climbing the stone stairs to the East Balcony, which housed an Apple Store, all glass and metal. There, scores of mostly affluent young people and New York professionals scoured the iPads, MacBook Pros, and shiny iPhones laid out on beautiful tables. He could almost see the love in their eyes as they held the devices.

He pretended to play with an iPad Mini. He could hear Ford at another table behind him, asking a female staff member about iCloud specs. Eventually, Ford left and headed back down the stairs to the concourse.

Reznick followed him out of the station and along East 42nd Street. Ford disappeared into the Capital Grille in the Chrysler Center, but Reznick walked on. Farther down the street, he stopped and took out his cell, pretending to make a call. He nodded as if listening, gave the occasional "Yup," and let the crowds surge by him. He waited twenty minutes before he turned around and headed into the Grille.

It had a clubby atmosphere—all dark mahogany, with red leather seats. A maître d' approached, but Reznick indicated he wasn't eating and was ushered to the bar, where he ordered a club soda. He looked around, and eventually saw Ford sitting alone at a booth. He was tucking into a steak, cornbread, and fries.

Reznick glanced up at the TV, which was showing the Weather Channel, tracking a hurricane heading up from the Caribbean, due to hit the Carolinas in seventy-two hours.

The man two chairs up from him was shaking his head. "It's gonna be a big one," he said. "Real nasty mother."

Reznick nodded as he sipped his drink and waited. He looked at Ford, and saw him paying for his meal with a credit card. The bespectacled waitress nodded politely as she swiped it and handed over a receipt.

After his meal, Ford went to the washroom before leaving the Grille.

Reznick finished his drink and went outside. He was just in time to see Ford climb into a cab and head uptown. Reznick caught a cab thirty seconds later, and managed to follow Ford all the way up Fifth Avenue, where the doctor got out at the glass-fronted Apple Store. Reznick waited a couple of minutes before he headed in.

Downstairs, he watched as Ford checked out the latest iPhone, spending a quarter of an hour discussing the device with the assistant. Reznick wondered why he hadn't bought the phone at Grand Central, but pushed those thoughts to one side as he observed Ford buying a brand-new phone before heading back to his friend's townhouse.

Back in his room at The Lowell, Reznick's cell vibrated in his pocket. He checked the caller ID and saw it was Meyerstein.

"How's it going?" she asked.

Reznick sighed. "Not much to give you."

"Any developments?"

Reznick took the next few minutes to outline the comings and goings of Ford in New York.

"Jon, I've got to be honest: all the analysis is pointing to the fact that this lead doesn't amount to anything."

Reznick stared at the unrelenting Upper East Side traffic outside his window.

Ten

Reznick was floating in a river of darkness, unable to breathe. He sensed he was not alone. The sky was inky black. The smell of rotting garbage drifted over him. He tasted dust, then blood. A humid breeze was blowing, helping to cool the fever. The sound of screaming. Yells. More screams. Gunshots. Then sirens blaring.

He bolted upright, heart pounding, and looked around. Semidarkness. He was still sitting beside the second-floor window of The Lowell, fully clothed, his cell phone ringing. He took a few moments to get his bearings, nightmares of Mogadishu still coursing through his brain.

He must have blacked out with exhaustion.

Damn.

Reznick picked up his phone, which showed it was 3:01 a.m.

"Yeah?"

"It's the night concierge, sir. You said if there was any movement from the townhouse up the street?"

Reznick rubbed the sleep from his eyes. "Ah . . . yeah, sure." Reznick had given the guy two hundred dollars to give him a call if he saw anything, so he could get some shut-eye.

"Well, there's a cab outside just now. Pulled up a minute ago."

"Good man."

Reznick went over to the window, and watched as Ford emerged from the townhouse and slid into the backseat of the cab. It pulled away and headed in the direction of Fifth Avenue.

Reznick bounded downstairs, thanking the concierge, who had already hailed him a passing taxi. He jumped in and followed Ford downtown, toward the East Village.

Ford's taxi pulled up outside the striped canopy of the Yaffa Cafe, and the doctor got out.

Reznick said, "Keep going. Drop me off in a couple of blocks."

The driver nodded, and stopped outside Paul's Da Burger Joint.

Reznick handed over a fifty-dollar bill. "That cover it for you?"

The driver grinned. "Damn right it does. Have a good night. And stay safe."

Reznick watched the cab turn onto Second Avenue before he headed back along St. Mark's Place. He passed a neon-lit cocktail place, a drunk sitting on the sidewalk outside as people walked on by. Then past a half-empty bar, some girls laughing raucously inside, and Jules Bistro. A cop car crawled along First Avenue, giving him the eye, windows down. Up ahead, he saw the sign for Yaffa. A few people were sitting and eating on the patio, but Ford wasn't one of them.

Reznick headed inside the restaurant. Out the back, there was a garden bedecked in lights hanging from trees. All around, people were drinking and smoking. He hung back by the door, and finally saw Ford at the farthest point of the garden, sitting by himself, talking into his shiny new iPhone, coffee on the table.

Reznick headed back inside and sat down alone at an animal-print booth. He ordered a double-shot Americano. A server brought it to his table within minutes.

His line of sight was good, with a view of everyone entering and leaving the bar. He sipped his seriously strong coffee. It felt good as the caffeine kicked in. Reviving.

He checked his watch—it was 3:42 a.m. He scanned the room, trying to appear disinterested. Everyone was very much in their groups and cliques, chatting, buzzing, and drinking.

Reznick nursed his coffee and listened in on conversations: the price of a room on Avenue A, relationships with unsuitable boyfriends, nightmare bosses.

He finished his drink and went to the washroom. A couple of minutes later, he peered through the doorway into the garden. Ford was reading a magazine, his phone on the table beside him.

Reznick got back to his table and took out his wallet. He wondered if he should stay put, order another coffee, or if he should wait across the street for Ford to make a move. Then, out of the corner of his eye, he saw Ford walk through the bar and leave. Through the window veiled by Buddha beads and statues, he saw Ford walk east along St. Mark's.

Reznick left a twenty-dollar bill on the table, waited a few moments, and headed out onto the street. Up ahead, Ford crossed over to the other side of the road before turning right onto Avenue A.

Reznick hung back. Satisfied he was out of sight, he pressed on past the bars and the metal-shuttered shop fronts scrawled with garish graffiti.

As Ford crossed over Avenue A at Sidewalk Bar and headed down East 6th Street, Reznick wondered what the hell the doctor was doing in the middle of the night, heading deep into Alphabet City. The area didn't seem like a natural haunt for a clean-cut, high-flying DC trauma surgeon.

He felt wired as he walked deeper and deeper into the East Village. His senses were fully switched on.

Ford crossed over at some lights on Avenue C. More residential. A vacant lot. More graffiti scrawled on buildings and trash cans. Then past a deli and across Avenue D. The Lillian Wald housing project towered over the east side of the street. But Ford turned right.

Reznick crossed over to the opposite sidewalk and stole a glance at Ford, who had stopped outside a nondescript brick building with a black door. He pressed a buzzer and waited. The number above the door was *45–51*. After a few moments, a woman opened the door, and hugged Ford before ushering him inside.

Reznick kept moving, crossing back over Avenue D and turning down Avenue C into a filthy bodega. There he bought an energy drink, a couple of candy bars, a gray Yankees cap, and a loose-fitting black T-shirt. He ditched his own shirt in the shop's trash can, pulled on the T-shirt, pulled the cap down low, and walked back to Avenue D.

Same person, different look.

He sat down on a bench in the shadow of one of the housing projects, in view of the brick building Ford had entered.

Reznick drank the energy drink and ate the candy bars. He took out his cell and looked up the address on his phone—the Bowery Mission Transitional Center.

Fuck. What was going on?

He mulled on that as a couple of tough-looking Puerto Rican kids walked past with pit bulls on pieces of rope, both giving him the cold eye.

"Yo faggot, what the fuck you looking at?" the smaller of the two said.

Reznick stared them down.

The kid and his friend tried to look tough for a moment, but they crossed over the street, pulling the snarling dogs behind them.

Reznick hung around for thirty minutes, then decided to go for a stroll near the homeless center. The black door was firmly locked, but there were a couple of lights on in the first floor.

He walked around the block and headed back down Avenue D, passing a panhandler huddled in a liquor store doorway under a pile of blankets. Farther north, the chimneys of the huge Con Edison plant billowed smoke into the pre-dawn air. He headed past the shelter and the sound of a loud TV from an open second-floor window.

At the end of the block, he bought a *New York Daily News* from a newsstand that was just setting up, and crossed over at the lights. He sat down on a bench in front of the huge Jacob Riis housing project.

He flicked through the paper as traffic picked up. Sidewalks were busier, early-morning workers on their way to the daily grind. A cop car cruised the main drag before edging up one of the adjoining streets. He heard the sound of metal shutters being opened.

Out of the corner of his eye, the panhandler shuffled into sight, a bottle of Night Train in his hand. Reznick took a closer look. The man was dirty, with wild blue eyes and bleeding bare feet. He sat down at the end of the bench, humming a show tune, then turned to face Reznick.

"Where you from?"

Reznick sighed. The last thing he needed was to engage with some broken panhandler. But he knew that to ignore him would attract the ire of the man.

"Just visiting friends nearby."

He pointed at Reznick. "There's no such thing as friends. Not here. Not now. Not ever. Not in this goddamn fucking stinking city."

Reznick said nothing.

The man glugged back some wine. "I don't want to go on anymore. You ever feel like that?"

Reznick nodded. "Yes, I do."

The man closed his eyes, bottle still clasped in his filthy hand.

For the next two hours, as the panhandler slept on the bench, Reznick alternated between walking around the block and taking up different vantage points farther down the street. He was starting to wonder how long he'd be waiting when the black door of the homeless shelter opened and Ford emerged and headed north up Avenue D.

Reznick waited a few moments before picking up Ford's tail. The sidewalks were starting to get busier. He passed a street vendor selling raspberry slushies from his cart, a cigarette hanging from his mouth. On the corner, a cop leaned against his cruiser, watching the world go by. The place was coming to life.

Ford crossed over Avenue B and headed past a nail salon and down East 11th Street. He walked past a dozen men standing in line for a soup kitchen and disappeared inside. Reznick stole a glance at the building as he walked by on the opposite side of the street. The sign said *Father's Heart Ministry Center*.

He kept on moving until he reached a deli fifty yards farther down the street. A Puerto Rican flag fluttered from a second-floor window of the building opposite.

Reznick bought a bottle of water. He took a few refreshing gulps, needing the hydration. Then he went outside and sat on the steps in front of the store.

He stared at the line of poor bastards gathering for breakfast. Handed a ticket and ushered in by cheery young volunteers.

His thoughts turned to Ford.

Two hours at a homeless shelter, and now a soup kitchen. The guy was either Gandhi or this was an elaborate cover. But if it was a cover, what was the purpose? It seemed on the surface as if the good doctor was doing his bit. Giving something back.

The thought depressed Reznick. It would mean that he was wasting his time, tailing a good guy.

He drank the rest of the water, walked around the block, and parked himself on a bench outside the 11 B Express pizza restaurant on the corner of Avenue B, diagonally opposite the soup kitchen. Partially obscured from view by the leaves of a huge tree, Reznick flicked through his newspaper.

He checked his watch. He walked around the block. He bought a coffee at the deli.

Finally, just before 10 a.m., Ford emerged onto the sidewalk, talking into his cell phone. He walked up East 11th Street and caught a taxi at Avenue A.

It was five minutes before Reznick got a cab, and he'd finally lost Ford.

⌣

A short while later, in the cab heading back to Lenox Hill, his cell rang. He didn't recognize the number.

"Yeah, who's this?"

"It's Meyerstein."

Reznick kept his voice low. "Any progress?"

"Nothing so far, Jon. Look, I'm going to be straight with you. I'm very tempted to do what everyone is telling me to do and haul you out of New York."

Reznick sighed.

"It's nearly two days and nothing, am I right? The general, besides threatening to haul me off the program, is at a loss to understand this obsession with Ford."

"I'll tell you why. There's something about this guy. His actions are—"

"What?"

The cab hit a pothole and Reznick was jolted in the back seat. "He got up and headed down to a homeless shelter on Avenue D, in the East Village. Then he headed across to a soup kitchen."

"And? Are you saying that's the sum of what you've got?"

"Look, I'm not buying this Mother Theresa crock of shit. It doesn't wash."

"Jon, this is a good guy. There are good people in the world."

"My gut instinct says that we need to keep an eye on him."

A long sigh. "Jon, listen to me. We've checked into this guy's background. We've gone over it. There's nothing to arouse suspicion. And what you say about helping out at homeless shelters and soup kitchens tallies with him working in Malawi for Unicef and in Haiti. He helped out down in New Orleans after Katrina. He's worked on vaccination programs for the World Health Organization. Jon, the guy's never had a ticket in his life. He's clean."

"I think we're missing something. What about the trip into the East Village in the middle of the night? Buying a new phone?"

"Buying a new phone? Gimme a break. What if you're just plain wrong?"

"What if I'm not? I'm telling you, there's a piece of the jigsaw that will pull this all together. But we're still missing it. We're not connecting the dots. I need to know for sure that this guy is legitimate."

Meyerstein sighed.

"I'm convinced we're missing something from his past. You've told me about the trips abroad. Are they accurate records?"

"Jon, I think you're reaching."

"Way I see it, we've made no breakthrough. He's the only link, no matter how tenuous, to Lieber and therefore O'Grady. I don't think we can dismiss him so readily."

"The problem is, Jon, no one on my team sees Ford as part of the jigsaw. Nothing about his past gives us any cause for concern. Counterterrorism did a separate trawl with the NSA, and it came back clean. You want me to go on? You're out on a limb here."

It wouldn't have been the first time in his career.

"Are you still there, Jon?"

"The guy is putting in some hours at a soup kitchen and a homeless shelter, while driving around in a car which could feed a hundred thousand people. Does that not strike you as out of place?"

"People do their bit in different ways."

"Then there's another scenario. Is it possible that these trips around town are a cover?"

"A cover for what?"

"Is he using a cutout?"

Meyerstein went quiet.

"Is he using an intermediary to pass or receive information?"

"I know what the hell a cutout is."

"Well, if he is, the cutout is based in the East Village. Look, I'm telling you, we need to start connecting the dots with this guy."

The silence on the phone was deafening.

Eleven

The conversation with Reznick had bothered Meyerstein. It added to the lingering suspicions she herself was having about the DC surgeon. She hadn't shared her thoughts with anyone on her team, not even Reznick. Her analysis was showing that Ford was clean. But the doubts Reznick had voiced mirrored her own, and they were beginning to gnaw away at her.

Meyerstein walked over to the team of senior strategic analysts who looked at any threats, vulnerabilities, and gaps in the special access program's knowledge. They sifted raw information from numerous sources and brought it all together. But nothing they had pointed to Ford.

Meyerstein called the office two floors below and asked for Roy Stamper, her trusted deputy. A man whose counsel she valued.

"Shut the door, Roy," she said when he appeared.

Stamper sank into the leather chair opposite and stretched out his arms and legs. He looked exhausted.

"O'Grady dead. Caroline Lieber still missing, not a trace. We're nowhere with this, Roy. Absolutely nowhere. What are your thoughts? And don't sugarcoat it."

Stamper sighed. "There is a link between O'Grady and Lieber. The call tells us that. Counterintelligence is telling us Iran is in the picture, what with O'Grady's area of expertise."

Meyerstein leaned back in her seat. She relayed the latest snippets of information Reznick had told her about Ford. "He thinks we need to focus more on our DC doctor. I'm wondering . . . What if . . . What if there's a chance—a chance—that Reznick's right and there *is* a connection with Ford? What if there's a thread we're missing?"

"Not one shred of intel on that, Martha. Look, I'm going to level with you. I think Reznick is wrong. We've checked Ford out. It's not possible that he's connected."

Meyerstein said nothing.

Stamper stared at her. "Can I be blunt?"

"Of course."

"I'm not too sure having Reznick on this team is a good move. Don't get me wrong. I like the guy. But he's making us take our eyes off the ball."

"Reznick made me look more closely at Ford. I've just been reading some analysis from one of the best behavioral guys we have—did you see that?"

Stamper nodded. "Malone? I thought that was a bit sketchy—part psychobabble, part pop psychology. It was all over the place."

"I agree, he can be out there, but he indicates there are personality traits he finds interesting in Ford. He thinks we shouldn't ignore him completely."

"And that's it? That's what we're going on? This is all we have—Reznick and Malone? Gimme a break."

Meyerstein sighed. "Roy, I don't feel like I know this guy. I want you to set up a dedicated team to analyze all data on his dates and times abroad, and recheck everything we have. Friends, family, lovers, acquaintances. Are we missing something—that's all I'm asking."

"You've gotta be kidding me."

"Do I look like I'm kidding?"

Stamper said nothing.

"I want us in every area of his life on a minute basis. Childhood, education, college, work. Top to bottom. I want to see documentary proof of each stage of his life—where he was and under what authority. I want pictures of him. But what I also want is a trawl of all foreign intelligence on Ford. Do they have anything on him that we don't? Any nugget at all."

Stamper blew out his cheeks. "I can't believe what I'm hearing."

"What the hell is that supposed to mean?"

"I think we're wasting our time, that's all."

"Maybe we are. Yes, you might very well be right. But I want to seal up every aspect of the investigation. I want Ford's new cell number, with all calls and messages analyzed by the NSA. I also want to know about his old phone. And the one before that. Is he running more than one phone?"

"Martha, I've got to say, I think you're taking a big risk with this."

Meyerstein leaned forward. "That's for me to worry about. Now listen, I've fed the info Reznick gave us into our system. He said Ford visited a place called the Yaffa Cafe just before four a.m. today, then the Bowery homeless shelter on Avenue D and a soup kitchen on East 11th Street. Find the volunteers—and all those who work there and have worked there—in the past two years . . . I want us to drill down into this guy and what he's all about."

"I don't understand your thinking on this."

Meyerstein felt anger tighten her stomach. "Roy, don't sweat it. I'll take the flack."

"I'm sorry, Martha, to appear so negative, but Reznick is barking up the wrong tree. The only thread holding it together is that O'Grady called Lieber shortly before they both disappeared, and Lieber was infatuated with a DC doctor. It doesn't stand up to the most basic bit of scrutiny."

"Look, the only thing we've got to lose is manpower."

"This is a dumb call, Martha—that's all I'm saying. I can't remember any dumb calls in all the time we've worked together. But this comes into that category."

Meyerstein was seething but she kept her cool on the surface.

"Have you forgotten, Roy, that I am an assistant director of the Federal Bureau of Investigation and I'm heading up this special access program? I won't have my judgment questioned by subordinates."

Stamper shifted in his seat.

"I've got to say, Roy, I thought I knew you better than that."

Stamper cleared his throat. "Look, I think we're all under pressure on this. But I think it's important that we can be frank with each other, Martha. I'm not the only one that thinks Reznick has no place on the team and is questioning why the hell we're even listening to him."

Meyerstein felt her throat tighten.

"Martha, the majority view from our analysts is clear. On the ground, we're looking for Eastern Bloc mercenaries, not some candy-ass doctor. You're giving too much credence to what Reznick is saying."

"That's enough! I've heard your gripes but—you know what, Roy?—I'm going to ignore them. Someone is working on the ground, probably at the behest of the Iranians or other proxies."

"So where the hell does Ford fit into that?"

"I don't know. He might *not* fit into it. But I need to be sure."

Stamper shook his head, looking dismayed. "Look, I didn't want to say this, but I'm going to."

"Spit it out."

"The guys on the team are busting their guts on this, and they don't like their boss, one of the most senior agents in the FBI, being made to look a fool over a has-been Delta."

Meyerstein bristled at the criticism. "In what way, precisely, am I being made to look a fool?"

Stamper's silence said it all.

"I don't give a damn what people think. Jon Reznick was brought in to augment the capabilities of my team. He offers something else."

"Like what?"

"He isn't afraid to go out on a limb. He doesn't take the safe path. He tells it like it is."

"And that's just what I'm doing, Martha. What if he's wrong? How are you going to explain how you wasted hundreds of man-hours on the say-so of Reznick? It seems the guy is answerable to no one."

"He's answerable to me."

"So why didn't he listen when you ordered us back to Washington?"

Meyerstein remained silent.

"What is it about this guy?"

"Do not call Jon Reznick into question."

Stamper raised an eyebrow.

"Now, you listen to me, Roy. We've worked together in harmony, as a team, for as long as I can remember. And I will not be spoken to like this by you, or by anyone. So here's how it's going to work. Do you want to be taken off this investigation and shipped back to HQ?"

It was Stamper's turn to flare. "I don't believe this!"

"Because that's what's going to happen if I hear one more word of insubordination. And that goes for everyone. You got a problem with that?"

Stamper shook his head.

"OK. You stay here and connect the goddamn dots. Updates, analysis feeds . . . I want it sent to me in real time."

"Where are you going?"

"I'm going to New York. I'm going to find out for myself what the hell is going on."

Stamper sat in silence, staring at the floor.

"When you come to lead such an investigation, you can make whatever call you like. But while I'm in charge, we're going to do this my way."

Twelve

It was late in the evening when Reznick's cell phone began to vibrate, as he hunkered down in his darkened room at The Lowell. A text message told him to make his way to The Fairfax, at East 69th Street and Third Avenue.

Reznick pulled out the SIM card from his cell and flushed it down the toilet, disposing of the battery in the trash on his way out of the hotel. He headed the six blocks to The Fairfax—a pre-war brick building—walked through the doors under the metal awning, and into a spacious wood-paneled lobby.

The guy on reception wore a dark suit and tie. He smiled. "Can I help you, sir?"

"Jake Smith. I'm visiting number eight zero nine."

"Very good, sir." He picked up the phone and punched in a number. "Reception here, sir. A Mr. Smith for you." A long pause. "Very good, sir. I'll send him up."

The guy pointed to the elevators. "Eighth floor. Right at the end of the corridor, sir."

Reznick rode the elevator to eight and headed along the carpeted corridor to 809. He knocked on the door. A few moments later, a heavyset man in a dark-gray suit ushered him inside.

The place had oak floors and high ceilings. He followed the man down a hallway and up some wrought-iron stairs. A duplex. On the next level, it all became clear.

It was a spacious, open-plan living area, like a converted loft. The smell of coffee permeated the room. Sitting at a table was FBI Assistant Director Martha Meyerstein, with a cell phone and MacBook Pro in front of her. At the other end was a middle-aged guy with a goatee, Ramones T-shirt, and jeans and sneakers, tapping away with one hand on an iPad.

"Good evening, Jon," she said.

Reznick wondered what was going on. He pulled out a chair and sat down.

She pointed to the other man. "Dr. Henry Malone. Behavioral analyst with the FBI."

Malone nodded, face impassive.

Reznick nodded back. "You mind me asking what's going on?"

"What's going on, Jon, is that I've decided to have a closer look at Ford."

Reznick smiled. "You kidding me?"

"No. I'll explain in a few moments. As of now, this will be your base in New York, along with four other members of a surveillance team attached to this program. Electronic monitoring has been set up in the bedroom."

"What is this place?"

"It's a safe house, of sorts. Used to be the FBI HQ in New York until 1980, when it was converted into apartments. We decided to keep a couple of apartments to use for special operations."

He looked around. "Interesting."

"The walls are soundproofed, and anti-jamming equipment and countersurveillance equipment is in place, so the place is clean."

"So where are we going with this?"

"I'm staying in an apartment down the hall while Ford is in town. I want to see for myself where he goes and what we have."

Reznick stifled a yawn.

Meyerstein looked him over. "You look like shit, by the way, Jon."

"I feel like shit, too, for what it's worth. So to what do we owe the pleasure?"

"I got a call from a counterterrorism specialist assigned to the team. He said something interesting. There was chatter on some Jihad Internet boards—encrypted—pointing to New York. Talking about something *special*."

Reznick went across to the window and stared out at the city, his back to Meyerstein. "We all know New York is everyone's top target. The economic power of Wall Street, media empires, the symbolism of Manhattan, all that stuff. Nothing new about that."

"Ford is in New York."

Reznick turned and faced her. "What else? I assume you're doing some digging on this guy."

"As we speak. I've ordered a comprehensive review of all the material we have on him. We've also spoken to Caroline Lieber's parents, but they've never heard her mention his name. So he means nothing to them."

"When this group was brought together, you said its objective was to find O'Grady. Well, O'Grady's been found—dead. And Caroline Lieber's still missing. Now you're talking about something going down in New York. And Ford's in the middle of this, I know it."

"We're rolling with this, Reznick. Bearing in mind O'Grady's work . . ." She looked at Malone. "Henry, you want to explain to Jon where we are and how you fit into this?"

Malone nodded. "I head up Behavioral Analysis Unit One focusing on counterterrorism and threat assessment. And I specialize in anticipated or active crisis situations."

Reznick nodded.

"OK, I've got to be honest—they all think I'm heading in the wrong direction wanting to look closer into Ford."

"So what's got you interested in Ford?" Reznick asked.

"A few aspects have piqued my interest. First, Ford's college and hospital assessments. He was clearly a brilliant student and resident. But when it came to what he was like as a person, common phrases that were used were *surface to a fault, glib, cocky* and *very arrogant.* Strong words for professionals to use about a brilliant student and doctor.

"In my work, we're trying to assess psychological constructs—you know, like cognitive and emotional functioning. The technical term, if you are interested, is psychometrics."

"Yeah, but I'm interested in how this relates to Ford," Meyerstein interjected.

Malone sighed. "There's a book I always found fascinating."

"And what's that?"

"*The Art of War* by Sun Tzu."

Meyerstein shrugged. "I'm more a Patricia Cornwell fan myself."

Malone cleared his throat. "What you said reminded me of a line. *Subtle and insubstantial, the expert leaves no trace; divinely mysterious, he is inaudible. Thus he is master of his enemy's fate.*"

"What are you saying?" said Meyerstein. "That Ford fits that description?"

"Perhaps. Know what Sun Tzu also said?"

Meyerstein shook her head.

"*All warfare is based on deception.*"

"I think you might be looking into this too much."

Malone bit his lower lip and looked at Reznick. "Maybe not. OK, let's see where we are. Psychologically?"

Meyerstein shrugged. "He seems, on the surface, to have it all. A very privileged background."

"On the surface, maybe," said Malone. "But I think he meets two out of the three criteria which interest me. A need for identity and a need for belonging. The charity work or god complex, call it what you will . . . Add this to his ego, and you have a very interesting case. And you begin to see a picture."

Reznick stayed quiet.

"On the surface, all is well. But something intrigued me about him after you described the inside of his house."

"What was so interesting about that?"

"Three things. Firstly, the fastidiousness . . . Nothing out of place. It was ordered to a meticulous degree. A man who—"

Meyerstein interrupted, her patience wearing thin. "That's a big leap, from being OCD to being a terror suspect."

"It's important to build up as full a picture as possible. It shows a type of personality. Obsessive–compulsive disorder is an anxiety disorder. People have repeated thoughts, feelings, obsessions, or behaviors that make them compulsive.

"The second aspect is that, according to recent research, modern terrorists are far more likely to be highly educated and come from wealthy backgrounds. This guy is, to all intents and purposes, a potential cleanskin. Ford is highly intelligent, rational, and can be dispassionate to ensure he can focus on the job in hand—namely, surgery. But, along with indications of Ford being superficial, glib, all surface, I believe there is a narcissistic element to his personality."

"Narcissistic? In what way?" asked Reznick.

"His fixation with self, an identity wanting to belong. I'm talking about the pictures of him in his house, the letter from the mother of the boy he saved. Your notes mentioned monogrammed towels in the bathroom. It reminded me of a case I'd worked on in the nineties."

"Which one?"

"Does the name Eric Robert Rudolph ring a bell?"

Meyerstein nodded. "The Olympic Park Bomber. A classic American lone-wolf terrorist. Set off the Atlanta bomb back in 1996."

"The very one. Narcissism was part of his psychological makeup, among a host of other things. With Ford, that may be part of his story."

Meyerstein pinched the bridge of her nose. "So, where the hell does some glib and arrogant doc with OCD and narcissistic tendencies fit into the plan?"

"Look, I'm not saying this guy is the one. However, he certainly needs further investigation. But that will take time."

"Something we don't have."

A member of Meyerstein's team shouted from the monitoring room, "Hey, he's on the move! He's carrying a bike, wearing cycling gear."

They all went to watch the real-time images from the van parked on East 63rd Street.

Meyerstein said, "OK, I want motorbike-courier surveillance activated."

The next hour was spent watching Ford cycling through the streets of Manhattan, weaving in and out of traffic. Midtown, downtown, and then the East Village. There, he locked his bike on the metal railings outside the soup kitchen on East 11th Street. More covert footage showed inside the soup kitchen. Ford was serving out big bowls of soup to men seated at long tables. He wore hygienic latex gloves like the rest of the volunteers.

Meyerstein dialed a number on her cell phone. "Roy, it's Martha. Are you watching the footage from the East Village?" She nodded. "Yeah, it looks like around a dozen young men and women, and four or five middle-aged volunteers helping out. I'm still waiting to find out who's on the list. And also at the homeless shelter. Get that info ASAP."

Reznick stared at the image of Ford on the screen.

"Who the hell *are* you?"

Thirteen

The sour breath and the smell of urine were making Ford feel queasy. He was twenty minutes into a ninety-minute stint at the East Village soup kitchen.

He looked down at the drugged-up panhandler in front of him. Pathetic. He was wearing a stained Obama T-shirt and filthy pants.

Ford kneeled down and checked the man's blood pressure, before pulling back his eyelids. No response. The eyes were glassy, pupils small. He held his breath so he wouldn't inhale the noxious chemicals circulating in the panhandler's system, and gently shook the man's shoulder.

"Michael, are you there?" He was glad he had his surgical gloves on.

The man tried to speak, but only a low moan emanated.

"Michael, you're at the soup kitchen on East 11th Street." He raised his voice. "Do you understand?"

Michael's sad eyes opened and began to focus as he came to. "I ain't got nowhere." His speech was slurred. "Got kicked out of the fucking Baruch. You believe that? I've been kicked out of shit-hole central." He began to laugh, exposing surprisingly white teeth.

"Obama sure as hell won't be living in the Baruch tonight. One thing we've got in common, right?"

Ford nodded politely, his empathetic mask on show for the world to see. "No, I don't suppose he will."

Michael closed his eyes and tears spilled down his face. He began to hum the tune to "The Lord is My Shepherd."

Ford stroked his cheek and smiled. "We'll take care of you, Michael," he said as he helped the man over to a chair.

His mind flashed back to his suburban teenage years. He remembered his father looking at a man in the same predicament, at a soup kitchen organized by his church. Ford had thought the whole setup was phony. He didn't give a damn about the downtrodden or those that had fallen on hard times. Darwin was right— it was survival of the fittest. The smartest and toughest would inherit the earth. The meek would inherit absolutely nothing. His father, by contrast, cared passionately about those less fortunate. He blamed society for people's ills and not the people themselves. It was his Christian faith.

Ford made sure Michael was safely on the chair. "I'll bring you over some nice soup."

Michael looked up at Ford, tears still streaming down his face. "The Lord as my witness, I will find the strength."

For a split second, Ford wanted to take a gun, press it to the man's head, and blow his brains out, putting him out of his misery. That's what people did to lame and crippled dogs. They put them out of their misery.

"I'm sure you will, Charles."

Ford's cell phone began to vibrate in his top pocket, and he moved across to a quiet corner to take the call, facing a wall.

"I wanted to let you know," the familiar voice said, "we're on track with preparations."

"When will I know the final details?"

"When we know, you'll know. Leave us to worry about that. You're doing great. How do you feel?"

"Alive. I want to do this."

"We know."

The line went dead.

Ford stood staring at his cell phone for a few moments. This was real. He felt wired.

He breathed in deep and let it out slowly. He breathed in deep again.

"Who was that?"

Ford spun around and saw Michael staring at him, a stoned grin on his face.

"I—"

"You got a secret girlfriend, is that what it is? I knew it!"

Ford managed a grin. "You know how it is."

"I heard what you said. That you want to do this." Michael winked conspiratorially. "Wanna do what? You leading a secret life, huh?"

Ford stared into Michael's dark eyes. His stomach knotted tight. He realized he would have to call this in and get it taken care of. "I'm sorry, I don't follow."

Michael leaned in close to Ford and flung his arm around his shoulder like a long-lost college friend. "Your secret's safe with me, man," he whispered, the sour breath impossible to escape.

Ford felt revulsion and a dark anger begin to consume him. He stared into Michael's stupid eyes for what seemed an eternity. But he kept his emotions in check.

His thoughts turned to what awaited the panhandler.

And slowly, the anger began to dissipate, a sense of calm and wellbeing washing over him.

Michael was as good as dead.

Fourteen

Just after six in the morning, in a bedroom in the upper part of the duplex apartment within The Fairfax, Jon Reznick was woken by a burly Fed on the early shift. "Hey, Jon, we got lattes and cappuccinos delivered up from Starbucks," he said. "What do you like?"

Reznick rubbed his eyes and groaned as he came to. He looked through into the apartment's living area and saw Malone tapping away on his laptop. "Latte for me."

The Fed smiled as he handed him a cup.

Reznick pulled off the lid and sipped the piping hot coffee. The caffeine jolt was just what he needed. "Damn, that's nice."

The Fed left him alone to get ready, shutting the door behind him. He pulled on a pair of jeans, a T-shirt, and sneakers, and headed through into the improvised intelligence hub with his coffee.

Reznick sat down on a sofa and looked over at Malone. "So, what's the latest on Ford?"

Malone leaned back in his seat, biting his lower lip. "Good morning, Mr. Reznick. After an hour or so at the soup kitchen, another trip to the Yaffa Cafe. He feels comfortable there." Malone was handed a coffee. He took a sip. "Thanks. Here's the thing. This café is like a hipster haunt, an alternative culture HQ . . . has been since before the East Village became more gentrified. But his profile doesn't fit it at all."

"What about a list of those working at the café? Photos, names . . . that kind of thing? Has that been checked?"

"Yeah, Assistant Director Meyerstein has just sent over photos and bios of those who've worked there in the last eighteen months. A team is trawling them now."

"So, what angle are you working on now?"

"I'm looking at this from a physiological point of view, as well as the psychological perspective. From what you've reported back, and going on what I've seen in the last twenty-four hours, this guy is not getting his sleep. He might be getting some during the day, but with two kids in that apartment, it won't be the quietest."

"Is he speeding?" asked Reznick.

"Could be."

"What else?"

Malone sighed. "I got a statement from an old college friend. He said Ford let slip one day that his father beat him as a child if he flunked a test. He said he couldn't wait to get away from home."

Reznick said nothing.

"By all accounts, he was a model student. He knuckled down, did the work, but wasn't the most sociable. Very private."

A knock at the door. The burly Fed answered and let Meyerstein in. She had a huge tote bag in one hand and a Styrofoam cup in the other.

"Morning, boys," she said. She sat down at the table, pulling an iPad out of her bag and placing it alongside her coffee. "Three hundred and twenty-four separate photos and bios. Soup kitchen, Yaffa Cafe, steakhouse waiters and cooks, and also volunteers and employees at the homeless shelter. Three have been flagged as having skipped bail on drug charges, two for outstanding speeding tickets, but all the rest are upstanding citizens. On the surface, no red flags. But we're working on it."

Reznick headed into the living area. "You mind if I take a look?"

Meyerstein pushed the iPad toward him. "Be my guest."

Reznick pulled up the gallery of color photos and short bios of everyone employed by or linked to the establishments. He clicked on the first of the soup kitchen volunteers: a fresh-faced young woman named Candice Olsen, a nineteen-year-old student at Columbia. She'd been volunteering every weekend for the last year, after moving to New York from Cleveland. He scrolled down. The second volunteer he clicked on was a twenty-two-year-old art student from Brooklyn, Leroy Burnett.

"What are you looking for?" Meyerstein said.

Reznick gulped down the rest of his coffee. "I don't know. Just like looking, I guess. No harm, right?"

Meyerstein shook her head. "You're an obsessive, Jon, do you know that?"

Reznick grinned and looked across at Malone. "Is that a psychiatric disorder?"

Malone raised his eyebrows, deadpan. "Oh yeah."

Reznick stifled a yawn. He was restless. He didn't want to just sit about and twiddle his thumbs. Even during his Delta days, the waiting was the worst. Waiting for the green light. Waiting for the go-ahead. Always waiting. He couldn't stand that. He'd much rather be doing something.

He switched his attention back to the photos on the iPad. Over the next couple of hours, he scrolled through the pictures and bios while Meyerstein videoconferenced in the next room and Malone researched more into Ford's background and upbringing.

Reznick rubbed his eyes as he reached the list of Yaffa Cafe employees, past and present. They were mostly young, predominantly in their early twenties. Quite a few were earning extra money while they studied at the Cooper Union—a private college specializing in architecture, art, and engineering—or at NYU, which had dormitories for undergraduates in and around the Village.

Reznick yawned.

Malone said, "You need to get more sleep, Jon, for Chrissakes! You look like shit."

"I'm fine."

"You can't be fine. You had four hours' sleep last night, and barely any in the previous forty-eight hours. You're gonna have a heart attack."

Maybe Malone was right. He didn't even know why he was scanning the photos. What was the point?

His mind was beginning to wander as he got to the last images, of staff employed at the Capital Grille restaurant. But then he pulled up the photograph of a very pretty young woman, Joan Wilson. Her hair was straight and long, her makeup subtle, and she wore tortoiseshell-framed spectacles.

Something about her face made him stop and stare. She looked familiar. Very familiar. His mind flashed back to the night Ford was served at the Grille, as Reznick ate at the bar, watching the Weather Channel. He remembered the waitress nodding politely as she took Ford's card and handing him a receipt.

"Pretty girl," Meyerstein said, looking over his shoulder.

Reznick shrugged. "Yeah. She served Ford in the Grille when I was there."

Meyerstein sat down. Almost immediately, her cell phone rang, and she got up again and went back into the adjacent room to take the call.

Reznick kept staring at the photo. His gaze lingered on the brown skin, dark eyes, and gentle smile. He'd seen her in the flesh, which was why he recognized her, but there was something else. Some other reason her face was stuck in his head.

He scrolled back to the top and started looking at all the photos again. Then he came across the reason why she looked so familiar.

A twenty-something girl named Stephanie Young, who worked at Yaffa—hair tied back, a dimple on her chin, wearing no makeup and no glasses, yet she was the double of Joan Wilson.

He scrolled back down to the photo of Joan Wilson: made up, hair down. More attractive. Glasses, which made her look older. He clicked on the image to make it bigger.

A dimple on the chin.

Reznick showed Malone and they compared the pictures.

"How weird is that?" Malone said.

"They could be the same person."

Malone winced. "I don't know—the girl in the restaurant looks a bit older, more mature, different eyes."

Malone called Meyerstein over. "Come and have a look at this. Are we talking one and the same?"

She studied the two pictures for nearly two minutes, side by side. She said nothing, her gaze fixed on one image, then the one beside it. "Son of a bitch."

"You think it's the same person?"

Meyerstein tilted her head slightly, as if looking at the face from a different angle. "I think we need to feed this into NGI."

"What's NGI?" Reznick said.

Meyerstein stared at the screen. "NGI? Next Generation Identification."

"The FBI's most sophisticated facial recognition software," Malone interjected. "Basically, it can distinguish between twins, and the 3-D face captures take us way beyond two-dimensional mug shots. It's also got some interesting face-aging elements."

Meyerstein called up Stamper. "Hey, Roy, pull up the shots of Joan Wilson and Stephanie Young. You got them?" She waited a few moments. "Yeah, that's them. Run them over to NGI, will you, and get back to me ASAP." She hung up and stared again at the images.

Twenty minutes later, her cell phone rang.

Meyerstein answered after one ring. "Talk to me, Roy." She nodded. "Get on it. Don't pull her in just now. Let's just do some more digging. Find out who she is and what she's all about. And when we do, get a twenty-four seven surveillance wraparound for her." She ended the call and looked first at Malone, then Reznick. "The photos are a hundred percent match. Without a shadow of doubt."

Malone leaned back in his seat and blew out his cheeks. "This just got a helluva lot more interesting."

A few minutes later, Meyerstein's cell phone rang again, and she switched to speaker so everyone could hear.

"Yeah, Roy?" she said, pinching the bridge of her nose.

Stamper sighed. "We're looking over the CCTV footage from the steakhouse on 42nd Street. I'm sending it over. Take a look for yourself."

They scanned the enhanced footage as the woman handed the check to Ford on a silver tray and left. He picked it up and looked over it for a few moments. He smiled as he took a ten-dollar bill out of his pocket and slid it under the tray, then got out his credit card. The waitress returned with a card machine and put Ford's card through the system, giving him the receipt with a smile. She took the money from under the tray, slipped it into her pants pocket and walked away to the next table. "She seemed to know there was money, despite it being covered," Meyerstein said.

Reznick folded his arms. "She's the cutout."

Meyerstein screwed up her face. "I don't think you can say that at this stage."

"I just did. Who the hell is she?"

Meyerstein leaned back in her seat and closed her eyes.

"What if she's a cutout and a cleanskin?" said Reznick. "Someone who doesn't arouse suspicion."

"You remember Richard Reid?"

Reznick nodded. "The would-be Shoe Bomber?"

"Not on anyone's radar."

Reznick rubbed his eyes, feeling tired.

Meyerstein looked at her watch. "In approximately fifteen minutes, I'm videoconferencing with the team back at McLean for the latest briefing. I'm sure we're going to get a fix on who this young woman is. She might be an illegal, using a false identity." Her cell phone rang, and again she switched it to speaker mode. "Yeah, Roy."

Stamper cleared his throat. "Our investigation is still ongoing into this woman, but I wanted to flag something."

"What is it?"

"The social security numbers have something in common."

"What?"

"They're both genuine numbers assigned to two women, neither of whom is the woman in the picture."

"I don't follow."

"I just got off the phone with the Social Security Administration. It does not invalidate or destroy original social security numbers when a new social security number is assigned."

"And?"

"Two separate women, victims of domestic violence—one in Ohio, the other Kansas. They both changed their names and were assigned new social security numbers. But their old numbers, these two separate numbers, are being used by the woman in this picture."

Meyerstein stared at the screen and ran her hand through her hair. "So who the hell is this woman?"

"That's the thing. We just don't know."

Fifteen

A tiny green light in the corner of the screen signaled that Meyerstein was hooked up to videoconference with McLean. The stern faces of Ed Froch of the State Department and Lieutenant General Black stared back at her as they hunched over a conference room table, papers in front of them.

Meyerstein sighed. "Gentlemen, you'll have had time to see the update we've sent through. It's more than a coincidence, her working in two places Ford has visited. Special Agent Stamper will draft an affidavit justifying the need for a search warrant. It may take time. But I think we need to close down this line of investigation and identify who this young woman is. It might be nothing, but we're not exactly inundated with strong leads."

Froch said, "I'm a State Department guy, Martha. My knowledge is foreign policy, terrorist threats. Do you mind if I play devil's advocate for a moment?"

Meyerstein shook her head. "Go right ahead."

"I think you're on the wrong track with this."

"I'm with Ed," Black interjected. "I just don't see where this New York angle is heading, Martha. The doctor is clean. She might just be a scam artist."

"That's a pretty sophisticated scam, if you don't mind me saying, sir."

"You want to know what the President's national security advisor said to me before I came into this conference?"

"What?"

"He wondered if I should hand over the reins to one of your colleagues within the Bureau. Someone with a counterterrorism background. But he also questioned your judgment."

"The national security advisor in question, sir, is an academic bed-wetter. He thinks because he teaches international security at Brown and he has the President's ear that he can run an operation like this. Well, you know what? He's wrong."

Black cleared his throat. "That may be." His voice had an edge to it. "But the national security advisor is concerned that Jon Reznick is on the team."

Meyerstein leaned forward. "Now, listen here. With respect, sir, I'm not going to take any lessons in procedure from some academic who has never investigated anything apart from chasing down students whose dissertations are a week overdue. And Ed, until the State Department gets a grip and comes up with any rationale or explanation as to why O'Grady contacted Caroline Lieber, I respectfully ask for you guys to stop the blame game. Do not try pointing the finger at a member of my team."

Froch shifted in his seat and his cheeks flushed red. "Look, we're no further forward than we were when O'Grady went missing. And now we're hearing about some young woman who served Ford in a steakhouse and might be using false ID? I mean, gimme a break."

Meyerstein inwardly seethed at the criticism. "It's not the fact that it's a false ID. It's the level of sophistication needed to obtain old social security numbers and the names of women—victims of domestic violence—who have assumed new identities. Standing alone, that information might not raise a red flag. But we need to run down this lead and see where it takes us."

Froch said, "How about the Iranian Interests Section? Isn't that where the focus should be?"

Meyerstein nodded. "That is where the main focus of our investigation is and will remain. We have that covered. Our teams are all reporting countersurveillance techniques being used. These are no dummies."

Froch steepled his fingers and turned to face Black. "I don't feel comfortable with Reznick being part of this. If this gets out, it'll be a mess."

Black nodded. "Martha, I expected his role to be more peripheral. Instead, reports have reached me that he was conducting a one-man surveillance operation in the Upper East Side. No backup, no plan, just him and this doctor. That needs to stop. And I say again, I don't want him on the team."

Meyerstein sighed. "I appreciate your concerns, and I'll make sure in future that there will be no more one-man operations. But I would say that without his surveillance, we wouldn't know what we know now."

On the screen, Froch stared back at her. She felt his withering look and shifted in her seat.

Meyerstein felt exhausted. The last few days had taken their toll on her. She was being touted as a candidate to be the first female director of the FBI. But she ignored all the internal political chatter about who was up or down within the Bureau. She was more interested the investigations, in bringing the bad guys down, than in schmoozing with colleagues after work. She drove herself hard. But she knew that she was gaining a reputation for taking risks, having previously used Reznick to work outside the rules. She had to be careful.

Meyerstein looked steadily at Froch and the others. She wasn't fazed. She didn't scare easy.

"So, any more questions?" she asked.

Froch leaned forward. "We're nowhere with this. I, for one, think Reznick should not be on this team. I don't see what he brings to the table."

Black nodded. "And you know my views on Reznick."

"Do I have your support, General Black?"

"I'll give you more time and support, but I want to let you know I'm reviewing your position."

Meyerstein went quiet for a few moments before she spoke. "I don't want distractions within my team. Everyone has to be pulling in the same direction. OK, I hear what you're saying. If you can leave it with me, I'll get back to you during our update meeting later today."

The screen went black as she ended the videoconference.

Meyerstein blew out her cheeks and picked up her cell phone to call home.

"Yeah, who's this?" The voice of her son Jacob.

"Hey, honey. I'm sorry, but I don't think I'm going to make your birthday party tomorrow."

"Oh, Mom, are you kidding me?"

"Sadly not. I want to say that I'll make it up to you."

"Mom, you promised!"

Meyerstein closed her eyes. She felt empty inside. "I know I did." The phone on the desk rang. "Listen, honey, I gotta go. Love you." She ended the call and took a few moments to compose herself before she picked up the other phone. "What's happening?"

"Ma'am, surveillance unit say the waitress with the false name is on the move. She's just emerged from her apartment in the East Village."

Meyerstein put down the phone and called Reznick into the room. She told him about the conversation she'd had with Black and Froch. "They want to fire your ass."

"You want me to walk?"

"Quite the opposite. I'm going to order a surveillance team to pick you up in fifteen minutes."

"Are you saying I'm still on the team?"

"That's exactly what I'm saying."

Sixteen

Meyerstein dialed Roy Stamper's direct line at FBI Headquarters in Washington.

"Roy, how far are we with the search warrant?"

Stamper sighed. "Martha, we got another problem."

Meyerstein had had her fill. "All you seem to be doing, Roy, is coming to me with problems. I need answers."

"Are you wanting to hear this or not?"

"Fine, go ahead."

"Look, I'm sorry. Here's where we're at. We drafted an affidavit justifying the need for a search warrant and sent it to the assistant attorney, who in turn drafted the search warrant. It was a real quick turnaround. But Judge Donald McCoy is refusing to sign."

"Are you kidding me?"

"Sadly not."

"On what grounds?"

"He said there weren't enough facts to give probable cause linking this woman to any national threat."

"Gimme a break, will you?"

"Wondering if we shouldn't just go warrantless. The Patriot Act allows search warrants to be issued without showing probable cause."

Meyerstein groaned. "Damn."

"What do you think?"

"I think you're forgetting the Mayfield case."

It was Stamper's turn to groan. Meyerstein was referring to an infamous warrantless FBI incident, when Portland attorney Brandon Mayfield, a Muslim convert, was mistakenly linked to the 2004 Madrid train bombings.

She remembered the case well. It was deemed that two provisions were unconstitutional. And the court ruled that evidence obtained through a Fourth Amendment violation was generally not admissible during a defendant's criminal trial.

Meyerstein's father had made her memorize all the amendments of the Constitution as a little girl, including the Fourth . . .

The right of the people to be secure in their persons, houses, papers, and effects, against unreasonable searches and seizures, shall not be violated, and no warrants shall issue, but upon probable cause, supported by oath or affirmation, and particularly describing the place to be searched, and the persons or things to be seized.

Stamper sighed. "Damn, of course. You want me to try another judge?"

Meyerstein looked across at Malone, who was tapping away on his laptop. "Wasting our time."

"What about the Foreign Intelligence Surveillance Court?"

Meyerstein closed her eyes for a moment. The Court oversaw top-secret requests for surveillance on suspected foreign intelligence agents. But since 2013, when it was leaked to the media that the court had approved a warrant ordering Verizon to provide all call-detail records to be sent to the NSA, it had been very difficult to get their approval without delays or modifications to the warrant. "Not an option in this climate."

"So I assume we just continue the surveillance on this woman?"

"Absolutely. Until we know who she is, we tail her."

He let out a long sigh. "Sure." He went quiet for a few moments. "You OK? You don't sound like yourself."

"No, I'm not OK. But thanks for asking." A long silence opened up between them as Meyerstein mulled things over, her mind racing. "We're missing something, Roy," she said. "We just aren't there."

Meyerstein ended the call. She sat down and closed her eyes, wondering if she had lost a sense of perspective. She ran through the options. Option one: they watch and wait. Option two: send in an FBI search team, who could undertake a sweep of the woman's apartment. Option three: send in Reznick. He could do the same as the search team, but if his cover was blown, he was just breaking into an apartment. He would give a false ID, and Stamper could get him out.

She called the head of the surveillance team, who were half a block from the woman's apartment in the East Village.

"Ramon, it's Assistant Director Martha Meyerstein."

"Ma'am, you looking for an update?"

"Very quick."

"She's been out for twenty-seven minutes. Mobile surveillance says she's just entered the Capital Grille."

"What do we know about her apartment?"

"It's in a brownstone on East 7th Street, just down the block from Tompkins Square Park. It's a walk-up, three flights. No neighbors on the same floor, so that's a plus. But it has video security."

"Damn."

"Don't worry about that. We got an electronics guy with us who can shut that off if required."

"Fine, do it right now. Jon Reznick will go in. I want you to be his eyes and ears. If she returns unexpectedly, that kind of thing."

Ramon sighed. "You want Reznick to go in?"

"I'll take the heat. Get him kitted out."

"What's the legal authority?"

"I'm giving you the authority. Have you got a problem with that?"

"No, ma'am."

"Hand me over to Reznick."

A few moments of silence before Reznick came on the line.

"Hi, how's it going?"

"Jon, I want a clean search, just by you. Nothing disturbed. We need an ID on this woman. Ramon will give you an ultraviolet light scanner to pick up latent prints. You know how to work it?"

Reznick cleared his throat. "Not a problem."

"Be careful. No one can know you've been in the apartment."

"You don't have to explain."

"You have fifteen minutes. Not a minute more."

Seventeen

Reznick sat crouched in the back of a van in the East Village, half a block away from the mystery woman's apartment.

"OK, Jon," a voice said in his earpiece, "you're good to go. Nice and easy."

Reznick picked up the backpack he'd been given and stepped out of the van, carefully locking the door behind him. Then he walked the fifty yards or so up to the entrance. He punched a preset code into the building's keypad and the door clicked open. He'd been told that the surveillance camera used inside had been deactivated remotely, giving him a clear run. He got inside, glad to be out of the sun, and walked up the three flights of stone stairs.

He knocked at the door to apartment 7 and waited. Silence. He examined the lock. It was a basic double-cylinder deadbolt, as he'd been told. He knocked again. No answer.

Reznick took out a bump key, slid it into the lock, and turned. A soft click, and it was open.

A long hallway with whitewashed walls, modern art, and dark hardwood floors. He stepped inside and shut the door. "That's me inside," he said.

Ramon said, "Nice and careful, Jon. We want to keep it as it is."

"Yeah, I got that memo."

Down the hallway and right into a loft-style lounge. Two beige sofas, and bookcases filled with books on two walls. A glass table in the center with a Madonna biography, and neat piles of art history books and issues of *Vogue*.

Through a door at the far end of the room was a tiny kitchenette. A stainless-steel refrigerator and freezer, small stove, and two cabinets. Dirty dishes were strewn on the white-oak worktop. He picked up a used glass, ideal for a set of prints.

Reznick opened up his backpack and pulled out the ultraviolet light, which looked like a home projector. He ran the fan before he switched on the power. The Luma Lite had a high-intensity arc tube. It detected blood, semen, fingerprints, and trace evidence.

He put on his orange-tinted glasses and began scanning the glass. Almost immediately, the blue light picked up fingerprints.

"Bingo," he said.

He did the same on the stainless steel kettle, once again picking up numerous fingerprints. The images were then wirelessly downloaded to an iPad for analysis by the Feds.

He packed the equipment away and headed through to the small bathroom, painted aqua blue, with navy and white mosaic tiling throughout and a shower in the corner. He noticed a hairbrush beside a small mirror. He tweezed a hair sample into a plastic evidence bag, and packed it in a side pocket of his backpack.

Then he went into each room, photographing the layout, the books, the artwork, the family pictures. It would all help build up a profile of the woman who lived there.

Lastly, he got to the bedroom, which doubled as a study. A Dell desktop computer on a small worktable was switched on.

Reznick hooked it up via USB cable to an external hard drive he'd brought with him. The screen came to life, and he downloaded all the files on the computer in less than two minutes. He disconnected the cable.

"How you doing, Jon?"

"One minute and I'll be out of here," he said, packing the hard drive and cable into the heavy bag. He searched the closet and rifled in the dresser. Nothing of note.

Reznick took one final look around the apartment before he left, relocking the door, no one any the wiser.

He checked his watch. It had taken him just eleven minutes to complete the black bag operation.

Eighteen

Meyerstein was staring at a mug shot of a haggard young woman on her laptop when Reznick returned.

"Very good work, Jon," she said. "We got a match."

Reznick leaned forward and studied the woman's face. "Jeez, has she had a face transplant?"

"Funny. This is Chantelle McGovern, aged twenty-eight. A former drug addict and dealer. The Integrated Automated Fingerprint Identification System confirms the match."

Reznick shook his head. "What's her story now?"

"She's now a political science student at NYU. Five years ago, aged twenty-three, she pleaded no contest to heroin possession with intent to sell. Police found more than thirteen thousand dollars' worth of drugs in her rented car during a traffic stop in Queens. But she's been clean since."

Meyerstein signaled across to one of her team. "Jimmy, where are we with the full picture on McGovern? How long has she been living in the East Village? How is she affording the tuition?"

Jimmy looked up from his computer screen. He looked as though he hadn't slept in days, dark circles around his eyes. He was one of

Meyerstein's trusted technology experts, and she knew he would push himself to the edge to get what the strategic analysts needed.

"I'm on it, ma'am."

"I want computer analysis back to me ASAP." She turned to Reznick. "Roy is also working this, from a different angle. We'll have something to go on soon. I know it."

They didn't have to wait long. Ten minutes later, Roy Stamper was on the line. Meyerstein switched it to speaker mode.

"Chantelle's place of birth is down as New York City on her student records. But we've checked. That's not correct."

"And?"

"Her brother spent ten years in Stateville Correctional Center in Illinois for armed robbery. That's where he converted to Islam. Now goes by the name Jamal Ali."

The news sent a buzz of excitement around the room. It was the first possible break.

Meyerstein looked across at Reznick, who was deep in thought, brow furrowed.

"She's the cutout," he said.

Meyerstein looked across at Malone. "What are you thinking, Dr. Malone?"

Malone was biting the end of his pen. "A picture could be emerging, Martha. We still have nothing on Ford. But the obscure connection to this woman—in two separate places—and now her brother . . . We might be on to something."

"How long will we have to wait on computer analysis of McGovern's laptop?" asked Reznick.

"That'll take time," Jimmy said. "Initial analysis shows it's heavily encrypted. We believe there are hundreds—maybe thousand— of photos, documents, bits of correspondence, perhaps diaries. And we'll have to check for embedded data. Steganography experts are looking through what we've got as we speak."

"A Muslim connection, huh?" said Reznick.

Meyerstein closed her eyes for a moment. "It's important we don't get too carried away at this stage."

"Where does this leave us?"

"We need to know more about Chantelle. Her time in jail is important. She's vulnerable. Impressionable. Angry. A very potent combination. And with an Islamic convert brother, a picture is emerging."

"You think she's a convert?"

"Could be."

"No sign of headscarves or anything like that."

Meyerstein sighed. "Please."

"We need to locate the brother. And fast."

Meyerstein's cell phone rang. She saw from the caller ID it was Lieutenant General Black, and she got up and went through to the small windowless room she had been using as an office. She shut the door and sat down, the air conditioning growling low in the background. She closed her eyes. She knew what was coming.

"I want to see you now," he said. "Face to face. Right now."

"Robert, I've got a hundred and one things to deal with."

"Now."

Meyerstein sighed.

"I think you know why I want to speak to you, Martha. This is getting out of hand. And you're breaking the law."

"Under the Patriot Act, sir . . ."

"I don't want to hear about the Patriot Act. This is serious. I want answers."

"Robert, I'm in New York. I need to be here. We have a developing situation—we could have a cutout. I need to chase this down."

Black sighed, long and hard. "I don't like the methods you've employed."

"The judge refused to sign and I didn't want to risk a warrant-less search. This was a third way."

"An illegal way, Martha."

"Sir, that's the call I made. And it's the call I'll stand by."

Black hung up.

Meyerstein felt more isolated than she'd ever felt working for the FBI. She was starting to wonder when and if the investigation would ever end. But the more she thought about it, she more she knew that she had to do things on her terms.

"Son of a bitch," she said, walking out of the office and back to the table where Reznick and Malone were hunched over a laptop, reading a file on Chantelle's brother.

Reznick looked up at her and smiled. "Someone bustin' your ass?"

"We live to fight another day."

Norris, one of the Feds in the monitoring room adjacent, shouted through, "Ma'am, she's back in the East Village."

"Back home?"

"Nearby. Come and have a look."

Meyerstein and Reznick crowded around Norris's screen. They watched Chantelle enter a Laundromat and pick up a bag of laundry. She smiled and struck up a conversation with a middle-aged man wearing traditional Muslim dress.

"Coin-operated Laundromat," Meyerstein said. "Where exactly is this?"

"At the corner of First Avenue and East 11th Street, ma'am."

"Who runs it? Who owns it?"

"Pulled it up already. One-man operation. Owned by a Mohammed Akhtar. Came from Bangladesh in the early seventies."

Meyerstein clicked her fingers excitedly. "Get the surveillance team to split up. Two on Chantelle, and two on Mr. Akhtar."

Norris picked up a headset and cleared his throat before repeating the message. Then he turned to Meyerstein. "You're gonna love this."

"Love what?"

Norris spoke into the headset. "Team Two, give me a diagonal line of sight from the Laundromat."

Meyerstein watched the camera pan around a busy intersection and then zoom in on a redbrick building on the corner diagonally opposite. She read the words on the sign.

"Islamic Council of America. You gotta be kidding me."

"It's one of the few mosques in Lower Manhattan. Akhtar attends this mosque. He lives above the Laundromat with his wife and five kids."

"Is he clean?"

"As far as we can see."

"This changes everything, people. I want Team Two on him around the clock. I want to know who he meets up with, where he goes, what he has for dinner."

Reznick leaned in closer. "It's perfect cover. She drops off laundry, she picks up laundry. How easy would that be for messages to be exchanged? No need to worry about electronic surveillance. It's old-school tradecraft."

Meyerstein sighed. "Let's not get ahead of ourselves, Jon."

"This is a clear Islamic connection."

"But there's a difference between Islamic and Islamists."

"Nuance was never my thing," Reznick said.

Meyerstein turned to Norris. "We need to feed this into counterterrorism and carry out an urgent review of what we have."

Norris nodded. "You got it."

Meyerstein pointed at the real-time footage of the Laundromat. "Is she still in there?"

Just as Norris was about to answer, on screen the door opened and Chantelle McGovern emerged, wearing sunglasses and carrying a bag of laundry. The surveillance switched to footage from Team 1, who tailed her back to her apartment.

Meyerstein turned and looked at Reznick. "What do you think?"

"I think we need to wake the fuck up and smell the coffee."

An hour later, as Meyerstein was reviewing new intelligence analysis from her team, Assistant Director Sam Chisholm—the FBI's most senior counterterrorism official assigned to the special access program besides Meyerstein—was on speakerphone. "Martha, we're getting up to speed with what you've got, and we've done some preliminary analysis."

"Where are we at, Sam?"

"I think the watch-and-wait was the right call. But there are enough elements to seriously concern us. I think there's something here."

"What?"

"It could be a clandestine cell structure. The problem is how Ford fits into this. We just don't get him. He's not on our radar."

"What about Chantelle McGovern, or her brother Jamal?"

"It's interesting. I've got people trying to find out where this guy Jamal is . . . Nothing. The last known address was in DC and that was three years ago. Since then? Nothing. As for Chantelle? Just what we know already. Nothing new."

"Sam, what have you got on this mosque?"

"Well, this Akhtar guy we know about. He's a long-standing, senior member of this mosque. We have a source in there. Today's Friday, so after evening prayers they'll head to an apartment down in one of the projects along the East River, for Koran discussions and study."

Meyerstein sighed. "Yeah, I bet. OK, we need more from your source, Sam. I need to know about everything and everyone linked to Akhtar and Chantelle. We need to integrate our two efforts. Let's hook up our teams for this and I'll oversee operations. I'll send Reznick to meet up with you."

Nineteen

The sky was darkening as the SUV headed down East 10th Street and turned right onto the FDR. Reznick sat in the back and stared out at the redbrick housing projects that towered over the area. FBI Counterterrorism Division Chief Sam Chisholm sat next to him, radio crackling in the background. It had been less than forty-eight hours since Reznick had followed the DC surgeon down to this nearly forgotten part of the East Village. The projects on Avenue D were ugly, no getting away from it. And they seemed like a stark reminder of the crime-ridden 1970s and 1980s, when this part of Manhattan was not synonymous with cool bars and bistros.

Three separate surveillance crews were working the area that night, all concentrating on Akhtar. Reznick's job was just as an extra pair of eyes and ears.

Chisholm pressed his earpiece in tight. "Our guy is heading toward one of the houses on East 6th Street. Mobile surveillance is on him. He's on foot, with two other guys from the mosque."

They turned onto East 6th Street and pulled up outside a side entrance to one of the Riis houses. Chisholm pointed to the green door of another Riis house, across the street.

"That's the one. Third floor."

Reznick focused. "So what do we know?"

"Well, it seems like every Friday night, after sunset prayers, a handful of the regulars at the mosque, including Akhtar, pop in here. Our guy inside is wired up. Let's see if it's just a Koran class or something we need to worry about."

"How long till they turn up?"

"Matter of minutes."

Reznick listened to the surveillance team setting up in an empty apartment directly opposite the address being used by those under investigation.

A man's voice said, "They're all heading up the street now—Akhtar and his usual bearded friends from the mosque. Our man is already there. Sit back and enjoy the show, guys."

They watched the shaky surveillance footage as the trio pressed the apartment buzzer beside the green door and went inside. A few moments later, footage appeared on Chisholm's iPad showing the group hugging each other.

The sound of *as-salaam alaikums* filled the vehicle.

Reznick sat and listened. For a few moments, the voices took him back to Afghanistan. To talking to village elders in the mountainous tribal areas. The taste of the tea that was passed around. The smells.

The sound of uproarious laughing on the iPad snapped Reznick back to the present. The men under surveillance were now sitting cross-legged on the floor in a circle as tea was served.

Eventually the meeting came to an end, and Chisholm instructed the driver to pull away and park on First Avenue, with a clear line of sight to the Laundromat.

Chisholm said, "The guys in the apartment are the same crowd every week. Same talk. But it never goes any further."

Reznick nodded.

A short while later, a car dropped Akhtar off outside his shop. He waved goodbye to his friends and headed to his apartment upstairs.

Chisholm sighed. "Got a feeling that's it for another night."

He was right. A couple more lights went on upstairs, but less than an hour later the apartment was in darkness.

Just before 2 a.m., a backup night shift surveillance vehicle pulled in one hundred yards up the street. "Time to refuel," Chisholm said, and he ordered their driver over to Sunny & Annie's, a 24/7 deli on the corner of Avenue B and East 6th Street, one block from Tompkins Square Park. There they bought sandwiches, Vietnamese soup, and huge Styrofoam cups of coffee.

As they sat in the back of the SUV having wolfed the food, drinking the dregs of the strong coffee, they saw a crowd of around a dozen teenagers, nearly a block away on the opposite side of the street, attacking a young guy. They rained down punches and kicks as he lay helpless on the ground, and ran off with his cell phone and wallet. It was over in seconds. No one stopped to help.

Chisholm shook his head. "What a fucking sewer."

Reznick sat and stared at the poor kid writhing on the sidewalk, only yards from a neon-lit bar. He'd just been a guy heading home after a night out. Now he was another casualty of the street.

The team drove back to First Avenue and resumed their position near the Laundromat.

Shortly after 5 a.m., a light above the Laundromat went on. An hour later, Akhtar emerged onto the street. He headed across to the mosque and opened it up, turning on the lights inside.

The night shadows disappeared like ghosts as dawn broke. Just after 6:30 a.m., men began to arrive at the mosque for the Salat al-Ishraq post-sunrise prayer.

The sidewalks became busier. The hustle and dirt and grime of a blazing hot day, kicked up by passing cars on First Avenue. The SUV's driver cranked up the AC a notch. The cool air felt good.

After early-morning prayers, the worshippers went their separate ways with handshakes and hugs. Just before eight, Akhtar emerged, locking up the mosque before he turned and walked down East 6th Street.

"Where's he headed now?" the driver said.

Chisholm yawned and leaned forward, and tapped him on the shoulder. "Just stay where we are, and let Team One cover him." He held a radio to his mouth. "Team One, do you copy? It's over to you."

The driver nodded. "Got it."

Half an hour later, a voice crackled on the radio. "OK, he's headed into the Baruch Houses at the corner on Delancey Street. Overlooking the Williamsburg Bridge."

"How far's that?" Reznick asked.

"Mile and a half, give or take. Lower East Side."

Chisholm spoke into the radio again. "Keep on his tail."

"Yeah, I got that. Stand by."

Chisholm tapped the driver on the shoulder again. "Let's drive over there, park up on Delancey."

The driver nodded and pulled away from First Avenue, heading over to the FDR. In the distance, the giant steel shadow of the Williamsburg Bridge loomed large over the neighborhood. Reznick could see the grim, crime-ridden Baruch public housing, almost identical to the Riis projects.

Chisholm dialed a number on his cell. "Karen, it's Sam. Baruch housing project . . . I need to know if there are cameras either inside or outside any of these apartment blocks." A brief pause. "Shit. OK, thanks."

Chisholm shook his head as the driver cut right onto Delancey and pulled into a parking space near a side entrance door. "Not one damn camera for seventeen separate Baruch buildings. Not one."

The radio crackled into life. "We have no number for the building—been ripped off—but Jeff is in. He's identified it as having the word *BOYZ* in black spray paint across the blue door. And he's on eleven."

The minutes passed by but there was no word from Jeff Morales, the agent on the ground. Chisholm tapped on his cell phone's plastic casing. Reznick stared at the graffitied blue door of the side entrance. He wondered if Morales was in an elevator, unable to talk or relay where the target had gone.

Reznick's mind was racing. He wondered if something had gone wrong. Why was it taking Morales so long to respond?

Chisholm bit his lower lip. "Where the hell is he?"

A voice over the radio said, "Stand by." Time seemed to slow down.

Chisholm began to grind his teeth and tap his fingers. "It's taking too long. This doesn't feel right."

Reznick turned to him. "Let me go in and have a look."

Chisholm nodded. "You packing?"

"Yup."

"Just be careful."

Reznick headed across to the blue door and found it was open, despite having a controlled entry system. Inside was graffiti all over the walls and the smell of piss and bleach and old booze and smoke. Even the ceiling had a black blotch of graffiti emblazoned on the concrete.

"You OK, Jon?" The voice of Chisholm in his earpiece.

"I'm fine. I'm taking the stairs."

Before he entered the stairwell, the elevator lights showed that it was making its way down from the eleventh floor.

Ten. Then nine.

It stopped at nine, then kept going.

Eight. Seven.

His senses were all switched on. He positioned himself in an alcove so whoever came out of the elevator wouldn't see him.

Six. Five. Four. Three. Two. One.

The elevator didn't open. Reznick waited a moment before walking over and pressing the button. The doors remained shut. He pulled a penknife out of his back pocket and tried to pry the doors open. Again, nothing.

Reznick headed up the stairs. The soft rubber soles of his Rockports meant his steps were virtually noise-free. His breathing quickened as he climbed higher. Step by step. He reached the third floor and saw that the elevator was still stuck on eleven—or, more likely, was just broken.

The light in the stairwell was bad. The smell was musty, damp, and smoky; cigarette butts, trash strewn everywhere. Graffiti scrawled on doors: *Lower East Side Boys, Baruch Boyz.*

The names of girls; phone numbers for "girlz."

The sound of hip-hop from a nearby apartment. Higher and higher he climbed. He was on seven, heading up to eight.

Onto the landing at eight, and two tough-looking kids were smoking, hats at an angle, pants down low.

"Yo, whitey, you got a lightey?"

The kid grinned like an imbecile and stepped in front of Reznick.

Reznick reached into his back pocket as if to give them a light. Instead, he pulled out a 9mm Beretta from his waistband and pressed it to the kid's forehead. "No, I haven't got a fucking light."

The kid's eyes went wide. "Man, I don't want no trouble."

"Disappear, you dumb fuck."

They scrambled downstairs.

Reznick headed up to the ninth. It was deathly quiet. Up to ten and then toward eleven.

He was in the zone.

Each step, he was edging closer. But closer to what? The silence was bad. He sensed Morales was in trouble. He reached eleven and went into the hallway. His brain sent the signal but it short-circuited for a split second.

Lying sprawled on the floor inside the elevator door was a man, blood pouring from a wound to the neck. It was Morales.

Reznick shouted into his lapel microphone, "Man down, immediate assistance on eleven!" Then he rushed over to Morales and checked his pulse. Weak, but still alive. He ripped off his shirt and pressed it against the fallen Fed's neck.

Morales tried to open his eyes as blood seeped through the light blue shirt, the top of which had already turned dark red.

"Don't move, man," Reznick said. "We're gonna get you out of here."

Morales opened his mouth to speak. "N . . . Ni . . ."

"What is it?"

"Nine." The word came out gargled, thick with blood. "Ninth floor. White door. I tried to escape. Black guy. He's the—"

A man ran past them and darted downstairs.

"I need help, eleventh floor!"

"We're coming in, Jon." Chisholm's voice.

Reznick squeezed Morales's hands. "Help's on the way. I gotta go, man." He didn't want to leave.

Morales managed to nod, eyes glassy.

"Hang in there."

Reznick headed down the stairs after the figure, two steps at a time. "I'm coming down, Chisholm. Suspect may be heading your way. Get a paramedic up to the eleventh, right fucking now!"

The sound of a gunshot.

Shouting. Screaming. The smashing of glass.

Reznick careened down to the first floor, where he carefully swept the area with his 9mm. He saw the body of a burly surveillance guy from Team One lying motionless beside an exit door, blood pouring from a neck wound.

Reznick didn't have to check. He knew the guy was dead.

He ran out of the building just in time to see a man running toward the thundering traffic on the FDR, out of sight of Chisholm's team.

His lungs were burning, his sinews nearly snapping.

The man was about fifty yards ahead of Reznick. He wore dark clothing. He turned around and saw Reznick gaining ground.

He hurdled concrete barriers and ran onto the freeway, cars screeching to a halt or swerving to avoid him. He climbed over a fence and was on the East River bike path.

Reznick's mind was racing as fast as his heart. He had to catch this guy before he disappeared for good.

He hurdled the metal divider and narrowly avoided being hit by oncoming traffic. Then under the Williamsburg Bridge and hurtling toward the smokestacks in the distance.

He was now thirty yards behind.

Up ahead, on a green metal pedestrian bridge that spanned the FDR, four Feds were heading toward the bike path, blocking off an escape route.

They had him.

Reznick was closing in. The man glanced back at Reznick, desperation in his eyes. He knew Reznick was going to catch him.

Ten yards. Heart pumping blood.

Suddenly, the guy darted off to his right, vaulted back over the fence, and ran straight toward an oncoming truck.

The screeching of tires, the blare of horns, and screaming from bystanders as the man was crushed under the wheels of the massive truck.

Twenty

The seconds that followed seemed like a lifetime to Reznick. It was as if he were unable to wake up from a bad dream. The horrified faces of the motorists, snarled-up lines of cars, the truck driver being sick on his knees beside the twisted, partially limbless body still under the wheels of his truck. Blood spilling onto the freeway.

Reznick leaped over the fence and crawled underneath the truck. The smell of warm blood, gasoline, and oil. He rifled through the pockets of the man's pants. He pulled out a wallet from the back pocket and looked inside. A driver's license. *Walter Irving. May 4, 1981.*

When he crawled back out, blood on his hands, a passing jogger screamed.

Reznick vaulted back over the fence and headed in the direction of the surveillance van. He held his lapel mike to his mouth. "Chisholm, he's dead. Got his ID—Walter Irving."

Chisholm sighed. "What the fuck happened?"

"I found Morales on eleven. Heard the guy make a run for it and went after him. Where's Akhtar?"

"We got him. Hiding in an apartment on the ninth."

"How's Morales?"

"Touch and go. Special Agent Tim Mallory from Team One didn't make it."

"Fuck."

"You better get the hell out of there before the news choppers catch you on the scene. We'll take it from here."

Less than an hour later, Reznick was back at The Fairfax, and had showered and changed into new clothes. The blood-soaked clothes he'd been wearing had been bagged for forensics.

When he went through to the hub of the apartment, Meyerstein was pacing the room on the phone. "Call me back when you have anything, Roy. We're on the right track."

She ended the call and stood, hands on hips.

"What the hell happened out there?" she asked.

Reznick went through the story again.

"What a fuck-up."

"It is what it is."

Meyerstein said nothing, eyes hooded. She looked like she was close to physical collapse. But she also had a determination etched on her face he hadn't seen before.

"Look, I know we lost a man and Morales is fighting for his life. These things happen."

"Don't you think I know that? I knew both of them. Good men." She sighed. "We're hoping Morales pulls through."

Reznick slumped onto a chair, head in hands. "Goddamn . . ."

"I think we're all hurting."

He looked up. "A guy like Morales doesn't want sympathy. He'd want us to hunt down these bastards."

Meyerstein sighed. "I know that."

"OK, tell me about this guy that was living on the ninth floor."

"We've got a laptop, which we're analyzing as we speak."

"What about Akhtar?"

"Not a word. He wants a lawyer, that's all he's said. No explanation of why he was at the apartment. Was that man a friend? What was his real name?"

Reznick nodded. "We're peeling this back."

"We have nothing. We have a dead guy with a false name, a Laundromat Muslim, and—" Her cell phone rang. She listened to the call, expressionless. Then she screwed up her face. "Are we sure about that?" She nodded. "Good work. But I don't want any delays. Get it to me ASAP."

She ended the call and Reznick said, "Who was that?"

"Forensics lab. Fingerprints were taken at the scene. They could have a result in less than an hour." She shook her head. "This is just a mess."

Reznick sighed. "There was a link, and it had to be chased down."

"Couldn't he have been taken down before he reached the freeway?"

"I didn't foresee the fucker running straight into oncoming traffic."

Meyerstein closed her eyes. "Tell me about Morales."

"Knife wound to the throat."

She stared back at him, glassy-eyed. There was a haunted quality to her look, as if the whole investigation was bearing down on her. Morales fighting for his life seemed to have been the final straw.

"He has a wife and four kids. His superior has just visited them in Brooklyn to give them the news. I can only imagine what they're going through."

Reznick was silent.

"Just doing his job." She threw the pen she was holding down on the table. "Just doing his goddamn job!"

"Take it easy."

"No, I won't take it easy, Jon. He's a highly decorated special agent. I know him. I worked with him shortly after I joined the Bureau. He was always there when the deal went down. Always."

Half an hour later, her cell phone rang. She answered on the third ring.

"Meyerstein. Talk to me." She nodded a few times. "Are we certain? I mean, one hundred percent certain?"

She hung up and blew out her cheeks. "We got something. The lab has a preliminary result. It's not conclusive at this stage, as they still have to do more tests. But there's a high probability it's who we're looking for."

"Who is he?"

"You were right, Jon. You were right all along."

"Who?"

"Jamal Ali. The older brother of Chantelle McGovern."

A buzz spread around the room. Meyerstein clapped her hands together and brought the room to order.

"People!" she said, raising her voice. "Time to refocus. There are clear Islamic links, but still nothing to tie Ford in. So, let's recap what we have. O'Grady, Lieber, Ford. Then McGovern, Akhtar, and Jamal Ali. What's their game? And why did Ali decide to take his own life?"

Reznick was handed a coffee by Malone. "Thanks. Almost certainly indicates a radicalized mindset, perhaps part of a group about to target New York. And he'd have been trained to die, rather than be captured and give up any secrets or information." He looked at Malone. "What's your take on this? You've gone all quiet."

Malone sat down at a desk. "I'm interested in this thread from Ford to McGovern to Akhtar and Jamal."

"Give me some odds on what you know," said Meyerstein.

Malone blew out his cheeks. "I'm not a betting man, as you know. But if I was, I'd say that the odds are we have a sleeper cell, and perhaps O'Grady woke them up, either by accident or design."

"We need Akhtar to talk."

Reznick moved to Meyerstein's side. "Let me try."

She was tempted. "We're in New York, not Guantanamo, Jon. Let's bring in his wife and two eldest sons. See if that shakes him up." She looked across at Malone. "What do you think?"

Malone nodded. "Depends on the state of mind of the individual. Sometimes, if the detainee believes their loved ones are under duress or suffering, they'll tell us what we want to know."

"Yeah, I'm well aware of that, Malone," Meyerstein snapped.

"What about McGovern?" Reznick asked. "We need to bring her in? Confront her with Jamal's death?"

Meyerstein ran a hand through her hair. "Let's not rush things. We have a media blackout on this. Let's see what her next move is."

Malone smiled. "Makes sense."

Meyerstein looked at her watch. "Look, I need to bring everyone back at the National Counterterrorism Center, including General Black, up to speed. Jon, I want you to sit in on this."

Reznick shrugged. "Fair enough."

They went through to the adjoining room and sat down in front of the screen as Meyerstein tapped in the encrypted video-conference code to link with the team in McLean.

She outlined the recent developments in a cool and rational manner. They listened. This time, there were no threats to take her off the investigation. An Islamic link was emerging. The big problem was still Ford.

Black didn't mention Reznick's presence at all, but he belabored the point about Ford. "On what we have so far," he said, "it could strictly be a coincidence that Ford had contact with McGovern."

Meyerstein avoided responding to the general's concerns. "Gentlemen, we have work to do. I will update you at eighteen hundred hours. Thank you."

As she was disconnecting the videoconference call, the desk phone rang. She switched it to speaker mode.

"Martha, it's Roy. It's all happening."

Meyerstein grimaced. "What's up, Roy?"

"Something's cooking."

"Tell me, for Chrissakes." She looked at Reznick and shook her head, as if she were used to Stamper being long-winded.

"I've just been told by the team looking into Ford's history, personal, and employment, that there is, in their words, a 'discrepancy.'"

"What kind of discrepancy?"

"All I know is that the timelines don't appear to be accurate."

"In what way?"

Stamper let out a long sigh. "That's all I know. They're still piecing it together. But it's his time working for the Red Cross that doesn't tally. Perhaps it's an administrative error, perhaps a wrong date given by him . . . we just don't know."

"When will they be able to confirm?"

"They're working flat-out on this."

"How long?"

"Honestly? I have no idea."

"I'm updating General Black and the rest of the team at eighteen hundred hours, Roy. So I want to know everything there is to know about this discrepancy by seventeen thirty at the latest. Understood?"

There was no response. Stamper had already hung up.

Twenty-One

It was dark and the air was like a steam bath as Ford stood on the Gapstow Bridge in Central Park. He was partially concealed by the canopy of leaves from the overhanging trees beside the pond.

He took a few moments to drink in the scene. The New York skyscrapers towering in the distance. He marveled at the city—this place where America met the world. It felt great to be cloaked in a pleasing darkness in the beating heart of America.

The park was still busy: night joggers, tourists, and people taking photographs of their friends with their cell phones.

Ford took off his backpack and reached inside for his Nikon camera, which sported a huge paparazzi-sized telephoto lens. He took off the lens cap and pressed his eye against the viewfinder, focusing on a terrace high up at The Plaza. He brought it into sharp focus. The infrared night vision showed two loungers, a dark table bathed in a warm light from the penthouse, and no drapes or blinds to block the view. Inside, he could make out the edge of a white sofa, and flowers in a vase on a bookshelf. He couldn't believe his luck. This was a perfect spot. Would this be the one?

The more he thought of what lay ahead, the more a raw energy surged through his body like an electric current. Something primeval.

He thought of the headlines to come. He could see his name in bold black print. He could see his picture. They would remember him. But, more than that, they would remember what he stood for.

He carefully replaced the lens cap and put the camera back in his bag, slung it over his shoulder, and walked off deeper into the park. He sensed people were watching him. But nothing more than that. He hadn't actually seen any tails. He'd been too careful.

His cell phone rang.

"Your first trip to the drop zone awaits."

"Are we all set?"

"It's all been taken care of. We just want you to go there, acquaint yourself with the surroundings and people." A silence opened up for a few moments. "How are you enjoying New York?"

Ford smelled the cut grass and the moisture in the air. The blossoms from the trees. And the smell of hot dogs, drifting across the park. "Not a city in the world like it. What a place."

"It just feels so right, doesn't it? You're a very lucky man."

Ford took a deep breath, and felt his heart swell with pride. "I know."

"Some of your backup team had some useful target practice with that panhandler from the East Village. He won't be clogging up any more soup kitchens."

Ford smiled but said nothing.

"OK, this is the one word you need in the drop zone."

"Shoot."

"The city of your birth."

Washington. "Got it."

"We're going to keep mixing things up but will reach you whichever way we have to."

Ford smiled, and looked back at the lights of The Plaza in the distance. He knew what that meant.

"Whatever it takes, I will not fail you. I will not fail America."

"We're counting on it. Till the next time, my friend. Stay safe."

Twenty-Two

Reznick was floating on a black sea, an inky sky overhead. He heard ringing and wondered where it was coming from. He opened his eyes and realized he was in The Fairfax, and it was dark outside. The ringing had stopped.

He sat up in bed and heard voices outside his room. Meyerstein was talking in hushed tones. But there was also the gruff voice of counterterrorism expert Sam Chisholm, his voice slightly raised.

He splashed cold water on his face, cleaned his teeth, showered and shaved, and pulled on a clean set of clothes the Feds had provided. Chinos, black T-shirt, and his Rockport shoes. He put on his watch. It showed 10:42 p.m.

He went through to the main room and poured himself a coffee. Chisholm nodded at him. "Hey, Jon, how you doing?"

"Felt better. What's the latest?"

Chisholm looked across at Meyerstein, who was sitting beside Malone, eyes scanning her laptop. Then he stared at Reznick. "What happened this morning has changed a lot of our thinking . . ."

"In what way?"

"Our guys are working around the clock on this. And we're beginning to see a threat. O'Grady's call to Caroline Lieber, her disappearance, and her friendship with Ford. We just couldn't figure it out. But after what happened earlier, things are becoming a bit clearer."

"You wanna explain?"

Chisholm scratched his clean-shaven chin and looked across at Meyerstein. "Am I OK to give this out?"

Meyerstein nodded. "Jon is part of this team."

Chisholm pulled up a seat and sat down. "Ford was assigned as a junior doctor to the UN's Office for the Coordination of Humanitarian Affairs in April 2005. He worked in Rwanda, Albania, Angola, Burundi, Eritrea, Sudan . . . you name it. The guy is considered to be a great humanitarian as well as a brilliant surgeon and doctor. Saved children's limbs. Saved countless lives. We have plenty of photographic and documentary evidence to back up that he was there at the time he said."

"So where's the problem?"

"This is where it gets interesting. We've checked the United Nations' records of their field staff, and there's a three-month assignment where he was in Somalia from June to August 2005."

"That's impossible. The UN withdrew in the nineties. I know all about Somalia."

Chisholm nodded. "We've spoken to Franz Topping, a senior official within the Office for the Coordination of Humanitarian Affairs, and he insists there definitely was not a UN presence in Somalia. But this contradicts the field records of Dr. Janice Sanderson, from Ithaca in upstate New York, who was working for a Christian medical charity. Her records state that Ford was working in Mogadishu. He was mentioned in her diary. And here's the kicker. Sanderson was killed in a car crash three months ago."

Reznick rubbed the top of his head. "So either Ford or a third party wants to hide three months of his life. We need to know why."

Chisholm nodded. "We're still working through the records of the other humanitarian agencies. It's a lot more fragmented. Fewer computer records, so that's causing a problem."

"But it's this three months we need to be concentrating on. Can we rule out that he was in a training camp somewhere?"

Chisholm stared at him. "We can't rule out anything at this stage."

Meyerstein looked up from her computer. "Sam, what's the latest on Ford's movements?"

Chisholm leaned over and checked a nearby laptop. "Team Two has him back in the park. Alone. Taking pictures."

"At this time of night?" Reznick said. "Same place?"

Chisholm nodded. "Same as when you were watching him."

"The exact same?"

"The exact same."

Reznick shook his head. "Consider this. The main object of surveillance is to check a possible target for security measures, vulnerabilities. Is this what's going on here?"

"Perhaps."

"Are we talking a high-profile target, or a target in the park? A spectacular?"

Meyerstein rolled her eyes. "Complete supposition, Jon."

"So what's your take on what he's up to and who he's linked with?"

Meyerstein was leafing through some papers. She leaned back in her seat and sighed. "I've got some analysis that we're working on. It's pretty raw, but it's showing that perhaps Ford is sympathetic to the aims of some of our homegrown militias. Extreme libertarians. Anti-government hard-liners. Perhaps in the Timothy McVeigh mold."

Reznick blew out his cheeks. "McVeigh? Christ. He was a whack job."

Malone cleared his throat. "McVeigh, huh? Interesting."

Chisholm shook his head. "Gimme a break. He was a cold-blooded bastard. The Oklahoma bombing killed a hundred and sixty-eight people, including children in a day-care center. More than six hundred injured. Nothing interesting about that."

"Hey, keep it down. I'm not disputing that. But I studied McVeigh at close quarters. Psychologically, he wasn't insane. Not by any means. I can remember he had an IQ of 126."

"I don't give a shit what his IQ was."

"Neither do I," Malone replied. "Tell me, Sam, have you ever read *The Third Terrorist* by Jayna Davis?"

"Yeah, and it's bullshit."

"The author said McVeigh and one of his accomplices—a guy by the name of Nichols—had significant ties to an Islamic terror group."

"She's wrong."

Malone shrugged. "Maybe. But we can't rule such thinking out when we're figuring out where Ford fits in."

"We can feed that into our analysis, sure, but I don't see that theory getting beyond first base. I think the book didn't give credible sources for this hypothesis that there was a Middle Eastern connection to Oklahoma."

Malone shook his head. "The book calls into question why the FBI turned a blind eye to eyewitness testimony that suggested McVeigh had a Middle Eastern accomplice. Twenty-two eyewitnesses gave written affidavits confirming there was a third terrorist—a guy called Hussain Hashem Al-Hussaini, an Iraqi soldier in the first Gulf War. All the eyewitnesses say that this man accompanied McVeigh to the federal building."

"Malone, I've got to stop you there," Meyerstein interjected. "I know the case very well. Investigation didn't back that up."

"Terrorism makes for strange bedfellows. Unforeseen alliances are not uncommon. Even in prison, the Mexican Mafia and Aryan Brotherhood have a loose alliance against their common enemies.

Outside, the Tijuana Cartel operates in alliance with the Aryan Brotherhood at various levels."

Chisholm sighed. "I think we're getting a bit off base. The thing that strikes me most about Ford is that he's lily white. He has no criminal history and no obvious links to Islamic terrorist groups or militias. He just doesn't fit the profile."

Reznick cut in. "We need to know where he was for those three months."

Meyerstein shook her head. "We'll chase that down, but I feel like we're going in circles. And I always come back to the same thing . . . How is it that the State Department doesn't know anything about why O'Grady was contacting Caroline Lieber? Surely they have to have something."

Chisholm nodded. "Something's wrong there. To me, the State Department is withholding information."

Meyerstein sighed. "It's frustrating. I know from personal experience how one agency jealously guards the very intel they should be sharing the most freely. But unless we get access to their files, it's on a need-to-know basis."

"That's dangerous."

"I know. Look, Froch isn't the most cooperative, I'll give you that. But I guess that comes with the territory." She caught Reznick's eye. "What's wrong, Jon? You've gone quiet on me."

"What about the ninth-floor apartment at the Baruch Houses?"

Chisholm shook his head. "We sent in forensics and specialist search teams. They scanned every inch of the apartment—drilled through walls, partitions, pulled off crown molding, lifted the tiles, and checked in all dead space. Not a goddamn thing."

"What about Akhtar's place in the East Village?" Reznick asked.

"We've had to rehouse the wife and kids, but same again—we've drawn a blank."

"Which leaves a deep search of Chantelle McGovern's place," Meyerstein said. "We've only done a fifteen-minute sweep of the place. And we're still waiting for the computer analysis to come through."

Chisholm stifled a yawn. There were dark shadows under his eyes.

Meyerstein looked across at him. "What do you think? McGovern's apartment—we go in again. But this time we go over it inch by inch."

Chisholm grimaced. "Tough call. If she's involved, I doubt there would be anything there."

Meyerstein looked across at Reznick. "What do you think, Jon?"

"That would make sense."

Meyerstein closed her eyes. "We could do with having Morales here."

Chisholm put his hand on her shoulder. "Looks like he's going to pull through, Martha."

"How the hell did they know Morales was in the building?" Reznick asked.

"Maybe they got spooked. There was no knife found. Akhtar's taking the fifth."

A voice shouted through from the adjoining room, "OK, we got something. He's out of the park and he's hopped in a cab. We're on him."

Meyerstein rubbed her hands together. "Where to now, Dr. Ford?"

A short while later, surveillance footage showed him getting out of a yellow taxi and buzzing a door on East 81st Street.

"Where is this? Locale?"

A short pause. A young systems expert checking the computers said, "Neighborhood Coalition for Shelter. It houses sixty-five formerly homeless men and women, most of whom are mentally ill."

Meyerstein sighed. "Shit. OK, I want a list of all volunteers over the last eighteen months. And also the names of the homeless who've stayed there."

Chisholm rubbed his eyes. "Goddamn, what is this guy playing at? I mean, what the hell is all this bouncing around shelters and soup kitchens at this time of night?" He put on a headset, adjusting the microphone in front of his mouth. "Surveillance, we need a female inside the facility. Agent Ferez. Get her made up as a panhandler ASAP. I want her in there and let's see what we've got."

* * *

The rest of the night was spent scanning the surveillance footage coming from inside the shelter. Reznick and the rest of the team monitored the screens as Ford talked with the undercover Fed about her alcohol use and asked when the last time she'd used the facility was. He was attentive. It was a master class in compassion.

As the hours passed, Malone grabbed a nap on the sofa. Reznick, Chisholm, and Meyerstein drank strong coffee after strong coffee. Reznick went to the bathroom and popped a Dexedrine. The chemicals hit his system.

Just after four, Special Agent Ferez was sent on her way, with hot soup, a sandwich, and a few dollars, and asked to come back the following night when they would have a spare bed.

It was strange to think that, less than twenty blocks away, Ford was oblivious to the sophisticated surveillance operation that was tracking him.

What was he really up to?

"Hold on," one of the surveillance operatives said. "Who's this? Check this out. We got movement out front of the facility."

Reznick and the others checked the footage. A figure—clearly female, wearing tight dark pants and a dark shirt, hair tied back, and sunglasses even though it was dark.

Reznick peered at the screen. "Is this a volunteer?"

Then the woman turned, as if spooked, and stared straight up into the camera, unaware she was being watched.

The woman took off her glasses, and Reznick recognized her face straight away.

"You gotta be kidding me," Meyerstein said.

It was Chantelle McGovern.

Twenty-Three

Just after 6 a.m., Meyerstein was getting ready for a secure video-conference with the three most senior members of the special access program. She had managed to snatch an hour or so of uninterrupted sleep and—after a shower, fresh clothes, and applying new makeup—she was served an Americano and a croissant. She scarfed them down and felt immeasurably better.

She got a rushed, five-minute briefing from an exhausted-looking Chisholm, who hadn't slept, before sitting down in front of the screen. She punched in the encryption code and found herself staring at the stern faces of Lieutenant General Black, who was in McLean, and Lieutenant Colonel Froch, who was on the eighth floor of the State Department office in New York, directly opposite the UN.

Over the next ten minutes, she gave a situation update. "Bottom line, gentlemen, our analysis is pointing to Ford being linked in some way. Otherwise, the statistical chances of him going to the same homeless shelter as McGovern, in addition to being served by her at a Midtown steakhouse and East Village café, are too ludicrous to contemplate. That's three separate locations. And that's in addition to her brother Jamal, an Islamist convert, being holed up in one of the Baruch buildings on the Lower East Side."

Black leaned back in his seat. She could tell he wasn't convinced. "You have not given one iota of evidence to show that he is in any way linked to anything. And there's no forensic proof linking him with anything."

Meyerstein sighed. She hadn't expected to be dismissed so readily.

Froch cleared his throat. "Can I jump in here?"

"Sure, Ed," Meyerstein said.

"I've got to say, I feel uneasy when people talk about a person—in this case Ford—being linked in some way. In what way is he linked, other than these bizarre coincidences? I'm not ruling out the possibility, but come on . . ."

Meyerstein leaned forward, hands clasped, as she felt the anger rise within her.

"Counterterrorism strategic analysts, military intelligence, and behavioral analysts all conclude unequivocally that Ford is far more likely to be involved than not. We're talking probability."

"Involved in what?" Froch said.

"At this stage? We just don't know."

"Oh, come on, Assistant Director, that's not gonna wash. We believe someone may be involved in something we don't know anything about? Is that what you're telling me?"

Meyerstein kept her anger in check. "Ed, we're building a picture. It takes time."

Black said, "O'Grady is dead, Martha. Lieber is still missing. These are concrete facts. And we can't keep this from the media forever."

"I know exactly where we stand. Look, we're getting closer to this. The analysis favors our focus on Ford and Chantelle McGovern. We're peeling it back."

"What about the Iranians?"

"We have them covered. There's nothing, no chatter or movement, to indicate anything in the offing."

"Let's be honest, Martha. We've been playing catch-up since the get-go. And to make matters worse, consider this . . . I was informed that, last night, the parents of Caroline Lieber met with the President, begging him to allow them to make a public appeal, to see if someone out there knows anything. They're beside themselves. They believe it's the only way."

"If I can make a suggestion here, I'd like to talk this over with them, face to face."

Froch nodded. "I think that's a good idea. The State Department should be able to open up some diplomatic channels to reach out to the Liebers."

"When are you free?"

Froch scratched his chin. "I've got a meeting with the Secretary of State at eight a.m. How does nine thirty sound?"

Meyerstein nodded. "I'll be there."

Black was also nodding. "Let's keep this tight. I want a goddamn breakthrough. And I want it real quick."

The monolithic concrete tower on First Avenue housed the US mission to the UN. Hundreds of diplomats and support staff worked behind thirty-inch concrete walls specially designed to withstand explosive-laden trucks. There were no windows on the first seven of its twenty-six floors.

Meyerstein was dropped outside a side entrance on 45th Street at 9:26 a.m. "I won't be long. Twenty minutes max," she told Chisholm, who was sitting up front beside the driver, talking to one of his team on his cell phone. She turned to Reznick, who was sitting in the back seat. "Let's see what Froch has to say. Wish me luck."

Reznick stared at her, long and hard, before he smiled. "Good luck."

She strode up to the entrance, flashed her ID at the armed guard, and was ushered inside to go through security. She walked through metal detectors and was searched by a poker-faced female guard.

"Sorry for the inconvenience, ma'am," the woman said.

Meyerstein looked at her and smiled. "Not a problem."

She rode the elevator alone to the eighth floor and was escorted through a maze of corridors to Froch's office by an attractive, twenty-something intern.

Froch was sitting behind his desk, leafing through some papers. He stood up and pointed to the chair opposite. "One minute early. You want a coffee?"

Meyerstein smiled as she sat down. "Morning, Ed. Black coffee, please."

The intern left the room and Froch made small talk. The high humidity, plans for vacations. When the intern returned, she placed the cup on the desk in front of Meyerstein.

"Ma'am," she said.

"Thanks for that." Meyerstein sipped some coffee, enjoying the caffeine taking hold. She was so tired.

"Gillian, can you shut the door behind you? Make sure I'm not disturbed."

The door closed, and Froch let out a long sigh.

"Thanks for making it at such short notice." He leaned forward and steepled his fingers. "Firstly, I want to say that any State Department involvement does not impinge on your role leading this investigation. I was briefing the Secretary of State and she is being kept in the loop, as you can understand."

Meyerstein nodded. "I would expect nothing less."

"There are one or two people within the State Department who say this should be led by Counterterrorism. But the feeling is that you have that base amply covered with Sam Chisholm being on board."

Meyerstein smiled but said nothing.

"Here's where I'm at. I've already dispatched an old family friend of the Liebers to calm the waters. He heads up the State Department's Office of Global Intergovernmental Affairs."

"Charlie Stanton?"

"The very man. He's known the Liebers for over thirty years. He'll be asking for seventy-two hours' grace."

Meyerstein sighed. "You kidding me? Ed, I need more time."

"That's all that's on the table. Charlie believes we can get that seventy-two hours. Nothing more."

Meyerstein shook her head. But she knew it was a take-it-or-leave-it situation. Not up for discussion. She was tempted to fire off a volley of criticism in his direction on how unforthcoming they had been with regard to O'Grady, his undefined role within the State Department, and who he had or hadn't been in contact with. But she knew, from long experience, it was better to try to be constructive, or at least appear to be.

Froch averted his eyes from her direct gaze. "The State Department's intelligence bureau and our counterterrorism people are studying the developments closely. They're pretty smart."

Meyerstein knew that was correct. She only had to think back to the national intelligence estimate of 2002 on whether Saddam possessed weapons of mass destruction. They were about the only intelligence agency who had emerged with any credit, primarily because of their dissent.

"They're very nuanced. I like that," she said.

Froch gave a thin smile. "I'll pass that on. We pride ourselves on the rigor of our reports and the quality of our staff."

"So has Stanton spoken to the Liebers?"

"Not yet. He's due to meet them around midday. We don't think there will be a problem. But we're on the clock now."

Meyerstein rubbed her eyes. "I appreciate your help. And, trust me, we need every bit of help we can get."

Froch's desk phone rang and a red light lit up. "I must take this. The President's national security advisor."

Meyerstein nodded and got up from her chair. "Let me know as soon as you hear from Stanton."

"Count on it."

Meyerstein left Froch's office and felt a migraine coming on. She headed to a bathroom and popped a couple of Advil, then washed them down with a small bottle of water she had in her bag. She looked at her reflection in the mirror. The shadows under her eyes. She applied some fresh Touche Éclat. Then she touched up her lipstick.

She closed her eyes for a few moments, hoping the pain would subside. There were so many things going through her head, it was unreal. Analysis, counterterrorism briefings, Reznick's presence on the team, pressure from Black, missing the kids. The more she thought about it, the more she knew she needed a vacation when it was all over.

The door opened behind her. Standing there was a fresh-faced, dark-haired woman. Her high cheekbones and peachy complexion made Meyerstein envious.

The woman gave a insipid smile and approached the mirror. She took a small bottle of perfume from her bag. Then she turned to Meyerstein and sprayed the cold spray into her left ear.

"What the . . ." was all Meyerstein managed to say before the words couldn't come.

"Take care now," she said as Meyerstein collapsed to the floor, struggling for breath, the woman staring down at her, smiling.

Then she was swallowed up in a spiral of darkness.

Twenty-Four

Reznick checked his watch as he sat in the back of the SUV parked outside the State Department's office in New York. He glanced at the clock on the dashboard. It showed 10:45.

"What's taking her so long?" he said to the driver. "She's been away for over an hour."

The Fed just shrugged. "Relax."

Reznick felt his foot tapping. He'd never been good at waiting. "Wasn't she supposed to be in for twenty minutes?"

The Fed nodded. "It happens. Meetings run over all the time."

That was true, Reznick thought. But Froch didn't seem like the sort of person who allowed meetings to run over. A stickler for detail. A small-print kind of guy.

The waiting went on. He looked at his watch at least a dozen times in the space of fifteen minutes. And still nothing.

He wondered what was keeping her. Neither the FBI driver nor Chisholm, sitting in the front seat, seemed unduly bothered.

Reznick leaned forward and tapped Chisholm on the shoulder. "That's an hour and a half she's been gone. Is that normal?"

Chisholm was checking his emails on his BlackBerry. He turned around and grimaced. "No idea, Jon."

"Look, do you wanna at least send her a message asking her how long she'll be?"

"I don't think that's a great idea."

"Why not?"

"Well, if she's in a meeting with Froch and some of his State Department buddies, you can rest assured she won't want to be disturbed by us, asking her where the hell she is. I know Martha. Have for a long time. And she doesn't like being disturbed in meetings."

Reznick sighed. "She had a twenty-minute meeting, Sam. She's now been gone a while."

"You need to get out more, Jon. Here in the real world, meetings run over all the time. It's a pain in the ass. But we roll with it."

Reznick remained unconvinced. She'd said earlier that she wouldn't be long. But here they were, an hour and a half later, and she was still inside.

He pondered on that. He'd always been strict about time-keeping, especially back in his Delta days. If you were given forty-five minutes to do a task, it meant forty-five minutes max. Not a second more. A night run for thirty miles over rough terrain had to be completed in less than twelve hours. And on and on it went.

He was obsessive about the time. It kept him focused. But anything that ran over jarred with him. He liked order. Precision.

The minutes dragged. He checked his watch again.

"She's been gone an hour and fifty minutes, Sam."

"What do you want me to do? She's an FBI assistant director. I can't just go marching into the goddamn office, asking what the hell is taking her so long."

Reznick tried to keep his natural aggression in check. "Can't you at least call Froch's assistant or secretary? Ask how long she'll be?"

Chisholm shook his head and smiled. "You're wound up too tight, Jon, do you know that?"

Reznick said nothing.

"OK, OK, I'll deal with it," Chisholm said, and he made a call. "Hi, sorry to bother you. This is Sam Chisholm of the FBI." A long silence. "Yes, Counterterrorism. Thank you. Can you put me through to Ed Froch's secretary?" A pause. "Hi, could you tell me what's keeping Assistant Director Meyerstein?" Silence. "Are you sure? I'm sorry, how long ago? Are you positive?" He nodded and closed his eyes before ending the call.

Reznick leaned forward. "So, where the hell is she?"

"She left more than an hour ago."

"What?"

Chisholm dialed another number. He waited for a few moments and left a voice message: "Martha, it's Sam. Where the hell are you? They said your meeting finished way before ten. It's now eleven seventeen and no sign of you."

"We need to get up there," Reznick said.

Chisholm gritted his teeth. "What the fuck is going on?"

They got out the SUV and rushed through the security door, where they were patted down and given temporary passes to enter the building. They rode the elevator with two security guards to the eighth floor, and headed straight to Froch's office.

The secretary let them in while Froch was on the phone. He hung up immediately.

"I've just been alerted that Assistant Director Meyerstein isn't with you," he said. "So where the hell is she?"

Chisholm ran his hand through his hair. "Shit."

"I've just ordered the security cameras to be reviewed. Something's not right."

"No fucking kidding." Reznick began to pace back and forth. "Did she say where she was going?"

"I assumed she was heading back to base."

Froch's desk phone rang and he picked up on the first ring. "Yes?" He nodded. "On this floor? Put the building on lockdown. Right now!" He hung up. "Security says the footage shows she went into the restroom on this floor. No sign of her since then."

"Fuck!"

Reznick ran out of the office with a security guard in tow, and headed back down the corridor in the direction of the female restroom. He barged inside. It appeared empty, but he saw one door partially shut. He spread-eagled himself on the floor and saw legs and shoes—it was Meyerstein, crumpled in a heap.

"End stall!" Reznick shouted at the guard. "Call 911! Now!"

He pushed back the door with his left hand and kneeled down. He gently cupped a hand behind her head and felt the pulse in her neck. "Very faint, but alive." He touched her cheek. It was getting cold. Clammy. Her lips were turning blue. Then he spotted some crystalline residue in her hair.

He pushed back her hair and saw the same residue on her earlobe. It reminded him of a hit by the Israelis on a Palestinian terrorist on the West Bank.

He turned to the guard. "Seal this place off! Don't let anyone out of this building, do you understand?"

The guard nodded and passed on the instructions over his radio.

Reznick turned his attention back to Meyerstein. "Stay with me, Martha!" He tapped her cheek, trying to rouse her, and began to shake her.

He turned to face the guard. "Where the hell are the paramedics?"

A few moments later, Chisholm came in with a female paramedic, who took Meyerstein's pulse.

"Not good . . . Very faint. Is this an overdose?"

Reznick pointed out the drug residue. "Someone got to her."

"With what?"

"Opiate, almost certainly. Try for fentanyl."

"How do you know?"

"Just do it! Naloxone, you got it?"

The paramedic nodded. "I'm on it!"

Reznick turned to Chisholm and cocked his head. "Let's go."

"We can't just leave her."

"She's in medical hands. Leave two of your team with her. We need to act fast."

Two Feds were called up to stay with Meyerstein as the paramedic fought to revive her. Reznick and Chisholm headed down to the building's security room, which contained banks of CCTV monitors covering entrances and exits.

The head of security pointed to a freeze-framed image of a young woman wearing a dark pantsuit, perhaps in her late twenties, long brown hair, State Department ID hanging around her neck.

"We've checked. This woman entered the bathroom, just after Assistant Director Meyerstein. She left twenty-two seconds later. Precisely."

Reznick stared at the woman. High cheekbones, a fresh face with dark, deep-set eyes. He leaned closer. "Zoom in on her ID!"

The head of security did as he was told. The ID read *Sacha Hall*.

He typed the name into his computer and it came up blank. "There is no Sacha Hall with State Department accreditation."

"So how the hell did she gain entry to this building?"

The man flushed a dark crimson. "We're checking it out."

Reznick stared at him. "When did she leave this building?"

He clicked a button and it brought up another image, this time showing the woman leaving via the main entrance at 10:05 a.m.

"I need those images," Chisholm said.

"I'm sorry, I'm going to have to run it past—"

Chisholm pointed at the man, hand inches away from his face. "You get those images to my guy right fucking now! You got it?"

The head of security nodded, visibly shaking. "Yes, sir."

"OK." Chisholm handed him an FBI business card with an email address on it. "Send them to Andrew Livingston, FBI Counterterrorism. Right now. But send them secure. Do you understand what that means?"

The security guy just nodded. "Encrypted, yes. You got it." He keyed in the email address and sent it across. "Consider it done."

Chisholm turned to Reznick. "What a fucking mess."

"Tell me about it."

They headed out of the building and into the waiting SUV. Chisholm's cell phone rang. He answered and listened. "Hold on." He covered the mouthpiece and looked at Reznick. "It's Livingston. He's got our mystery girl. Facial recognition has just made a hundred percent match at Grand Central's food court. They've been tracking her via security cameras. There's a shadow with her. A big guy. Jeans, shades, Yankees hat."

Reznick tapped the driver on the shoulder. "Let's move it!"

Chisholm ended the call as the car sped through the Midtown traffic, until it pulled up outside Grand Central. Reznick and Chisholm headed through the soaring main concourse. They rushed down to the food court, knocking people out of the way, scanning faces, trying to block out the announcements, earpieces relaying the command and control from Livingston.

"She's on the move, headed for the platform. Yeah, she's on Track Three on the 42nd Street Shuttle."

Reznick sprinted down a ramp to the platform, only to see the train pulling away.

"Damn!"

He heard Livingston's voice in his ear. "Reznick, next train will be along in thirty seconds from Track One."

Reznick and Chisholm headed across to the waiting train.

A minute passed. Then two.

"What the fuck is going on?" Reznick said, frustrated at the delay.

Chisholm called Livingston and ordered the lockdown of Times Square station—less than a mile away—so no one could exit. Eventually, nearly five long minutes later, the 42nd Street Shuttle thundered away from the station into the tunnel.

A minute later, they were there.

Reznick and Chisholm squeezed off the car, along with hundreds of others. Bustling and shoving and moaning into Times Square station. Down badly lit corridors, down stairs, avoiding street kids and homeless musicians, until they got to one of the lower platforms.

"Where the hell has she gone?"

Livingston's voice in his earpiece. "We got her. She's on the Seven platform."

Reznick saw a sign and sprinted for it, careening down more stairs. He heard the roar and rumble of a train.

He descended onto the platform, scanning the faces. He spotted her. She turned and stared straight at him.

Reznick moved toward her.

The huge man appeared from the crowd behind her, eyeballed Reznick, and calmly pressed a gun against the back of the woman's head. He stared at Reznick with cold eyes as he shot her dead.

The noise was like an explosion in the confined space. Blood and brain matter splattered everywhere. Crowds screamed. Panic ensued. The sea of people parted.

It was then that time seemed to stop for Reznick. Shocked faces. Blood. Screaming. He was in the moment.

Reznick drew his 9mm and aimed at the man, but the target had already made his move.

The gun was already in the man's mouth, his fierce eyes locked onto Reznick.

Then the man calmly blew his brains out on the platform, the back of his head exploding in an eruption of blood.

Twenty-Five

Reznick somehow managed to block out the noise and chaos that followed as people scattered amid the carnage. He felt detached. Part training, part instinct. His mind seemed to have split from what he had just witnessed. He began to think rationally. He got a Fed's iPhone and zoomed in, photographing both faces.

Reznick stood above the man's body as blood pooled around his shoes. He was surprised that the front of the man's face was remarkably intact. But the woman was a different matter, a gaping hole where half of her face had been.

He stared at them for a few moments. The woman's face was virtually unrecognizable, torn to shreds by the bullet, but he had already seen her Slavic features on the surveillance footage. Her mouth was slightly open, as if aware only for a split second that she was about to die. The man looked Russian—perhaps Slavic, too. Pieces of his flesh, fragments of bone and brain matter were all over the platform. Eyes pale blue, still open.

He wondered what had driven the man to kill the woman and take his own life. What did he want to hide? What was worth dying for?

Reznick saw Chisholm in his peripheral vision but didn't let on. He bent down and rummaged through the man's pockets. Nothing.

Inside the woman's jacket pocket there was an iPhone. He put it in his pocket and disappeared into the fleeing crowds—with Chisholm and two Feds who'd joined them—before anyone could ask any questions.

His mind raced as he ran from the chaos of the station and stepped into the steam-bath humidity on street level, the sound of car horns, the neon advertising of Times Square. Hundreds of people all around, cop cars pulling up.

Chisholm's driver hailed them from the SUV, and Reznick, Chisholm, and the two Feds climbed in.

Safely inside, Reznick handed Chisholm the woman's iPhone. "This is her phone. We need to download everything on it. Let's get back to The Fairfax."

The driver hit the gas and they sped away.

Chisholm held the cell phone gingerly and dropped it into a plastic evidence bag.

"What the hell happened?"

Reznick breathed out as Midtown Manhattan flew by. "They eyeballed us. The guy shot the woman first. Then he shot himself. You wanna tell me what's going on?"

Chisholm's face drained of color as he stared at the phone. "We're using facial recognition to try to establish who they were."

"And?"

"We believe they may be Russians."

"Working on whose orders? The Russians I know don't shoot each other. I think you need to look at that again. Is this Boston all over again? Are we talking Chechens?"

"Distinct possibility. We're working this from all angles."

"What's the latest on Meyerstein?"

"Not good. She's unconscious, on a ventilator. Doctors believe it's an offshoot of China White, a form of fentanyl. Two hundred times more potent than morphine. The Russian mob's very involved in the importation of the drug."

Reznick put his head in his hands. "Fuck."

Chisholm held up his hands as if to pacify him. "Take it easy, Jon."

"Look, Chisholm, they might be Russian, they might even be Russian mob, but why the hell would he kill the woman and then kill himself? They don't want us to get below the surface."

Chisholm closed his eyes for a moment. "Here's another problem we're facing. Who the hell would target Meyerstein? Counterterrorism thinks we might be compromised in some way."

"Communications?"

"Should be impossible, but . . . it can't be ruled out."

Reznick stared at the streets as they headed uptown. "How the hell did they get to her?"

"Too early to say."

Chisholm's phone rang. "Yes, sir. We got the female's phone. Computer forensics will copy over the contents of this phone and we'll have the analysis within the hour. You'll have the results as soon as I get them. Sir, I'm well aware of that." He nodded a few times before he handed it to Reznick. "General Black wants to talk to you."

Reznick hesitated.

"Don't worry, it's encrypted."

Reznick cleared his throat and took the phone. "Sir."

"I just heard about Meyerstein. This is quite outrageous."

"Indeed it is, sir."

Black let out a long sigh. "Jon, your photos of the two dead individuals will be very helpful. Save us a lot of grief with NYPD. We're strictly in-house on this. And that's the way it's going to stay."

"What the hell is going on, sir?"

"You know as well as I do, Jon, that nothing is straightforward in our world. We could be dealing with a terrorist cell, Russian Mafia . . . who knows? Take your pick."

"Sir, with respect, how the hell could someone get to an FBI assistant director in broad daylight, within a secure complex? This is an inside job, isn't it? Someone wanted to derail this investigation. Throw us off the scent."

"There's a lot of questions we need answered, Jon. And whoever is behind this will be taken care of. But as of now, as I've just told Sam, I'm taking charge of this program. Now, I know there were one or two objections about your inclusion on the team, and I was one of the objectors, but I want you to know that I want you to stay. That is, if you want to. If you want to walk away and get back to your life, I understand. Your call."

"I don't do walking away, you should know that. I want to help you find out who did this."

"Very well. So, what's your take on this?"

"We have definitely been compromised, that's goddamn obvious. My question would be, who knew Meyerstein was heading to Froch's office?"

"Half a dozen people directly, but then another half a dozen who'd get to know by association."

"The key players would be me, you, Chisholm, Froch, and Stamper."

"The person would need to know her every move well in advance to plan this."

The car hit a pothole and the suspension shuddered. Reznick looked at Chisholm, who was receiving an update on his iPad. "It happened on Froch's patch. He was the last person to see her. It happened only yards from his office."

"I've known Ed Froch for two decades. He's beyond reproach."

"Check his phone records. Check his home phone records. Check the dead woman's phone."

"Jon, Froch is connected to very powerful people within the administration. We can't go pointing the finger."

"I'm not asking you or anyone to point the finger at him. We need to do some checking."

"I suppose I could call him up . . ."

"Assume the worst, sir. If we call ahead, he has prior warning, if he's been compromised."

"And if he's not been compromised?"

"Then we're only being thorough."

"Jon, this isn't how we work."

"Sir, we need to speak to him and he needs to answer some questions."

"Jon, he would never harm Martha."

"We don't know that."

"You're saying we give him no prior warning and just turn up at his office?"

"You got it."

A sigh, and then a grunt. "Pass me over to Sam, will you, Jon?"

Reznick did as he was told.

Chisholm took the phone, nodded twice, and ended the call.

"Straight back to Froch's office," he told the driver.

Fifteen minutes later, they were back outside the State Department's office. There was a heavy police presence. The exits were covered.

Chisholm and Reznick rode the elevator to Froch's floor. Cops and forensics were milling around the restroom. They headed down the carpeted corridor and toward his office.

His secretary looked up at them.

"I need to speak to your boss," Reznick said.

"He's not here."

"Where the hell is he?"

"I don't know."

"What do you mean, you don't know?"

The young woman flushed pink. "He left the office ten minutes ago and didn't say where he was going."

Twenty-Six

The heat was almost unbearable as Ford pounded the paved track around the Central Park Reservoir. He felt the spray—whipped up by the gusts of wind from the choppy water—cooling him as the temperatures climbed into the nineties. He wondered how long it would be until the day. He mused on that as he passed red-faced joggers pushing themselves in the stifling New York heat.

The thought of what lay ahead sparked a new rush of endorphins.

He ran on, and looked across the water. The sky was pale blue, only a few wisps of white cloud drifting past.

He was in the zone. He was in the right city at the right time. It was all coming together.

The voice of his mentor on the tape ran through his head. He was playing it three or four times a day now. Everything was becoming clearer. More focused, as they said it would.

It was remarkable to think that he was going to be remembered. That's what his father had wanted for him. His name would live for a thousand years. Echoing down the years like a dark whisper. Infamy.

Satisfied with the workout, Ford slowed down and stood beside the steel fence that surrounded the reservoir. He stretched out his legs, feeling his calf muscles tighten. He was cocooned in the after-glow of exertion, sweat dripping down his neck.

He closed his eyes, listening to his breathing, as the runners pounded past him.

He loved this moment. Being still.

His cell phone vibrated on his waistband, snapping him out of his relaxed state of mind.

Ford pressed the phone to his ear.

"We got a new location," the familiar voice said.

"At this late hour?"

"It's all in hand."

"Why the change?"

"It's still in New York."

"Who changed the plans?"

"That was beyond our control."

Ford went quiet for a few moments as he mulled it over.

He liked order. He liked visualizing what he was about to do. Now that wasn't possible.

"Not ideal."

The man said nothing.

"When will I know the venue?"

"All in good time."

"And my wingman?"

"He's watching your every move. We got you covered. You're going to have a clear run."

Ford afforded himself a smile at a beautiful jogger, and she smiled back.

"This is going to happen, right?"

"It's gonna happen because you're going to make it happen."

Ford detected a slight tension in the man's voice, as if he weren't telling the whole story.

"What about an exact date and time?"

"The date is still the same. The time is changing. We'll let you know."

Ford said nothing.

"One final thing."

"What?"

"It won't just be the main event at the venue."

Ford's stomach knotted. "The wife?"

"You'll get a clear shot at both."

Ford closed his eyes. He could see the whole scenario unfold in his head.

Twenty-Seven

It was nearly dark when the Feds, with Reznick in tow, pulled up outside Terminal 4 at JFK. It had been less than an hour since Feds at the airport had seen the FBI circular that had been sent out to law enforcement agencies with Froch's details. Facial recognition software running on surveillance cameras had pulled up a perfect match. And they had alerted Chisholm that the missing State Department official had been spotted. But Chisholm had instructed them that under no circumstances were they to approach Froch unless he boarded a flight.

Reznick knew that was the smart thing to do. The last thing they needed was for airport security, outside of the secret program, to haul Froch in for questioning. They had to bring him in and let Chisholm's guys interrogate him.

They were ushered through the arrivals hall by airport security and onto Concourse B, past a myriad of shops and restaurants.

Finally, they headed toward the gates.

Reznick spotted Froch in a line at gate B20, talking into his cell phone.

He turned to Chisholm. "How do you want to work this?"

Chisholm stared as the line slowly moved forward. "We don't want a scene. The last thing we need is for passengers to be pulling out their goddamn iPhones and filming us taking him down. We want to do this slow and quiet."

"What about Customs?"

Chisholm shook his head. "The less they know, the better. OK, approach him, nice and gentle, and explain that he needs to come with you. If necessary, make something up."

"And if he says go to hell?"

"Then haul his ass out of the line. The last thing the FBI needs is for me to be filmed dragging some State Department guy out of an airport line."

"Got it."

Reznick turned and walked across the concourse and straight up to Froch. He stood in front of him, smelling liquor on the man's breath, sensing looks from the other passengers.

"Sir, you need to come with me." His voice was low.

Froch flushed a dark red and took a few moments to speak. "What's going on? Why are you here?"

"Your wife, sir."

"My wife? What about her?"

"I'll explain on the way there."

Froch went quiet for a few moments, as if mulling over his options. "Is she OK?"

"I'll explain on the way over. You need to come with me now, sir."

"And if I don't?"

Reznick inched closer to him, eyeballing him. "Don't make this more awkward than it has to be."

Froch visibly blanched. "I see."

Reznick cocked his head in the direction of Chisholm. "OK, now we're clear, let's get a move on."

Froch stood still for a few moments before his shoulders slumped. He then headed over to Chisholm, shadowed by Reznick. He was frisked by the Feds, his cell phone confiscated, and led away to the waiting car. He didn't say a word during the twenty-five-minute journey, sat sandwiched between Reznick and a rookie Fed.

Reznick looked out of the window and saw a sign for Brooklyn. He wondered where exactly they were going. It looked sketchy. The area was post-industrial, with junkyards and auto body shops standing like rusting reminders of the area's past.

The car headed toward an unmarked redbrick building and into the parking lot, screeching to a halt.

Froch was taken out of the car by the rookie Fed and the driver, and led into the building via a steel door. Reznick and Chisholm followed behind.

Inside, it was a different world. Gleaming steel, with countless large-screen TVs. Al Jazeera, Arab TV stations, BBC World, CNN, and Fox—watched by terrorist-threat experts with headphones. Others were reading classified intelligence briefings. In an adjacent room, language specialists were poring over Farsi, Arabic, and Pashto jihadist chat rooms, translating hundreds of hours of audio recordings.

Froch was taken on ahead to an interview room.

Reznick pulled Chisholm aside beside a water cooler. "What the hell is this place?"

"The Feds have an arrangement with the NYPD. Their counterterrorism guys run this. We stripped it out and reconfigured a few things."

"So this is run as a separate FBI New York field office?"

"We're in New York, and yes, it is an FBI office of sorts, but this runs strictly parallel to both the FBI and NYPD. We use it for high-value targets we pick up in Manhattan. Need-to-know investigations."

Reznick could see what he was getting at. "I see. You run special counterterrorism operations in and around New York, answerable to who exactly?"

"You think too much, Jon."

Chisholm popped out of the room for a few moments, and returned with two Styrofoam cups of coffee. "Get this down you, Jon. You must be running on empty, too."

Reznick nodded. "Tell me about it." He took a gulp.

Chisholm sipped his own coffee. "Follow me."

He turned and walked toward the far end of the room and the keypad-operated doors, Reznick in tow. He punched in a code and the doors clicked open. They headed along a long corridor and entered a tiny room with one large window, through which they could see Froch sitting, head bowed, drinking a cup of tea.

Reznick stared through the one-way mirror. He watched Froch tap his feet as if agitated. He wondered what part Froch had played—if any—in the attack on Meyerstein.

He felt helpless, knowing that the FBI would use their own interrogation techniques on Froch, and certainly nothing enhanced.

He turned to Chisholm. "So what's the lowdown on Froch?"

"We're working on the assumption that he may have been compromised. If so, we need to know in what way, and by whom." Chisholm sighed. "The problem is, we have nothing. We're chasing shadows. They're fucking with us."

"Who is *they*? Do we know who those two dead Russians were yet?"

"All we know is that they entered this country on Russian tourist visas."

"There's someone behind them, Sam. They're not just Russians. This has echoes of Boston. I'm talking Chechens."

"We're working with the Russians, trying to connect the dots."

Reznick cleared his throat as he stared at Froch, who was picking at his fingernails.

"We're also forgetting something," he said.

"What?"

"Ford. How does he fit into this? And what about goddamn Jamal Ali?"

Chisholm looked through the glass as Froch leaned back in his chair, arms folded and eyes closed. "We're checking the two Russians to see if there's a security or military background. We've got search warrants for an apartment in Queens and a suburban house in DC."

Reznick shook his head. "They might be Russian. But this sure as hell isn't the sort of operation sanctioned by Moscow."

Chisholm said nothing.

"What about Meyerstein? You think Froch knew anything about that?"

"For his sake, I hope not. Look at the poor bastard. How the hell did it come to that?"

"I'm convinced, and this is just me talking, that someone got to him, pure and simple. Either that or he's lost his goddamn mind."

Within the first few moments of the interview beginning, Reznick could see through the glass that Froch was going to talk frankly and freely. In fact he talked incessantly.

He'd been blackmailed. It began, he said, with a trip to MIT to recruit talented math and computer graduates to work for the State Department.

Reznick wondered where this was going. He watched as Chisholm nodded empathetically, listened carefully and occasionally took notes.

It wasn't long before Froch had his head in his hands. He began to cry. He'd been staying at the Mandarin Oriental in Boston, he explained. His drinks had been spiked. He'd had sex with two different women. Prostitutes, he was told later. He'd passed out. He remembered half waking, and looking up as his picture was being taken, and seeing lights from a video camera.

It was a lost weekend.

He flew back home to his quiet life in McLean, to his wife and family. Life went on as normal for months. He thought that he'd never hear any more about it. But then he received a phone call at his home one evening, just hours after the special access program had been set up. The red flags were all there. But he'd been too frightened to tell anyone.

The phone calls continued. They escalated to threatening his wife, family, and friends. His carefully ordered life was going to fall apart if he didn't do as he was told.

Reznick felt sorry for Froch, but everyone knew the rules. Never succumb. Never put American national security at risk. Tell your superiors. No matter what you've done, there can be a fix.

He listened as Froch begged Chisholm not to tell his wife.

Chisholm retorted, "Your wife is the least of your problems."

Then he turned the screw. He wanted to know if Froch had received any kickbacks and from whom. Froch said absolutely not. Chisholm said, "We're going to scour every bank account in your name, your wife's name, your kids' names, your mother's name, and every goddamn relation in the world. We'll check your cell phone records, home telephone records, office phone records, and we will get to the bottom of this, so if you want to stand a chance, you better spill the beans."

Froch shook his head. He said he hadn't received money. He'd been frightened for his family and his career, not to mention his reputation getting trashed in the press.

"Why didn't you alert your superiors at the State Department?

Froch bowed his head. "I'm in the Church. I believe in God. My family . . . what sort of man would I have been made to look like then?"

Chisholm rubbed his face as Froch began to cry again. He stopped for a coffee break, and joined Reznick in the observation room.

"What do you think, Jon?"

"Hard to say. What about a polygraph?"

"That's next. You know what all this reminds me of?"

Reznick shook his head.

"The book by Dulles, *The Craft of Intelligence*. He said that honey traps—bar girls and all that—were classic moves favored by the Russians. And such lures were sent to trap targets."

Reznick stared through the glass as the sobs from Froch got louder. "Russian tactics, absolutely. But as I've said, there's something more at work here."

"Well, whatever the purpose, the end result is that two of the senior members of the special access program, Meyerstein and Froch, are both now off the team investigating the disappearance of O'Grady."

"They're sending us a message."

"And what's that?"

"*We know who you are. We know what you're doing. We can get to you.* I'm telling you, these guys are something else."

Chisholm went quiet for a few moments. "The whole thing—O'Grady, Lieber, Meyerstein, and now this Froch business—it's like a slow-burn nightmare. You think you're getting close to something, and it disappears."

"You know as well as I do, we need to refocus this investigation."

"Jon, gimme a break. We're working around the clock. Scores of FBI, Homeland Security specialists, NSA, counterterrorism specialists, all desperately trying to figure this out."

"Either wittingly or unwittingly, that fuck in there has endangered the life of Assistant Director Meyerstein and threatened the integrity of this investigation. I want to rip him to shreds."

Chisholm sighed. "He's weak and he should've seen the signs. But he could have made it OK by just reaching out to someone in the State Department and saying what had happened. It would never have gone this far."

"What about his bank accounts?"

"We're checking those."

Reznick shook his head. "To think that a few hours after he sat down with Meyerstein in his office, he was selling her down the river."

"Froch was compromised many months ago," Chisholm said. "So this operation is a long-term thing. And the planning would've gone on for at least a year before it started."

"Which brings us back to Caroline Lieber and Ford."

"The Liebers will go to the press and try to publicize their daughter's disappearance."

"Can you blame them?"

"No, I don't blame them. Not in the least."

"Got any theories as to what happened to her?"

Chisholm shook his head.

"We're missing something, Sam."

A phone rang. Chisholm pulled his BlackBerry out of his pocket and answered it. "Yeah." He nodded. "Three cars on him, cell phone tracking, everything we have." He pressed the red button to end the call.

"What's up?"

"Our guy's on the move."

"Ford?"

"Yup. Picked up his car and he's heading out of the city." Chisholm bit his lower lip, the red light blinking on his phone. He pressed the button and opened up the message, eyes quickly scanning the words.

"There's a girl."

The words were spoken as if in a trance.

"Who?" Reznick asked.

"Stamper and his team have discovered that Ford had a girlfriend. Hilary Stapleton."

"Why the hell has this taken so long?"

Chisholm ignored Reznick, and stared at the message on the screen. "Jesus H. Christ."

"What is it?"

"Says here she's in a psychiatric unit in Baltimore."

Twenty-Eight

The next morning, Reznick and Chisholm found themselves on the fourth floor of a building on the Johns Hopkins Medical Campus in East Baltimore. They were led down tiled corridors, then through locked doors, before they reached the office of the director, Ron D. Franklin. The receptionist knocked on the door and they entered.

Franklin was waiting for them. He introduced himself, shook their hands, and sat down behind his desk. He was in his mid-sixties, tall and slim with wispy white hair. His shirtsleeves were rolled up as if he were ready for business.

He waited until Reznick and Chisholm pulled up a seat opposite before he spoke. "I believe you're interested in talking to one of our patients."

Chisholm cleared his throat. "That's correct, Dr. Franklin."

"Do you mind me asking why?"

"It concerns a major investigation. Counterterrorism."

Franklin furrowed his brow as if deep in thought. "I'm ultimately in charge of the medical care of all those within the inpatient unit. Patient confidentiality is paramount, so unless she consents, there's nothing I can do."

Chisholm shifted in his seat. "Dr. Franklin, I'd ask you to bear in mind that we have already applied for an order requesting access to her records, under Section two fifteen of the Patriot Act, and this has been approved." He pulled out the signed paperwork and handed it over to Franklin.

The doctor glanced at it. "How very thorough."

Chisholm didn't reply to the barbed comment.

"So, what do you want to know?"

"We want to know more about Ms. Stapleton and why she's being kept within the Mood Disorders Center."

Franklin let out a long sigh. "Bipolar disorder. Self-harm. A mental breakdown."

"How long's she been here?"

The doctor pursed his lips. "Three months, give or take a few days. She was a highflier. Then she crashed."

"What line of work?"

"Hedge funds. High pressure."

"What about a boyfriend?"

"Interestingly, just after she was admitted, she talked about her boyfriend." He flicked open a file on his desk. "Adam Ford. She mentioned that he was seeing another woman. She also mentioned that she thought she was being followed. Calls to her office, telling her to be careful, to stay away from Ford. People watching her. It could've been paranoia. Who knows?"

Chisholm nodded. "Did she know the person or people who were calling?"

"No. All she said was that it was a man's voice. An American. But we believe she was suffering from hallucinations. Voices in her head."

"When was she diagnosed with bipolar disorder?"

"When she was twenty-one. But she was a high-functioning bipolar. She would work manically for four days without sleep, and then crash. But then the hallucinations started earlier this year. She said her boyfriend was lacing the joints she was smoking with PCP."

Reznick wondered if Adam Ford, with his knowledge of drugs, was trying to get her hospitalized, knowing the devastating impact of PCP on someone with bipolar. And if so, for what purpose?

"Ms. Stapleton said the hallucinations were off-the-scale frightening."

Chisholm allowed a long silence to open up before he spoke. "We really need to speak to Ms. Stapleton, if that's all right with you."

"I would ask that you please bear in mind that her mind wanders, and she is prone to flights of fancy. Her moods can be dark, but also, by sharp contrast, she can go manic. Very excitable. Chatty."

"How is she just now?"

The doctor arched his thick eyebrows and smiled. "Go and see for yourself."

The room was all beiges, with gentle watercolors on the wall, two terracotta sofas, and a coffee table in the middle. Hilary Stapleton was standing with her back to them, staring out of the window, dragging hard on a cigarette. She didn't turn around when Chisholm and Reznick were ushered in by a nurse.

"FBI to see you, Hilary. You OK with that, honey?"

Stapleton turned around and beamed a wide smile at the nurse. She was very attractive, even without any makeup. "Thanks." She wore faded jeans, a tight-fitting pink T-shirt, and sneakers.

The nurse smiled. "I'll be waiting outside, Hilary," she said before shutting the door behind her.

"You wanna take a seat, guys?" she said, pointing to the sofa nearest the door.

Chisholm nodded and they sat down.

Stapleton remained standing. "First goddamn visitors I've had. You believe that shit?"

Chisholm smiled empathically. "I'm sorry to hear that, Hilary."

"You have no idea. I'm going out of my mind." She closed her eyes and laughed. "Do you know how that feels, huh?"

Chisholm shook his head.

Stapleton seemed to Reznick to be ricocheting between depression and mania, unsure where the mood was going to take her.

She sat down on the sofa opposite and crushed the cigarette out in a glass ashtray. She looked at them for a few minutes. "I'm sorry."

"You've nothing to be sorry for, Hilary," Reznick said.

Tears filled her eyes. "Thank you. I like it when people are nice to me. It's just that . . ." The words fell away, and she looked up and smiled. Her mood was changing by the second.

Chisholm leaned forward, hands clasped. "Hilary, we very much appreciate you seeing us. My name is Sam Chisholm, I'm from the FBI. And this is a colleague of mine."

Stapleton was still smiling. "Nice to meet you both."

"Now," Chisholm said, quickly clearing his throat, "we just want to chat with you. We don't want to write anything down and make you feel uncomfortable."

Her face relaxed. "I don't like it when people write things down when I'm here. It's like they're judging me. They don't know me."

"Absolutely, Hilary. We've just got a few questions about a guy you know."

"What guy?"

"Hilary, what can you tell me about Adam Ford?"

She closed her eyes for a moment, as if composing herself. Then she began to bite her lower lip. "Why do you want to know about him?"

"It's nothing major. We're just trying to find out a little bit about him."

Stapleton stood up. She was rigid, staring straight ahead. "I'm going to need more information," she whispered.

"What do you want to know, Hilary?"

"Do you think he still loves me?"

"I'm sure he does, Hilary." She nodded. "Let's sit down, Hilary, and you can tell me about him."

Stapleton sat down slowly, crossing her legs. "Things were great at the start. He was attentive. Caring. I was in love." She stared off into the middle distance. "But there were differences."

"What kind of differences?"

"I like music. I like to dance, have fun, drink, smoke pot, have a good time . . . you know what I'm talking about?"

Reznick nodded. "Sure."

"He didn't like my friends. He liked sports. He ran ninety miles a week sometimes. He rowed. He was down in his basement gym at all hours of the night. He meditated. I mean, for Chrissakes, I'm open-minded, but that's fucking nuts, right?"

Chisholm smiled. "So, you had different lifestyles. Did he take drugs of any sort?"

"Absolutely not. Categorically fucking not. He hated me smoking. He'd put me out in his backyard, like a dog, in all weather, while I smoked myself crazy."

"How did you meet?"

"My sister lives in DC. I visited and we went out to a few clubs. I was stoned and slipped on the floor and fell onto a broken glass." She pulled up her T-shirt and showed them a scar across the top of her breasts.

Reznick and Chisholm averted their gazes.

"When I went to the hospital, I was covered in blood, and then I met Adam."

Chisholm nodded. "And you hit it off?"

"I liked that he was so kind. I wanted to see him. I wanted more than that, to be honest. I think I'm a nymphomaniac, but I'm still to be diagnosed for that."

Reznick struggled not to laugh.

Chisholm cleared his throat. "OK, Hilary, so you wanted to see him again?"

"Yeah, so I started calling him, and eventually he agreed to meet me for a coffee. We talked. I had taken my Xanax, so I was OK."

"And it grew from there?"

"Slowly. Very slowly. I was working eighty hours a week on Wall Street, and by the time the weekend came, to see Adam, I was exhausted. But when I saw him I felt alive. Full of energy."

Chisholm pinched the bridge of his nose. "Can you tell me what he was like to be around?"

Stapleton shook another cigarette out of the pack that had been lying on the table and lit up. She inhaled deep into her lungs and blew the smoke out, away from them. "What can I tell you? He was nice and gentle. I think he was trying, at least in the beginning, to save me from myself."

Chisholm nodded but said nothing.

"He hooked me up with a therapist he knew. I didn't like him, but I persevered, because Adam wanted it for me so much. He really did. But then it all kinda, I don't know, started to change."

"What started to change?" Reznick asked.

"Him. At least I think it was him. He started paying less attention to me. He seemed very cut off, all of a sudden."

"When did this start?"

"Earlier this year. I was convinced he was seeing another girl."

"And was he?"

Stapleton rolled her eyes. "He's a guy . . . I don't know, maybe. It was hard to figure it out. I kept on asking him if he was happy, but he didn't want to talk about things. Not even his work, which he used to like doing. He really had a mission to save people. I don't know, this probably isn't making much sense, right?"

"Was there one trigger for you guys breaking up?" said Chisholm.

"It all started, I guess, when he came back from a trip."

"A trip where?"

"I don't know. He just said he went on a trip to find himself for a week."

"Go on."

"When he came back—well, about a week after he came back— I thought I was being followed."

"Followed by whom?"

"I had an apartment by Battery Park, and I reported a prowler on my block—a man acting suspiciously, as if he was checking on me, spying on me."

"Did you report this to the police?"

"Yes, I did. NYPD. Check it out if you don't believe me."

Chisholm reached forward across the table and patted the back of her hand. "We absolutely believe you, Hilary."

Stapleton dragged again on the cigarette and watched the plumes of smoke rise to the ceiling. "I looked out my window a few times and was convinced I saw people photographing me."

"Hilary, I don't want you to take this the wrong way, but was this just paranoia on your part?"

"No. This was plain as day. It was a man, sometimes in the shadows. I didn't like it. The police thought I was a crazy lady."

Chisholm smiled. "The doctor said you've been doing PCP. Couldn't this have led to paranoia?"

"I'm telling you, I didn't take PCP. You've got to believe me. It was Adam. He laced the joints. I know it."

"Why would he do that, Hilary?"

Stapleton went quiet for a few moments, a look of uncertainty crossing her fine features. "I think he was playing games with me. I think he's a monster."

Reznick smiled empathetically at her and then exchanged a knowing glance with Chisholm. The Fed went over to Stapleton and sat down beside her, taking her hand.

"Hilary," Chisholm said, "we need to know all about Dr. Ford."

"When I look back now, I can see that I was a toy for him to play with and then throw away. I think he arranged for me to be watched, to be followed, so that I would become paranoid. Maybe to keep an eye on me—I don't know for sure. Then the PCP to finish me off, cause my breakdown, and now I'm here." Stapleton laughed, tears filling her eyes. "No one believes me. Everyone thinks I'm a crazy loon who's trying to blame someone else for her problems. But believe me, Adam isn't the kind doctor type he makes himself out to be. There's something so dark and scary about him. I'm telling you, I get afraid even thinking about him."

"Go on."

"Within twenty-four hours of arriving here, I was self-harming." She pulled up her jeans and showed them cuts to her shin and the back of her calf. "I was losing my grip on reality and I needed to try to feel something. I felt the knife go into my skin. It felt good. For the first time in a long time, I felt at peace."

Chisholm nodded. "I think you've been through a helluva lot. And I'm glad you're getting the help you need here."

Stapleton stood up and walked to the window. "Feel like I'm in a fucking zoo. Fat-assed nurses talking about art therapy, cognitive therapy bullshit. I mean, gimme a break, I just need some quiet. Is that asking too much?"

"No, it's not."

"Thank you. Thank God somebody gets that. Since when has it been wrong for an American, in America, to want to shut the door on the world and just be left alone?"

Chisholm smiled and nodded along. "That's not wrong. I know where you're coming from. Every single day of my life, I want to shut the door on the world. I mean, who needs that shit?"

Stapleton flung back her head and laughed. "You guys are fun. Wasn't it Sartre who said hell was other people?" She ran a hand through her hair. "I always envisioned the Feds to be real cold bastards. You're not so bad."

Chisholm said, "You kidding me? Just ask my kids, I'm as soft as they get. Trust me."

Suddenly, Stapleton got a faraway look in her eyes. She'd changed. There was sadness in her gaze. "Always envisioned having kids. You know, cuddling up to them, being with them, nurturing them."

"It's not too late."

"I had visions of Adam and myself, me a stay-at-home mom, baking bread with my daughter, or son, take your pick . . . yeah, baking bread, that would've been nice."

"Did you ever talk to Adam about this?"

Stapleton turned and looked out of the window. "I saw, certainly in the early days of knowing Adam, a gentleness that I'd never encountered in a guy before. The way he looked at kids or expectant moms. He talked a lot about how America seemed to have lost its way. Its ideals had gone. It was all about the family, he would say. And I thought he would make a great father."

Chisholm nodded. "Did he ever talk about his friends or family? Did you ever meet them?"

"Never."

"What about old girlfriends? College buddies, that kind of thing?"

Stapleton turned and stared across the room at Chisholm. "Why do you want to know that?"

"We're just trying to build up a picture."

"Of who?"

"We need to know more about Adam," Reznick said.

"Is that right? But you've not answered my question. Why do you want to know about any old girlfriends?"

Reznick smiled. "What we're looking for is very important to us, and we're hoping you can fill any gaps in our knowledge. You've been very helpful so far."

Stapleton walked back to the table and shook another cigarette out of the pack before lighting up. "You're not telling me the full story, are you?"

Reznick said nothing as the room filled with tobacco smoke.

Chisholm pursed his lips. "Look, Hilary, if you can't help us any further, that's fine, we'll be on our way."

Hilary held up her hand as if to stop them. "I never said I couldn't help you. I want to help you. If you need this information, for whatever reason, then fine."

"So were there any old girlfriends that you knew of?"

"I asked him about that once. He said there was a girl a long time ago. He sometimes called out a name in his sleep. He would sometimes wake up in a cold sweat, panting hard, in the middle of a nightmare. I don't know . . ." She screwed up her eyes. "I think she had a foreign-sounding name. Russian."

Chisholm tried to appear disinterested, scratching his chin. "Russian, eh?"

"Yup."

"Did he talk about this girl?"

"Only the once. They were planning to get engaged but she died. He wouldn't elaborate. But I could sense a sadness there."

"What about a name? Can you remember the girl's name?"

"Kristina, I think."

Twenty-Nine

A couple of hours later, Reznick and Chisholm were at a conference table at the National Counterterrorism Center to talk to the rest of the special access group via video link.

Chairing the meeting with the Pentagon and three White House national security special advisors was Lieutenant General Black, who took off his spectacles and shrugged.

"Hard to know where to start."

Black looked at the huge screens showing the interested and tense-looking faces at the Pentagon and in the Situation Room at the White House. "If it's OK with you guys, I'll let Sam Chisholm give the update."

A Pentagon intelligence specialist called James McCormack said, "That's fine. Go right ahead, Sam."

Chisholm blew out his cheeks and looked at the screen, glancing quickly at the notes in front of him. "OK, people, anyone want to add anything, jump in. Here's what I know."

Over the next fifteen minutes, he outlined the revelations about Ford's latest girlfriend Hilary Stapleton, and the possibility that Ford's previous girlfriend was a Russian called Kristina. They listened in rapt silence, all taking notes. When he had finished, he opened it up.

Black looked at Reznick. "What are we missing here, Jon? I've got FBI Counterterrorism, the NSA, the CIA, Homeland Security, and every goddamn expert at the Pentagon scratching their heads on this." He glanced at the screens. "Jon is part of our team and has been working closely on this from day one."

A few nods.

"I'm thinking a cell," Reznick said. "Government backing."

A few murmurs from those in the White House Situation Room.

"What about Ford?" Black said. "I think it would be fair to say that there are some within the intelligence community who are not as convinced on Ford as you are."

"Well, there are strong indications of loose Islamic connections—perhaps cutouts—to Ford. Why is that?" Reznick shrugged. "Who knows? Let's chase down the leads—that's what I would do. *Was* there a former Russian girlfriend? Also, what about the missing three months?"

Black rubbed his eyes and looked at Stamper. "Are we still waiting for details of Ford's past?"

"Yes, we are. We're still filling in the blanks."

Reznick said, "Roy, what's taking so long?"

Stamper's gaze fixed on Reznick, who returned the look. "The FBI has allocated major resources to this investigation, and Ford is not the only avenue we are pursuing."

"Didn't Assistant Director Meyerstein ask for this forty-eight hours ago?"

A long silence. "Yes, she did. As I said, we're still working on it. Do you know how many aid agencies and government agencies provide medical assistance during natural disasters, wars, and other emergencies?"

Reznick shook his head.

"Hundreds. And we're checking and rechecking incomplete records as far back as two decades ago to see where Ford fits into this."

Reznick sighed.

"You don't look satisfied with the answer, Reznick."

"I'm not."

Stamper's face flushed. "Look, I don't take orders from you, Reznick. Are you clear on that?"

"This isn't about you, Roy. This is about this goddamn investigation. It's about the disappearance and murder of O'Grady. It's about a critically injured FBI special agent, Morales, a dead Islamic convert, his goddamn sister in the East Village. It's about a missing college student. It's about who took down your boss in broad daylight. And it's about trying to piece this jigsaw together. You want me to go on?"

"Who the hell do you think you are, coming in here, telling me what I should or shouldn't be doing?"

Black held up his hand to restore order. "OK, let's take this down a notch."

He looked at Stamper, who had flushed a bright red. "It's true that you don't answer to Jon Reznick. But he was only asking a simple question. He's part of this team in an advisory role."

Stamper shook his head, his lip curling into a sneer. "In answer to your question, we should get something within the next twenty-four hours. There's a hole in Ford's timeline in the 2000s, a period of three months spent away from the hospital in the US we can't account for. Once we know that, I can give the group what it's looking for."

Reznick nodded. "Appreciate that."

An awkward silence followed amid the rustling of papers.

"If we can leave Ford aside for a moment," Chisholm said, "I think it's worth noting that encrypted chatter on some hardcore, extreme-right, white-militia blogs is talking about bombing a syn-agogue on the Upper East Side. And also messages from Oregon and Michigan militias talking about Jewish blood flowing down Fifth Avenue."

A hand raised on the Pentagon feed. "Can I jump in, General Black?"

"Sure."

"Lieutenant Colonel Jack Anderson. I can confirm that Fort Meade has highlighted numerous channels going through several militias as well. We're working closely with Sam's team to track them down."

Black said, "As it stands, we have Islamists, militia, and a DC surgeon in our field of vision. It doesn't take an expert to see that something isn't adding up."

Chisholm piped up. "You're forgetting the Russians. What the hell are they doing? I just don't get it."

Reznick said, "I think they're proxies. Would they be dumb enough to use militias or Islamists to further their cause?"

McCormack put up his hand. "When it comes to Moscow, you can never rule anything in or out. You want me to remind you about Anna Chapman and those nice Russians living as American suburbanites? That was deep cover."

Black nodded. "Everyone around this table knows the Russians like to play the long game."

McCormack said, "I'll tell you what. This is a new Cold War. They're wanting to get us off balance. Islamists, militias, maybe they're the proxies. But the fingerprints of Moscow can't be erased."

Black interjected, "Look, I think we're going in circles. The question that I don't think we've really addressed is: what's the end-game for whoever is pulling the strings? Is there a target? Is there a mission?"

McCormack spoke first. "The anniversary of nine eleven is fast approaching. That's a clear red flag. And we'll have a lot of important people in New York on that day."

"Like who?" Reznick asked.

"The commander in chief himself, no less," Chisholm said, "But we have no indication as to who or what the target is."

A silence opened up for a few minutes.

"We're wondering if Ford was turned while overseas," McCormack said.

Black pinched the bridge of his nose. "Sam, what is the FBI saying to this?"

Chisholm flicked through some briefing papers before looking across the table at Black. "We concur with the 9/11 timeline analysis. The problem is Ford. We just can't get a handle on where he fits in. Does he have a hatred for the US government? Has he been radicalized? Ethiopia? Venezuela? Is he on the Moscow payroll? He's worked in the Third World: Nicaragua, across Latin America, Venezuela."

The red light on Chisholm's BlackBerry—sitting on the table in front of him—began flashing. He picked it up and scanned the incoming message.

"Any updates for us, Sam?" said Black.

Chisholm stared at the message for a few moments before he looked up. "That was the fingerprint guy at Port Mortuary in Delaware. There's been a development in regard to identifying the two Russians."

Thirty

The military mortuary in Delaware was run under the auspices of the Department of Defense and was one of the biggest in the world. Reznick had visited once before, when a Delta buddy was killed in Iraq. The mother wanted him to be there to ensure everything was above board. He'd never felt so empty in his life. He remembered when the boy, because that's what he had been, arrived in the aluminum transfer case, packed in ice inside a large freezer, along with a dozen other soldiers who'd been killed on duty.

Port Mortuary, officially called the Charles C. Carson Center for Mortuary Affairs, was where they'd brought the men and women killed on 9/11 at the Pentagon for processing. His own wife, who died on 9/11, had been turned to dust. No body for him. No closure.

His mind flashed back to the wailing of relatives as their dead loved ones arrived home from Iraq. Mothers and fathers sobbing, hugging each other for comfort. The crying echoing around the building as they waited.

Reznick was on edge as he followed Chisholm. They were ushered through an atrium with plants and a fountain. A motto on the stone wall read *Dignity, Honor, and Respect*, above a commemoration of those soldiers who had fallen in wars and terrorist attacks in modern American history.

The list seemed to go on forever. *Vietnam: 21,693 deceased . . . Mass Suicide, Peoples Temple in Guyana: 913 deceased . . . Terrorist Bombing, Marine Headquarters in Beirut, Lebanon: 237 deceased . . . Operation Iraqi Freedom: 3,431 dead or missing in action.*

He looked at two doors, one labeled *Counseling* and the other *Meditation.* He wondered which one a bereaved family was to choose.

They were led down a series of corridors until they got to the director's office. The door was open.

James Mulcahy was standing, stern-faced. He was tall, barrel-chested, with hair shaved to the bone. He wore a navy polo shirt and cargo pants. He stepped forward and shook their hands. "I believe one of your fingerprint specialists has already been in touch," he said.

Chisholm nodded.

Mulcahy shut the door before sitting down behind his large mahogany desk. "Look, I'm really sorry about this, but I'm afraid this journey has been a bit premature. Take a seat, guys."

Reznick and Chisholm sat down as Mulcahy adjusted the framed picture of his family on his desk.

"I'm sorry, I don't follow," Chisholm said.

Mulcahy sighed, huge hands spread out on his desk. "The fingerprint specialist who is one of your guys is quite new here. And by new, I mean wet behind the ears. A matter of days. He doesn't understand the protocols that exist. These protocols ensure that every process is done logically, with regard to the needs of the dead soldier's families taking precedence over everything."

Chisholm scratched the back of his head, obviously getting frustrated. "Of course, I appreciate there are protocols, that's only right. But I was told there had been an important development in the identification of the two bodies brought in from New York. It's vitally important that they are identified as soon as possible."

Mulcahy's eyes fixed on Reznick for a few moments. Reznick met his gaze and Mulcahy looked away. "Firstly, like I said, the fingerprint guy should not have contacted you directly. Secondly, the autopsies haven't even been started."

"Hang on, are you kidding me? They've been here nearly forty-eight hours."

"I appreciate that. But we have other priorities. A planeload of dead Marines—thirteen, to be precise. Blown up by a rogue Afghan army officer. That takes precedence, I'm afraid."

Chisholm leaned forward, forearms resting on his thighs. "Listen, I need these bodies identified. You can do it now."

"I don't think you understand how it works. We don't have to answer to the FBI. We answer to the parents and loved ones of the brave men and women who serve this country. The procedures are very detailed."

"Listen again. We're running a sensitive investigation that has implications for national security. And we need to find out about the two bodies which were brought in here."

"They'll be dealt with like all the bodies that arrive here. They carry the 'believed to be' status, meaning identity can be confirmed only here."

Reznick knew from bitter personal experience that all dead soldiers returned to Dover were tagged "believed to be" until their identity could be confirmed officially after a series of exhaustive forensic tests.

Chisholm said, "I appreciate that, but—"

"I don't know if you do. The fingerprints will have to be examined, dental and full-body X-rays carried out, DNA samples taken. Only then can the body on the table officially be given a name and formally identified."

"I hear what you're saying. But I want to speak to your fingerprint guy about what he knows."

"Look, he jumped the gun. I can't just go bumping two unknown bodies up ahead of our guys because you're running some investigation."

"Are you fucking kidding me? Are you saying we've come all this way—"

Reznick shifted in his seat, glad Chisholm had shown his displeasure.

Mulcahy put up his hand. "I run this place, not you. Do you understand?"

"You want me to go above your head on this? Do you want me to call up the Office of Special Counsel and report what you're saying? Do you want them to know that you're hampering a critical investigation which has, as I'll say again, national security implications?"

Mulcahy leaned forward. "Don't threaten me. I answer to the US Air Force and the Department of Defense. We do things our way, with respect."

Chisholm took a moment to compose himself. "Maybe I'm not making myself clear. While I understand that the autopsies have not been done, I would nevertheless like to speak to the fingerprint specialist who contacted us about developments. Now, I don't think that's asking too much, is it?"

Mulcahy leaned back in his seat and shook his head. "Look, I deal with a lot of requests, from pathologists and anthropologists, forensic photographers, and the Air Force Office of Special Investigations, all wanting priority access or information there and then, and it's just not possible. What you're asking for flies in the face of what we do. All I can say is that I'm sorry you've had a wasted journey, but as soon as we're in a position to conduct the full autopsies, including fingerprint analysis, and have the results, we'll let your team know." He fixed his gaze on Reznick. "It's protocol. First, last, everything."

Reznick sighed and slowly stood up. He stared down at Mulcahy. "Fuck your protocol, you desk jockey. We need to speak to your fingerprint guy. Right fucking now."

A sneer crossed Mulcahy's large face. "Are you threatening me, son?"

Reznick stepped forward and grabbed Mulcahy by the throat, pressing hard against the carotid artery. "Listen, you fat fuck, this is how it's going to work. You're going to give us access now, or you won't be able to swallow for a month." He squeezed tight for a couple of seconds and Mulcahy flushed, his teeth clenched with pain. "Am I making myself clear?"

Mulcahy struggled and gasped for breath.

Reznick held tight, then slowly released his grip. "So, I'll ask again. Can we see the fingerprint guy?"

Mulcahy gulped in air as Reznick held his throat. He nodded furiously.

"Is that a yes?"

"He's in his office," Mulcahy croaked. "By the water cooler."

Reznick turned and looked at Chisholm, who was nodding his head. "Thank you so much for your help, Mr. Mulcahy."

It was a long walk.

Chisholm spoke first. "That was out of line."

"He was out of line."

"That's not how I operate, Reznick. Do you understand?"

"Absolutely."

"Are we clear?"

"It won't happen again."

They took a right and walked down a long corridor until they reached a cubby-hole office by a water cooler. The door was open, and sitting at the desk was a baby-faced, dark-haired kid wearing a navy suit, white shirt, pale-blue tie, and shiny black shoes. He looked twenty-five, if that.

Chisholm approached the doorway. "Are you the fingerprint guy?"

"Sir, Special Agent Lee Horowitz," he said. "I'm from the Bureau but assigned to Port Mortuary."

Horowitz sprang out of his chair and offered his hand.

Chisholm shook his hand and smiled at the kid. "You mind if we come in and take a seat, son?"

Horowitz flushed crimson and pointed to the chair opposite his desk. "Please, but I only have two chairs."

Chisholm sat down. Reznick stood and leaned just inside the door, arms crossed.

The young agent sat down. "I'm sorry, I believe I've been a bit presumptuous contacting you guys about identification of the two gunshot victims from New York."

"We've smoothed it over with the director," Chisholm said. "You called us, Horowitz. You said there were developments. We're all ears, son."

Horowitz took a deep breath. "I had started preliminary work on the hands— photographing them, checking the fingerprints— before we got the dead Marines in from Afghanistan. That became a priority."

"So, let me get this straight. You had started work, but then this had to be stopped until after the autopsies and identification of the Marines?"

"Absolutely. It was only a few minutes I spent on them, but I saw similarities on the thumbs and forefingers of both victims."

"What kind of similarities?"

Horowitz turned his laptop around and tapped a couple of keys. Color close-ups of a male index finger appeared on the screen. "Look really close. You see it?"

Reznick saw a wafer-thin, gelatin-like sliver covering the small area where a fingerprint would be taken. "Shit."

"Indeed. I've still to do the analysis, but as a preliminary assessment, I would say that this is the residue from an attempt to thwart fingerprint-detection technology. It might be glycerin, but it might be a glycerin–gelatin hybrid."

Chisholm stared at the image. "So, how does this help us identify them, Horowitz?"

"Sir, in my opinion, this is the residue from a highly sophisticated attempt to fool a biometric fingerprint scanner."

"And?"

Horowitz looked up at Reznick and Chisholm. "Low-end optical fingerprint scanners can often be fooled with a simple image, but nowadays the scanners check for electrical current and blood flow. But there are numerous examples of how the characteristics of gelatin are similar to a human finger and can fool high-end scanners."

Reznick stared at the image and shook his head. "The clear gelatin allows the scanner to read a false fingerprint."

Horowitz nodded. "Precisely."

Chisholm picked up a pen and pointed to the gelatin residue on the photo. "What about liveness-detection technology?"

"This type of thing can spoof most of what we have at US airports. That's the reality."

"How the fuck have we not sorted this out?"

Horowitz shrugged. "Take your pick—design, cost, political will. As it stands, research is ongoing to find a balance between price, user-friendliness, and security of the system. But the bottom line is, the system is heavily flawed. And determined and sophisticated terrorists can circumvent fingerprint technology used in airports across America."

Chisholm rubbed his eyes. "OK, so what've we got? An attempt by these two individuals to conceal their identities, right?"

Horowitz nodded.

"Who are these people? What about their true fingerprints?"

Horowitz grinned. "Hoped you were going to ask me about that." He tapped the keyboard, and two side-by-side fingerprints appeared on the screen.

"What are we looking at?" Chisholm asked.

"Digitally enhanced fingerprints showing what we believe the full fingerprints would show, if the minute sliver of gelatin on the fingers was erased."

"Hang on, so the fingerprints we're looking at were scanned and signs of the gelatin residue were removed?"

"Right. With a 0.04 percent degree of doubt, these are the real fingerprints of the man and woman with the gunshot wounds."

"So you're 99.96 percent certain that these fingerprints on the screen are accurate. But there's been an attempt to conceal their true identity . . . am I keeping up with you?"

Horowitz nodded. "You got it, sir. And guess what else?"

"What?"

"We got a match. I contacted a source at the Russian Foreign Intelligence Service, and they said they had an exact match with our computer-generated fingerprints. That's why I wanted to speak face to face."

"Have they communicated the identities of these two individuals?"

"Not yet. They're waiting to get proper clearance to release that information. But they did tell me two things."

"What?" Chisholm said, grinding his teeth.

"Both the man and woman were Spetsnaz at one time."

Reznick's blood ran cold. "Russian special forces . . ."

"The thing is, they aren't just Russian."

"I'm sorry, you're not making sense."

The kid blushed.

"So what the hell are they?" Chisholm said.

Horowitz cleared his throat self-consciously. "Sir, they're also Chechens. Brother and sister. Islamists."

Thirty-One

Five hours later, the full IDs of the two Chechens were on big screens in a conference room back in McLean. The talk was of another Boston-style bombing.

Chisholm stood, hands on hips, chewing some gum. He glanced at the two sullen faces up on the screens. "This is Anatoly Umarov and his sister, Kristina. Is this the woman Ford knew?"

A deathly hush.

"We don't know at this stage." He cleared his throat. "Leave that aside just now. Anatoly is the one to focus on. He is the cousin of Caucasian insurgent leader Dimitri Umarov, and was one of his inner circle. And we believe he would have been acting on direct orders."

Black stared at the picture, eyes hooded.

"The Umarovs are notorious. They are part of a radical jihadist movement that the State Department has classified as a threat to the United States." Chisholm pointed at the photo of Anatoly Umarov. "This guy, along with his cousin, reactivated a dormant Chechen suicide battalion, Riyadus-Salikhin. They're guerilla fighters. They've been linked to a series of suicide bombings on the Moscow subway that killed forty people, the bombing of a luxury train that killed twenty-eight, and an attack that nearly killed the president of Ingushetia. He is wanted by Russia for kidnapping, homicide, and treason. And his cousin is the self-proclaimed Emir of the North Caucasus, an unrecognized Islamic state known as the Caucasus Emirate."

Black leaned back in his seat. "This changes everything." He looked across the room at Chisholm. "This is clearly an Islamist operation, right?"

"The problem is, General, we don't have a clear, definitive assessment."

"What do you mean? This is clear as day."

Chisholm sighed. "I think it is imperative that we keep an open mind. We've got to question assumptions, but also see different perspectives. We don't understand what the purpose of this mission was. Are they part of a cell? Are these two Chechens the cell? Is there something bigger going on behind the scenes? The analysis, as it stands, is not conclusive by any means, and we're still trying to see how Ford fits into the picture."

Black pointed to a senior FBI counterintelligence specialist, Miles Griffin. "How does Ford fit into this? And please, Miles, spare me any management-speak. I've had my fill of it."

Griffin took off his glasses and leaned his elbows on the conference table. "We're looking at this from multiple angles. Motivation, behavior, counterterrorism, threat analysis, source intelligence, and we're pulling in CIA and Homeland Security know-how. But, as Sam says, we just don't get it. The cutouts are there. Jamal Ali has visited Pakistan four times since he got out of jail. His sister is most likely the cutout, as Reznick alluded to from the outset. The most intriguing aspect of all this is—and we keep coming back to this—the role of Ford. How does he fit into this structure?"

Black's face reddened. "What the hell are you talking about? What structure? Are you saying he's part of this Islamist cell?"

"Not at all. Let's leave Ford aside for a second. The latest analysis I've seen, within the last hour, does show that there is an escalating risk of terrorist operation in the US in the coming days."

The color seemed to drain from the general's face. "What?"

"Timescale is pointing to a terrorist attack, almost certainly Islamist in nature. It's almost the anniversary of 9/11. That's flashing us red lights, big time."

Black nodded. "So all this—taking out O'Grady, Lieber's disappearance, Meyerstein, not to mention putting the squeeze on Froch . . . It's all to protect one man?"

"The majority view from my analysis is that this group or cell, whoever they are, are making sure their guy gets a clean run at this. At all costs. But Ford is causing us all a real headache. Who the hell is he? No one knows."

Chisholm said, "We need to pull him in. Right now."

Black grimaced. "On what grounds? We have nothing. If we jump on Ford, we don't know if there is a Plan B, C, or even D. Not to mention the network would still be in place—on the ground, in America. I say the sound strategy would be to watch and wait."

Chisholm sat down in his seat and shook his head. "With respect, sir, I don't concur. My concern is that all these signals are going to get lost in the noise from the data that's pouring in."

Black glared across at him. "I don't give a rat's ass if you concur, Sam, because—from where I stand—no one is able to give me a straightforward assessment."

Chisholm sighed. "This is not an exact science. We all know that. As it stands, the range of probability from analysis across the intelligence spectrum suggests that the possibility of a terrorist attack could be from as low as sixty percent up to eighty-nine percent, which can be translated into saying that there is a significant probability that an attack is imminent. Everyone believes Ford fits into this. But they're not sure how."

Black's face was like stone. "I'm finding it hard to get my head around the fact that Ford could be an Islamist. We have no concrete proof. Why the hell would an upper-middle-class white American head down this route?"

"A lawyer in Marin County whose son went to fight for the Taliban didn't understand either," Reznick interjected. "A middle-class guy from a good background in California—John Walker Lindh. Remember him? His father described him as a sweet kid. I was there when we interrogated him after the prison uprising near Mazar-e-Sharif. It happens. Good kids go bad. He wasn't a bad kid intrinsically. He was naive. He wanted to learn about Islam. He developed fluency in Arabic. And then he got radicalized. He took up arms against America. It happens."

Those around the table were listening intently.

"The possibility must exist that something has happened to Ford. Did he convert, and was he then radicalized?"

"There is no proof of that," Black said.

"The possibility exists. And think about it. What phenomenal cover . . . White middle-class American, covertly protected by white Chechens. Easy for them all to blend in, right? We all have the picture in our head of the Middle Eastern-looking guys with beards, toting machine guns or semiautomatics. Well, I've got news for you: the two Chechens in the morgue may just be the tip of the iceberg. These Islamists are willing to lay down their lives to avoid giving themselves up." He pointed at the pictures on the screen. "Anatoly Umarov shot his sister and then shot himself to avoid us getting them alive. They faked their fingerprints. That may point to a highly sophisticated operation. They may also be well funded. I'm telling you, we've got a major problem on our hands."

"Froch was set up and has confessed that he was being black-mailed. This may point to a foreign government," Chisholm said. "Russia? We don't think so, but we can't rule them out. We've got to focus on the possibility that the Chechens may be proxies for a Middle Eastern power. Syria? Iran? We just don't know. There might also be a parallel operation going on—the possibilities are endless."

Black said, "Let's focus on what we do know. Tell me more about these Umarovs."

Chisholm sat down and flicked through his papers. "A few years back, the Umarovs denied that the Chechen separatist movement was linked to al-Qaeda or any jihadist groups, and claimed they only wanted independence from Russia. But Anatoly Umarov's cousin—as recently as 2011—expressed solidarity in an intercepted cell phone conversation with, and I quote, 'brothers in Afghanistan, Iraq, Somalia, and Palestine.' Interestingly, his cousin has publicly attacked America, Russia, the United Kingdom, and Israel for oppressing Muslims. He believes in Sharia law. And he was implicated in the Beslan siege."

"Here's something else to consider," Reznick interjected. "We were identifying an Iranian Shia connection from early days. But I think we can say that, if Chechens are involved, this is far more likely to be a Sunni Islamist threat."

Black said, "Wahhabis, like al-Qaeda—is that what you're saying?"

"I'm not an analyst, but that has got to be a possibility. But I think you have to remember that bin Laden wasn't a Wahhabist. Most Islamic extremists follow the ideology of Sayyid Qutb, not Wahhabism."

One of the FBI intelligence experts was nodding. "That's a very good point indeed, and easy to overlook. Wealthy Saudis—and to an extent the Saudi government—are the paymasters for Muslim Brotherhood chapters and hard-line Islamists. And they're pulling the strings in Syria with their jihadist links."

Black's eyes were hooded.

"What about a foreign government pulling the strings?" said Reznick.

Chisholm stared back at him but said nothing.

"You know how it works, guys—a government doesn't want to leave their fingerprints on an operation. I don't think we can rule out the Iranians. The Chechens are nice cover for them. Look at Bosnia way back in the nineties. The Iranians were involved in supplying Bosnian Muslims with large numbers of multiple rocket launchers and huge caches of ammunition. This included 107mm and 122mm rockets. All made in Iran. The Iranian Revolutionary Guard was very active on the ground in Bosnia, and the CIA estimated that around four hundred had been detached for future terrorist operations."

Black frowned. "Chechens being used as proxies?"

Reznick sighed. "The problem with all this conjecture is that we still can't pin down how Ford is involved. The doctor who likes to do good. The doctor who likes to row. The doctor who saves lives. The doctor whose ex-girlfriend is in a psychiatric unit, accusing him of drugging her, and another girl who is missing. Wouldn't that bother you—if a girl you knew was missing?"

"But wasn't Caroline Lieber the one who was obsessed with him?"

Chisholm pinched the bridge of his nose. "Goddamn."

Reznick said, "If we're saying Ford may be an Islamic convert, when did this happen? His ex-girlfriend didn't mention any Muslim sympathies or ties."

Chisholm said, "I really think we need to bring him in."

"And say what?" Black said. "*Are you in the middle of a terrorist operation, doc?* I mean, come on. Besides, he's under surveillance twenty-four seven."

Chisholm stared at him. "We don't have to be so obvious. We could say that we're in the middle of an ongoing investigation, and ask if he could help us. Ask him to fill in the blanks of his past. If he can't—why not?"

A few nods from around the table.

Black said, "Look, we're watching him. His new cell phone is being tracked. We've got all the agencies working on this—"

Just then, there was a sharp knock. Everyone turned around as the door opened.

Walking in, ashen-faced, head held high, was Assistant Director Martha Meyerstein.

Thirty-Two

Reznick looked across at Meyerstein. Her face was drawn, and her carefully applied makeup could not hide the dark circles around her eyes and the pallor of her skin. She looked fragile, almost vulnerable. She took the seat next to Black and reached for a glass of water, her hand betraying a slight shake. She looked at those around the table and smiled.

"Against my doctor's advice . . . and probably my better judgment, I'm taking charge again," she said.

Some forced laughter, before a palpable sense of relief swept through the room.

Chisholm smiled. "Great to have you back, Martha. Are you up for this already?"

"I'm here. OK, so where the hell are we?"

A five-minute overview briefing followed, outlining the latest theories about the two Chechens and the blackmailing of Froch. Meyerstein listened intently but remained silent.

Then Black said, "This Chechen link, in light of what happened to you and with what happened in Boston still fresh in all our memories, has to make us wonder if there are others. I for one don't believe these two are acting alone."

Meyerstein nodded. "Look, I'm coming at this cold. I need to get up to speed—and quick. I'm going to read all the briefings, updates, and threat assessments we've got. So before I disappear for a couple of hours, what's the latest on Ford?"

Chisholm said, "He's on our radar. But we're still missing part of his history. Something's not adding up. Roy's guys are busting a gut on this. They'll get it."

Meyerstein's gaze went around the rest of the room. "But when? Look, this guy Ford, something's wrong, and I can't put my finger on it. So let's get some answers. And damned quick." A few nods. "OK, meeting adjourned. Let's meet up in four hours' time. Let's get to it." A shuffling of papers, and everyone began to drift out of the room.

Meyerstein approached Reznick and took him aside.

"Hey, I believe I owe you one. Thank you." She held his gaze for a moment and smiled. "I mean it."

Reznick felt uncomfortable and shrugged off her gratitude. "Forget it. All part of the service."

Meyerstein gave a tired smile. "I need to speak to you and Sam in private. Couple things I'd like to run past you. But not here."

Chisholm and Reznick followed her out of the building and into the back of a waiting car. Meyerstein sat up front. They were driven in silence all the way to FBI Headquarters in Washington, each lost in their own thoughts. Reznick sensed something was up. She knew something. But what?

Meyerstein stared ahead, occasionally glancing at her BlackBerry when its red light flashed, indicating she had a message.

The more he thought of it, the more he realized the investigation was in deep trouble.

The car pulled up at the security gate before being waved through. They took the elevator to the seventh floor of the Hoover Building and headed along a corridor to an electronic door.

Meyerstein punched in a four-digit code and they went on through. Down another corridor, flanked by the offices of the most senior FBI agents, until they reached Meyerstein's. Her name and rank were etched in silver on the glass door.

Meyerstein led them inside, where a young agent wearing a sharp suit and tightly knotted tie was standing by a window, waiting for them.

Meyerstein shut the door behind her. "Take a seat."

Reznick and Chisholm did as they were told. The young agent remained standing.

Meyerstein sat down behind her desk. "This is Larry McNair. Before you ask, he's new. He's a counterespionage expert. Electronic surveillance, all that stuff."

Reznick nodded at him, and McNair smiled.

"I've been doing a lot of thinking since I got out of the hospital. It's given me time to reflect on the investigation and how it has developed—or not, as the case may be. And I started thinking about how I'd gotten involved. It was right that I was assigned to head this, with the missing State Department official and all that. But then I started thinking about the special access program. What was the rationale behind that? I didn't give it much thought earlier. I just assumed the rationale was sound. Why wouldn't it be, right?"

Chisholm said, "It makes sense."

Meyerstein said, "Remember, Jon, we got the last number O'Grady called—Caroline Lieber—and I asked you and Roy to chase it down, which you did, and this led us to Ford. But initially, I kept that information from the main members of the special access program."

Neither Reznick nor Chisholm said anything.

"This is difficult to explain. But I've felt that . . . I've felt that we're being second-guessed every step of the way. Something isn't right . . . I was attacked, drugged, and left for dead in a goddamn State Department bathroom. I mean, how was that possible?"

"Froch. He was compromised," said Chisholm.

Meyerstein smiled. "Yes. But I believe there's someone not connected to Froch who's playing us."

Chisholm ran a hand through his hair. "Whoa! What are you saying?"

"I don't know. But yesterday, I sent a secure message to McNair, who visited me in hospital."

Reznick and Chisholm looked across at McNair, who stood looking slightly embarrassed.

"I asked McNair to help me out."

"In what way?" asked Chisholm.

"I wanted to make sure that none of the rooms and offices we had were being bugged."

Reznick sat forward. "You kidding me, right?"

Meyerstein shook her head. "You know what McNair found out? My office, which was allocated to me within the National Counterterrorism Center in McLean, and yours, Sam—along with the conference room we meet in—were all bugged."

"Bullshit," said Chisholm. "Those offices will be routinely swept for bugs."

"This is no bullshit, Sam. McNair? Do you want to jump in here?"

McNair blew out his cheeks. "Absolutely. The listening devices are in the walls. Don't know how long they've been there. But it's a sophisticated job."

"And that's why, gentlemen, I brought you here. Someone is keeping tabs on what we're doing and why."

The revelation had come clear out of the blue, and Reznick's mind was racing. The more he thought about it, the more he wondered if there was anyone around the special access program he *could* trust.

McNair said nothing and looked at Meyerstein.

She cleared her throat. "Sam, this bug doesn't emit radio waves. That's how high-end this operation is. We'd have to drill through the walls to retrieve the bug to identify it. That in turn would defeat the purpose, as we'd alert those listening in that we were aware of them."

Reznick looked at McNair. "What about General Black's office?"

McNair covered his mouth with his hand and coughed. "The tests were conclusive. Two covert listening devices in the walls of his office. This is something on a highly sophisticated level. Virtually undetectable with routine anti-bugging equipment."

Chisholm sighed, eyes closed.

McNair continued, "As Assistant Director Meyerstein said, these devices don't emit radio waves. Instead of transmitting conversations, they record the conversations within the room." He paused for a moment. "We've got military-grade equipment that can look for magnetic fields, or electrical noise given out by computerized technology in digital tape recorders, but most offices have photocopiers and computers, so the background noise is very difficult to deal with. But what we did was sweep the rooms using thermal cameras, and we detected the residual heat of a bug or power supply concealed in the walls. Simply put, our devices located hot spots where the bugs were."

"And you're certain of this?" Reznick said.

"In my opinion, it's one hundred percent conclusive."

"Covert ops, no question." Chisholm said, turning to Reznick. "Where would you start in figuring out where these recording bugs came from, and how they carried out the placement?"

"I think it could've been done by a two-man team—maybe three—in one night, under the cover of maintenance. I trained CIA guys in just such work. The whole place could be done . . . the plasterboard walls pulled off and drilled back into place with the bugs inside, then a lick of paint. But to answer your question— where they came from—you need to head back to the start of this investigation. The origin of the special access program, I mean."

Meyerstein shifted in her seat. "It began when I got a call."

"A call?" Reznick said. " From whom?"

"A three-star general in the Pentagon. I'm not at liberty to divulge who. He just told me that a special access program was up and running, and I had been tasked to head up the investigation with General Black."

Reznick smiled. "So this is from the Pentagon. Christ, that doesn't narrow it down much."

Chisholm sighed, as if weighed down with it all.

Reznick looked at Meyerstein. "They're assuming that we don't know they're listening in. So, I reckon we've got three options. Option number one: go straight to General Black and tell him what we know. The response? Who the hell knows? Option two: keep quiet and find out who is behind this. Problem is, that's time-consuming and moves the focus away from possible security threats. Option three: keep quiet and concentrate on the investigation."

Meyerstein looked at McNair for a few moments. "I'm instructing you, Special Agent McNair, not to reveal what you know to anyone. We'll deal with this. Do you understand?"

McNair nodded. "Yes, ma'am."

"Head back to the Office of the Director of Intelligence and get back to work. You understand?"

"Absolutely."

McNair left the room, shutting the door quietly behind him.

Reznick let out a long sigh. "This whole thing is getting under my skin."

Meyerstein said, "Me too. Sam, where would you go from here?"

"My feeling is that we should be up front. We have nothing to hide. We speak to General Black in private, letting him know and in the process also those who are listening in."

"Jon, what about you? What do you think we should do?"

"I thought it interesting that in the meeting, Sam, you said that you thought we should bring Ford in. I would have taken what you had to say very seriously. But Black flat-out disagreed." He looked at Meyerstein. "What would you do if you were in Black's shoes?"

"I'd haul in Ford. He has questions to answer. Yes, bringing in Ford would alert those within any cell that we're on to them, but I still think we should pull him in."

Reznick smiled. "So, you both agree that Ford should be brought in. I agree. I also think Black's option of wait and see is a risky strategy."

Meyerstein said, "So, how do we move forward in regard to the bugging of the offices? Do we speak directly to General Black?"

"Absolutely," said Chisholm.

Reznick sighed. "I'd go one step further. I'd say this should be raised with everyone else. Put it right up front."

Meyerstein shook her head. "That would be like I'd ambushed him. I think it's better to keep it restricted. But I'll speak to him myself. Face to face."

Reznick shrugged. "Whatever works for you. I agree you need to bring it to Black's attention, but there's another reason why. And it's this. He'll either sit on that information and do nothing, or pass it on to someone higher up within the Pentagon."

Meyerstein picked up a pen and began playing with it for a few moments. "And how would we ascertain if that information has been passed on, and to whom?"

"Track his calls and emails and messages. Electronic surveillance."

"Are you fucking crazy, Reznick?" Chisholm said.

Reznick shook his head.

Meyerstein said, "Are you seriously saying we should consider this?"

"Your investigation has been compromised, perhaps from day one. You need to get to the bottom of this. And General Black may provide the answer."

Thirty-Three

When they returned to the Office of the Director of National Intelligence in McLean, they went straight into the meeting with Lieutenant General Black and the other members of the special access program.

As she sat down, her train of thought was interrupted by flashbacks of the face of the woman who had carried out the attack in the State Department restroom. Knots of anxiety washed over her as she shuffled her papers. She took a few moments to compose herself, knowing all eyes were on her.

She began to think of how to broach the subject of the bugging with Black while she listened to three senior intelligence experts—from the FBI, the National Counterterrorism Center, and Homeland Security—confirming growing chatter about a real and growing threat, with New York as the target city. She wondered how Ford fitted into that.

Although there was a convergence of views among the intelligence agencies warning of an impending yet unspecified threat, no one could agree what the target was and who would be carrying out the attack. The discussions became heated, not surprisingly. Black listened intently, scribbling on his notepad, as the debates raged.

The President's national security advisor said, "I've got to let you guys know that the President is increasingly concerned that we have not established the exact nature of the threat. I mean, what is actually going on?"

Chisholm spoke up. "Like we've said again and again, there are numerous strands. The kidnapping, the attempted murder of Meyerstein, Froch, McGovern, and Jamal. Then Akhtar, who has decided to plead the Fifth, and the Chechens—and of course, let's not forget Ford."

"So why the hell aren't we bringing him in?"

Black sidestepped the question. "My main concern is that the Chechens are the proxies for Iran or Syria, Sam."

A red light started flashing on the phone in front of Chisholm. He picked it up and listened for a few moments before he spoke. "When . . . ? Keep with him." He put down the phone.

"Surveillance teams are saying Ford is now on the move. He just jumped into a cab on the Upper East Side. We have three separate teams—one on a motorbike and two in cars—tracking his every move."

Meyerstein looked at Reznick. "Jon, I want you back in New York with Sam and his guys until this is over. I think we're all agreed New York is the endgame target. You OK with that?"

"What's the brief?"

"I want you on the ground as we continue the surveillance on Ford."

She looked across the table at Black. "General, I agree with Sam. We need to bring in Ford. Right now."

Black cut short the meeting. "Not an option. At least for now."

***

Half an hour later, Meyerstein was on a Gulfstream heading for New York, with Reznick and Chisholm a row in front, deep in conversation. She perused the latest analysis but her thoughts inevitably drifted to the bugging.

The more she thought about it, the more she realized Black was out of step with the other experts working on the investigation. But she pushed those thoughts aside as she began to focus again on the myriad strands of the frustrating and complex investigation.

Why hadn't Stamper yet filled in the blanks on Ford's overseas work? But Stamper was meticulous and wouldn't leave any stone unturned. He would get to the bottom of it. She knew that.

Reznick sat down beside her and handed her a black coffee. "Drink it. You look like you need it."

Meyerstein smiled. "Yeah, I guess so."

Reznick looked at the papers covering the table in front of her. "You're snowed under."

"Tell me about it."

"So where do you go from here?" he said.

"I feel very conflicted. The investigation is paramount, and distractions are not good. But bugging the intelligence offices? Who did this? And why? How long have the bugs been there? Is this connected to the special access program? Have they been in place for years? The problem is, Jon, these questions are going to be almost impossible to find answers to." She sighed. "What would you do?"

"I've told you what I would do. I would find out what General Black is up to and work back from there."

"I need a judge to sign a warrant."

"Then get him to sign it."

"Might be a bit tricky, considering it's an unacknowledged special access program. Its very existence isn't acknowledged, so it's a catch-22."

"Then be more creative. Put him under surveillance without authorization."

Meyerstein closed her eyes. "I don't know. Where does that end?"

"It ends when you learn who authorized the bugging. Listen to me . . . all this smoke and mirrors—Froch, the murder of a diplomat, a missing student, Islamists—I'm telling you, this is not a cell-like operation by one terrorist group. There's something else at work."

"What are you getting at?"

"Nothing is what it seems."

"Jon, you're getting pretty obtuse, if you don't mind me saying."

"Sometimes, just sometimes, the story you see is not the whole story. It's not even the real story."

"What the hell is this, Jon—some philosophical discussion?"

"Maybe."

The phone on Meyerstein's armrest rang and she picked it up. She listened intently, nodding a couple of times. "You kidding me?" She closed her eyes. "Superb work, Roy. Send it over to me. Right now." She ended the call.

"Development?" Reznick said.

Meyerstein pressed a button on her laptop and checked her inbox. "You could say that." She clicked on the newest email from Roy Stamper and opened the attachment.

It was a grainy color picture showing bearded, battle-hardened Islamists wearing army fatigues. Reznick stared at the image, focusing on each and every face. Meyerstein took a pencil and pointed to the beautiful brown-eyed woman standing with them. "Kristina Umarov, the Chechen shot dead by her brother."

"Jesus."

"That's not all." She pointed with the pencil at a ruggedly good-looking, bearded Caucasian guy in the middle. "Take a closer look."

Reznick leaned forward. Cold blue eyes. Handsome face. Mid-twenties, perhaps. "Son of a bitch."

Meyerstein looked at the picture. "Dr. Adam Ford just outside Grozny, Chechnya."

Thirty-Four

It took a few moments for Reznick to get his head around it. "How the hell did we get this?"

Meyerstein sipped her coffee. "Russian security services raided the homes of Chechen leaders and their associates, as well as relatives of the Umarovs, in the last forty-eight hours. We'd circulated an image of Ford a few days ago. And they found this in an old FSB filing cabinet: Kristina Umarov in the same photo as Adam Ford. One of my team, Special Agent Brian Martin, has gone over it ten thousand times with the latest facial recognition software. It's a perfect match for both. One hundred percent."

"What was his cover?"

"Russians think he slipped into the country while working for an American medical charity which is now defunct—American Medical Aid across Frontiers."

"Never heard of them."

"Neither have I. But in the time he said he was working for the Red Cross in Somalia, he was with them."

Reznick stared at the image. "Adam Ford . . . Who the hell is this guy?"

Meyerstein shrugged.

Reznick looked out of the window as the plane descended through the clouds into perfect blue skies, as they began their approach to New York. His mind was racing. "We definitely have to bring him in."

A shudder from turbulence. Meyerstein said, "No. I want you to shadow him. I think there's a bigger picture here, and we use Ford to get to it. But we keep tight on him to make sure he doesn't cause trouble."

Reznick sighed but said nothing.

"The picture changes everything, Sam. But we'll keep this to ourselves. See where Ford takes us."

"What do you mean, *keep it to ourselves*?"

"I don't want Black to know about this development."

"Why the hell not, Martha?"

"When I met with him earlier, he said he'd get on to the White House about the bugging of the offices. McNair is monitoring Black's phones. The only call he's made is to an unlisted number at the Pentagon."

Chisholm crushed his empty Styrofoam coffee cup and threw it on the floor. "This is getting crazier by the second."

"It is what it is," Reznick said.

Chisholm let out a long sigh. "OK, leave it with me."

Meyerstein leaned forward and put a hand on his arm. "Thanks, Sam."

The phone on her armrest rang again. "Meyerstein," she answered. Then she nodded. "Are you sure?" A beat. "Shit. Keep on it. We'll be landing in less than five minutes."

She hung up. "That was surveillance on Ford. He's been dropped off in Queens and he's walking."

Reznick rubbed his eyes. "Walking? Walking where?"

"In the direction of Flushing Meadows. The US Open tennis."

"What?"

"We've got him covered. He'll get a priority search."

"That's irrelevant. There could be others inside. How the hell have we missed this?"

"The focus was on forthcoming nine eleven commemorations."

Meyerstein felt a headache coming on, drilling deep into her head. "Look, we're landing at LaGuardia. Virtually on top of Flushing Meadows. We'll be there in fifteen minutes. Jon, I want you inside with Phil Gritz and the red team."

"And what do you want me to do?"

"You watch and wait. If he makes a move, you shoot to kill."

Thirty-Five

Crowds surged all around Flushing Meadows Park. They pulled up half a mile from the larger stadium and stepped out into the early-evening heat.

Reznick felt the sweat run down his back.

Gritz put on his shades. "Weapons concealed at all times. We'll be waved through by security, OK?"

"Where's he going to be sitting?" Reznick asked.

"We're working on that."

Reznick pulled on a white Nike baseball cap. He'd been teamed up with a young FBI agent, Tom Blake—a muscular, preppy-looking kid. "OK, son, let's do this."

"You got it," the Blake said.

They disappeared into the crowds headed for the stadium, the smell of sweat and cigarettes mixing with the sound of laughter and excited chatter. A few minutes later, they were in a huge line at the South Gate, directly in front of the Unisphere. Fifteen minutes later, they were ushered inside the stadium by the security director, and into a crammed concourse.

Reznick and the kid headed up an escalator. His earpiece buzzed into life. "Jon, Ford has just gone through the gates. He's headed for the expensive courtside seats, where you'll be sitting."

"Where exactly?"

"You'll be situated behind the baseline on the south side. You'll be handed a courtside ticket from an usher. He's a Fed, Special Agent David Jackson. Big guy, can't miss him."

"OK, got that," he said as they made their way through the concourse as the crowds headed toward their seats for the match.

The Arthur Ashe stadium towered high, the promenade seats mostly empty. But in his area it was a lot busier.

A huge usher stepped forward. "Tickets, please," he said, slipping the tickets into their hands. He flashed them a smile. "Enjoy the game, guys."

They walked toward their assigned seats. The kid sat down about ten yards away, and Reznick headed farther down the steps to his row. He squeezed past a chicly dressed woman and her impeccably attired partner, who was wearing a sky-blue suit, speaking into a phone. Reznick sat down on his seat at the end of the row, eight seats from the front.

"Jon," Gritz said into his earpiece. "Three down from you. You got a fix?"

Reznick scanned the row and saw Ford wearing brown tortoiseshell sunglasses, a US Open Panama hat, white polo shirt, and khakis, talking into his cell phone.

"Have we got that number?"

"Must be using a new, untraceable phone. Fuck!" Gritz sighed down the line. "The section to your right. Can you see Special Agent Blake?"

Reznick turned around and saw Blake, pretending to read the *New York Times*. "Got him."

"OK, take it in turns. If Ford gets up, you follow him. Then alternate that with Blake. We've got plenty of cover beside the restrooms, and agents working in the burger vans and even the Heineken stands."

"Nice."

Gritz gave a throaty laugh. "We're keeping a nice overview of the area, Jon, and I'm watching you on a monitor. We're all set up."

Roars from the restless, noisy crowd. "Keep me posted."

The crowd whooped and hollered and high-fived as points were scored, and eventually sat down as the players took a two-minute break.

Reznick turned around and stole another glance at Blake. Then he looked over at Ford and saw he was still on the phone. It had been ten minutes.

The more he thought about it, the more uneasy he felt. It was a risky strategy to allow Ford free rein. But as he sat in the middle of this stadium in New York, the anniversary of 9/11 a couple of days away, he did see the logic of letting the operation continue.

The sun had dipped behind the stands. His shirt was sticking to his back. He drank some cold water from a bottle. It felt good. He poured some down his neck, which felt great.

Ford eventually ended his call and put the phone into his pants pocket. He lifted a pair of binoculars and focused on the action for a minute or two, despite having no need for them as he was sitting so close. Reznick watched as Ford pointed the binoculars higher, toward the nosebleed seats opposite.

His earpiece buzzed into life. "You see what he's doing, Jon?"

"Yup."

"You see the game fine?"

"Great line of sight. Perfect view of both players. Unless you're nearly blind, no need for binoculars. No one around here has them. Anything or anyone of note in that area?"

"It's nearly empty." Reznick stood up as a fat guy squeezed past. "Unless he's just curious."

The earpiece went quiet as the crowd cheered another point.

Reznick caught sight of a roaming Heineken vendor with a portable keg in a backpack, dispensing beers.

His earpiece crackled into life again. "Don't even think about it, guys," Gritz said. "Might be tempting. But let's focus."

Reznick smiled as more shouts, clapping, and stamping announced a point won. The smell of hot dogs and fries wafted over from a couple of huge kids sitting with their plump mother, who was sporting a diamond-encrusted watch. The place was like a zoo.

Half an hour later, Ford got up from his seat and headed up the stairs toward an exit.

"Blake, you take this," Gritz said.

Blake waited a couple of moments before he headed out to the concourse.

Gritz's voice. "Yeah, we got him." A long pause. "Blake's on his tail. He's on the escalators and is now entering the Aces restaurant on the club level, between gates three and four."

Over the next thirty minutes, as Reznick sat amid the hubbub, he got updates from Blake and Gritz on Ford.

The doctor dined alone. He drank chilled sparkling water with a slice of lemon, ate some sushi, and then had some strawberry frozen yogurt. He paid the bill with an American Express card.

A full forty-five minutes after Ford had left, he returned to his seat. He was immediately back on the phone.

Reznick saw one of the players fluff a shot, and groan and scream out loud. He felt like doing the same.

The noise levels cranked up a notch, the floodlights on and the action on the court hotting up. The stadium was now in shadow, but the humidity was high.

Reznick swigged some more water as the interminable match dragged on.

The voice of Gritz in his earpiece. "Jon, stretch your legs for ten minutes. Blake's got it covered."

"I'm looking at the back of the guy's head. Where are you?"

"Suite one ten, northeast of where you are, but behind court-side seats. Watching you and Blake right now. You wanna move?"

"Yup. I can't see shit."

"Get yourself freshened up, and one of my guys, Special Agent Curtis Montgomery, will wait for you outside the bathroom and bring you here."

"OK, I'll see him in a few minutes. Get someone to cover my spot."

"Leave it to me, Jon."

Reznick went to the bathroom and splashed some cold water on his face. He bought himself a large Coke from a concession stand and guzzled it down. The caffeine fix and sugar rush felt good. More alert. Then he spotted Montgomery, who cocked his head, and they headed to the suite where Gritz had set up base.

A quick knock and they went in.

Gritz was standing at the far end of the suite, staring through binoculars, as was his sidekick. He turned around.

"Any movement?" Reznick said.

Gritz offered his binoculars. "Take a look for yourself."

Reznick sat down and scanned the crowds where he'd been sitting. He brought the spectators into focus.

"You got it?"

A moment later, Reznick got a fix on Ford. "Yup." He focused on Ford's face for a few moments. "What the hell you up to?"

The game seemed to go on forever. The crowd got louder. More boisterous. The place was jammed.

Ford got up and climbed the steps to the exit, disappearing from sight.

Reznick's throat felt parched, and he swigged some water from a bottle. "Where's he going?"

A moment later, the voice of Montgomery in his ear. "We're on it. He's in the bathroom again. I got him."

Ten minutes later, Ford was back in his seat. Montgomery said, "OK, guys, probably nothing, but Ford just put in some contact lenses in the bathroom. This doesn't tally with his medical file. Twenty-twenty vision, by all accounts."

"Interesting," Reznick said.

Montgomery said, "We also didn't see him take any old lenses out, although this might point to him wearing prescription sunglasses."

Reznick looked at Gritz, who was shrugging. "OK, copy that."

"That's an anomaly," Gritz said.

Reznick watched as Ford slid his shades into his shirt pocket. "Maybe."

Half an hour later, Ford got up from his seat again and headed up the stairs to the nearest exit.

Gritz said, "He's on the move, people. Guy's got ants in his pants. Montgomery, you're on this."

Montgomery's voice. "Got him." A long pause. "He's picking up a coffee. Heading back to his seat."

A few minutes later, Ford returned and sat down. He blew on the coffee and inspected the side of the cup.

Reznick stared through the binoculars, focusing on the cup. "White Styrofoam cup. Why is he still inspecting it?"

Reznick watched as Ford opened his eyes wide for a few moments, as if his lenses were hurting. Maybe a bit of grit or dirt in his eye. But then again, maybe it wasn't grit. What if he wasn't used to wearing lenses?

He focused in on Ford's face with the powerful binoculars. Clean-shaven skin, glistening with sweat, chiseled jaw and steely gaze. "Green eyes."

"What?" Gritz said.

"He doesn't have green eyes."

"You sure?" Gritz punched in some keys on a laptop and pulled up the medical records. "Yep, color of his eyes is blue."

Reznick looked through the glasses for the umpteenth time. "I'm looking just now and see hazel-green eyes. You tell me what you see."

A pause. "What the fuck? Green eyes. Who the hell are you, Adam Ford?"

Reznick sensed something else was afoot. "People's eyes don't change color."

"Unless he's wearing colored lenses."

"The question is, why? Why the change in eye color?"

"Jon, I'm not a fucking ophthalmologist."

"Neither am I. Run it by your analysts. Put it into the system."

Gritz nodded, and relayed the change of eye color to his team.

Reznick's mind flashed to the image of Ford inspecting the foam cup. "Something's going down."

Gritz wiped his brow with the back of his hand. "What?"

"I think Ford's just been given a hidden message, written on the cup."

Thirty-Six

Ford stared again at the words scrawled in ultraviolet, pale-blue writing, invisible to the naked eye but clear as day through the specially tinted contact lenses. He could barely hear the noise of the crowd as he reread the short message to ensure he wasn't getting it wrong. The message said simply: *Treat yourself to a hot dog and Coke. Then wait. Then proceed to East 81st Street hostel . . . this is your base camp.*

His heart began to pound hard as his mind raced. The adrenaline was flowing, his true intentions hidden from all in sight.

He looked around and his heart sank. The American public in all their gory glory, unaware of the man sitting among them. His true intentions. Some waddling down the steep concrete stairs, carrying mountains of junk food and watching a sport they didn't understand or play. Pampered, morbidly obese, chugging back beer, wine, burgers, and whatever shit they could stuff down their throats.

The Land of the Free of his childhood had become the Land of the Living Dead. A nation of fuckwits, halfwits, and dimwits. People who worked their guts out so they could consume junk food and die premature, horrible deaths. A nation that had long ago given up the ghost.

He was not one of them. He hadn't given up the ghost. He was part of a new breed.

Ford had his orders. This was the moment he had waited for.

He took in a deep breath, dropped the cup onto the ground, and kicked it away from his seat amid the rest of the trash lying around his feet.

Ford clapped a winner down the line and jumped to his feet alongside everyone else. He felt like an automaton. A robot. Preprogrammed. He was following orders—to the letter.

He left his seat and bought a hot dog smothered in onions and mustard, and a small Coke from a vendor. Just like they wanted him to. He knew they wanted him to blend in. It was mission-critical. They knew he despised junk food. But that was a small price to pay.

His heightened metabolism would burn off the calories almost as soon as they were ingested. He finished the hot dog, wiped his mouth clean with the napkin, and washed it down with the sugary drink. He chucked the paper and cup in a trash can at the end of the row.

Ford sat down again and wondered if this was what it was like to be high.

His thoughts turned to the next step. The carefully planned exit from the stadium. Then his journey to the base camp.

He realized he was on the verge of greatness. But as he'd been reminded time and time again, patience and a clear mind were all that mattered.

He knew how it would all end. He could almost see it play out in his mind's eye.

Ford thought back to the sniper shot that had killed the man called O'Grady. The man who had jeopardized the mission, they said. He remembered the struggle with the ropes. But he also remembered the surge of excitement he'd felt. They had set him a challenge. And it had been carried out. Perfectly.

Ford's gaze wandered around the crowd under the full glare of the floodlights. One of America's great sporting spectacles. Little did they know how tonight would end in the smartest part of Manhattan.

Thirty-Seven

In a secure conference room in the FBI's New York field office in Lower Manhattan, Martha Meyerstein was standing in front of a huge screen beaming back real-time footage of Ford at Flushing Meadows. Watching with her were half a dozen strategic intelligence analysts assigned to the special access program, trying to establish what threat lay over the horizon.

She felt her mind wandering ever so slightly, thoughts flashing back to the attack on her. The woman's face. She still felt fragile. Her vision was blurring occasionally, but she didn't want to alarm those around her. She wished Sam Chisholm and Roy Stamper were with her. She always found it useful to listen to theories and ideas from those she trusted closely, to get a full appraisal of any given situation.

What she wouldn't give for them to be here now.

But Chisholm was convinced he had a lead and had left to meet with a "high-level source," as he called it, near Battery Park. She hoped he wasn't on a wild goose chase.

Meanwhile, Roy Stamper was working out of Liberty Crossing at McLean, chasing down leads on Ford.

Her gaze fixed on the video from Flushing Meadows. Ford was sipping a Coke, clapping occasionally, looking slightly distracted.

She shook her head. "I don't know, guys. Has a message been passed to him?" She sighed. "Maybe. But why such an elaborate setup just to pass on a message?"

A few minutes later, Meyerstein hooked up for a videoconference with Lieutenant General Black and other senior members of the special access program team back in McLean, as she prepared to give them an update.

Black said, "Martha, we're watching events in real time, too. We're in touch with the White House almost continuously, and we still don't seem to have this nailed down."

Meyerstein felt her blood pressure hike up a notch and her cheeks flush. "General Black, the strategic analysis is unequivocal. There appear to be elements in place for a possible attack, no question. We don't know where and by who, but we are of the view Ford is involved, and we need to know who he's communicating with. We have surveillance in place. We're doing everything we can."

"And yet, two days before the nine eleven anniversary, we are still no further forward in establishing what network is in place, if any, and who is involved and what the target is. Frankly, it beggars belief. Is this going to be a repeat of the Boston bombings?"

"Sir, I don't think we can wait any longer. I say we bring Ford in right now. That's also the view of Sam Chisholm. I think it is important to—"

Black slammed the palm of his hand down hard on the table. Papers scattered everywhere. "May I remind you that—"

A national security advisor put up his hand. "Sorry to butt in, General, but from what we know, and the revelation of this picture of Ford in Chechnya—"

"We don't know how authentic that is. Christ, it came via the Russian security services. Are we really to believe what those people say?"

"General, I know Russia very well. I was stationed there for the best part of a decade. I know how they think and operate. And I must now concur with Assistant Director Meyerstein and Sam Chisholm. We need to bring this guy in, now. We can't afford any fuck-ups. It might be tenuous, but we cannot take the slightest risk with national security."

"What about the network? How are we going to find out who's involved?"

Meyerstein spoke up. "General, I appreciate your candor, and your rationale can't be faulted, but this is a fast-moving situation and we all believe this is a real and credible threat."

Black's face darkened.

She continued, "Sir, with respect, I would ask that we apprehend Ford right this instant."

Black stared straight at her from the screen before looking at those around the table in McLean.

"We need to be sure. Besides, what we don't want to do is create a panic or alert others that he's being taken in. Remember this match is being shown live, around the world." He let out a long sigh. "So, how about we apprehend him when he leaves."

"But, sir, that could be hours. As long as he remains in place, there's going to be uncertainty. Far better to just get him out of there right now."

"As I said, apprehend him when he leaves and the stadium is thinned out. Am I making myself clear?"

The screen went black.

Meyerstein felt her anger mount. She wanted to move in on Ford now.

She had begun to pace the floor of the conference room when the phone on the oval table rang. The caller ID showed it was Sam Chisholm.

"Talk to me, Sam."

"I got something you need to see."

"What is it, Sam? I'm kinda busy."

"Face to face. I have some crucial information."

Meyerstein wondered why he wouldn't just tell her what he knew. "Sam, where exactly are you?"

"I'm not far. Battery Parking Garage—you know it?"

"Sure. Not far."

"I'm on the fifth level. Black Lincoln. I need to talk. Right now."

"Sam, I'm real busy. Come in and we'll talk here if it's that important."

"No." His tone was strident. Not like him. "A source of mine . . . he wants to speak to you face to face. He has some documents."

"Documents? What sort of documents?"

"Martha, they concern . . . they concern General Black."

Meyerstein sighed. She knew Gritz, Reznick, and the dozens of agents in and around Flushing Meadows had Ford's every move monitored. "OK. Give me twenty minutes."

It should have been a short drive down Broadway, but evening traffic had snarled up.

"Goddamn, what is this?"

The driver shook his head and pointed farther down the street. "Looks like a bad one."

She craned her neck and saw a cyclist had been knocked over, and was now surrounded by paramedics. She considered walking the mile or so on foot, but within a few seconds they were on the move again, and the driver somehow managed to weave around the accident.

They skirted the periphery of the World Trade Center site, turned right onto Liberty Street, and then hung a left, down Greenwich Street.

The red neon sign of the parking garage was up ahead.

"Up to the fifth level," she said to the driver.

"Sure thing, ma'am."

A few minutes later, they arrived on the fifth. The dimly lit, concrete catacomb was jammed with cars. She got out of the vehicle, her minders never more than a yard away.

Meyerstein spotted a black Lincoln in the far corner of the garage. She thought she saw two people inside. She headed straight for it, past the other agents. As she got closer, her stomach tightened and her heart rate quickened.

Bad thoughts crept into her mind. Alarm bells were ringing. Why the sudden call from Chisholm? Why the urgency? Why face to face?

She strode on toward the Lincoln. Ten yards away, she stopped dead in her tracks. The smell of cordite hung heavy in the air.

Then she saw it. Specks of blood splatter across the inside of the driver's window. She felt her insides move as she stepped closer. Time seemed to slow down. Then stop.

Gray brain tissue and dark blood were sprayed all across the side and back windows. Inside was Sam Chisholm, eyes open but no life in them. His face frozen in shock, as if he knew in that split second what fate awaited him. One bullet hole in the forehead, the back of his head splattered across the passenger window and beige leather seats. Another man, not known to Meyerstein, with two shots drilled into the right temple—double-tap, execution-style. Blood congealed around the entry wounds; sinews, tiny fragments of bone and brain matter on the man's ashen face.

The news about the double murder spread like wildfire throughout the FBI. Meyerstein had gone back to the nearby Manhattan office, where she had fielded more than a dozen calls from everyone—including Langley, the Department of Homeland Security, and the national security advisor to the Office of the Director of Intelligence. But the one person who did not contact her was Lieutenant General Black.

She began to focus her thoughts. The NSA had pulled up the call from Sam Chisholm and the verdict was clear. The call was genuine. It was made from his FBI cell phone. Video analysis from within the parking garage showed him arriving with an elderly man.

It took the FBI exactly fifteen seconds to identify the man formally as Marcus Belling, a rear admiral who had worked out of the Pentagon since the 1960s, until he retired in 1986.

The more she thought back to the call from Chisholm, the more it was clear he had something on Black. A connection, perhaps. Information about his Pentagon past. Belling would have worked with or come across Black at the Pentagon at some point during the height of the Cold War.

The shock and the adrenaline were still coursing through her veins, and they propelled her on. She hooked up a secure video link to Roy Stamper and they talked.

"Martha, I'm so sorry about Sam. I know you knew him well. I mean . . . I don't know what to say."

Meyerstein was determined to be all business. She cleared her throat. "Sam's deputy, Special Agent Jamieson, is leading the counterterrorism team on this. But I need to speak to General Black right now."

Stamper grimaced. "Might be a problem. He's not here, Martha."

"What do you mean he's not there? I was just speaking to him a little while ago."

"I mean, he's been out of the office the last thirty minutes or so."

"Shit."

"I've tried his cell but there's no reply. I was just about to trace his phone via the GPS."

"Do it now."

Stamper pressed a few keys on his laptop in front of him, eyes locked on to the screen.

"We've got him near us. Gated community in McLean."

"That's where he lives."

"He's back home now? That doesn't make sense."

"None of it makes sense."

"You want me to go and speak to him?"

"No, you focus on your own work. We've got Ford. Leave the general to me. I want to speak to him myself. Face to face."

"Be careful, Martha."

———————

Meyerstein's mind raced throughout the one-hour flight to Reagan International. She popped a couple of Advil with a glass of water. When the flight touched down in DC, it was late.

She picked up her car from the near-deserted economy parking lot and drove across to West McLean. Fifteen minutes into her journey, her phone rang.

"Meyerstein," she said, focusing on the GPS.

"Martha, it's Roy. We really, really have to get this guy out of here."

"The order is to wait until he leaves."

"Listen to me. We've got something—it's all beginning to take shape. But not in a good way."

"So, what is it?"

"Firstly, Black's a member of the Trilateral Commission. Did you know that?"

Meyerstein was aware of the organization set up by Rockefeller in the early 1970s. It included powerful banking, corporate, political, and military interests.

"I didn't know that."

"He's not on any public list, but he's attended the last dozen or so meetings. I have it on good authority that he's a very influential member of the Commission."

"What else?"

"Here's the kicker. Our computer guys, along with the NSA, have accessed heavily encrypted Department of Defense files, including redacted secret files, relating to General Robert Black."

Meyerstein was getting butterflies in her stomach. "I'm listening."

"We believe Sam Chisholm had access to the same files."

"And?"

"Black was on the periphery of a cabal at the Pentagon that was at the center of setting up an unauthorized plan to try to replicate Operation Northwoods."

Meyerstein's blood ran cold. He was referring to an infamous and highly secretive false flag operation—planned by the American military during the Cold War—to carry out apparent terrorist attacks on the US, hoping to blame the Cubans.

"Goes way back to the early sixties, the Northwoods plan, apparently."

"Cuban missile crisis-era, right?"

Meyerstein's mind was racing ahead. "Just to be clear, we're talking about the same Operation Northwoods? The one way back in the time of the Kennedy administration?"

"Precisely."

"So the question is—is what we're dealing with a false flag? Americans bombing or shooting Americans?"

Stamper said nothing.

"What else? I need to know more about Black's part in this."

"Black was a young officer at the time, but—along with others of the same political outlook prevalent at the time—he became aligned with a hawkish grouping. This group was led by General

Lyman Lemnitzer, Chairman of the Joint Chiefs of Staff way back in the sixties, but his plan to launch bombings in the Miami area and in Washington was thrown out by Robert McNamara."

Meyerstein felt her heart beat faster, her mind going into overdrive as she got closer to Black's home.

"I've got more. Black wanted to recast the Northwoods plan once in the eighties. This was based on the original blueprint of the work of Brigadier General William Craig and other right-wing patriots, as they saw themselves. Lemnitzer and Craig thought Kennedy was a no-win president. They thought he was soft on Castro. Black was trained by Craig."

The oncoming headlights made Meyerstein wince. "Craig?"

"Yeah. Black was mentored by William Craig. And Black in turn proposed an Operation Northwoods-style plan, including bombings, shootings, and plane crashes, to blame on the Iranians and galvanize public support for bombing Tehran to dust in 1981. Black's plans were codenamed Operation Dustbowl. That's what they wanted to turn Iran into. Dust."

"Are you serious?"

"It was how part of the senior military was thinking at the time."

"So how does this relate to Belling?"

"Apparently, Belling got wind of the 1981 blueprints that Black had circulated as a secret briefing paper. Belling worked out of the Pentagon—but, ironically, it was Belling who was edged out toward retirement. Black had numerous backers, both military and political, no doubt through his Trilateral Commission contacts, although the plans were never acted on and were finally scrapped after the Iran–Contra scandal broke."

Meyerstein's brain was racing ahead of her as the lights of the oncoming cars sped by.

"So how did Sam Chisholm find out about this?"

"Chisholm had an old Pentagon source, a friend of Chisholm's late father. Both were in the army. And he pointed him in the direction of Belling. Said Belling had something on Black, or words to that effect."

Meyerstein's mind was in overdrive. Scenarios ran through her head at breakneck speed. "Roy, I want you to relay this information directly to the President's National Security Council."

"They already know."

"Good. OK, this kind of puts a different spin on the analysis pointing to Islamists, right?"

"Counterintelligence and Counterterrorism are still working on this. They are up to speed with this information about Black. But I'm awaiting the latest from them. Expect an update within the hour."

"Is that everything?"

"Not quite."

"Not quite? You got something else?"

"Yeah, on Black. Martha, it's true General Black works out of the Pentagon and has since the eighties. But we're drilling down. He's not reporting to anyone within the Department of Defense. I have that on good authority from three separate people."

"What are you talking about?"

"Martha, he's CIA. Always has been."

"Since when?"

"Since forever. Vietnam, Korea, Laos—he's been on the ground every time. You name it, he's been there. And then some."

"It's all pointing one way, Roy."

Thirty-Eight

As Meyerstein drove along the tree-lined streets of McLean, her mind tracked back to the numerous confidential reports she'd read about the true nature of the Islamic threat to the United States and how it had really emerged.

Geopolitics. During Soviet rule in Afghanistan, it was American policy to use mosques to recruit those who would fight the Russians. She knew about Camp Peary, also known as "The Farm," the CIA's covert training facility. It trained clandestine officers. But it was also where young Arab nationals from countries like Egypt and Jordan, along with young Afghans, were taught strategic sabotage skills. And so the blowback went on. And on.

The jihad that the US had created and fostered and nurtured was engulfing large parts of the Middle East, and those same jihad-ists were turning their gaze on America. Bin Laden himself had been linked to a jihad refugee center in Brooklyn.

But her investigation was now not about jihadists. They were going to be the patsies, while the true nature of the emerging threat would lie undiscovered.

She felt a terrible emptiness within her. Was this her country? Was this her government? Was this how it had always been?

She turned onto a deathly quiet residential street and saw the house. Floodlit garden, shielded by massive trees and hedgerows. Lights on in the upstairs windows. She walked up to the front door and knocked three times.

Her heart was beating fast as she waited. Inside, footsteps. A small, gray-haired woman wearing an orange blouse and long skirt answered the door.

Meyerstein flashed her ID. "Sorry to bother you, ma'am. I'm looking to speak to General Black."

The woman stared at Meyerstein. "This is most irregular, is it not?"

"Indeed it is, Mrs. Black."

"Do you mind me asking what this is about?"

"I'm sorry, that's not possible."

The woman sighed. "I see."

"This isn't about me. This is about your husband. Now, are you going to invite me into your house or do I have to go and get a warrant from a judge?"

Mrs. Black's eyes bored into Meyerstein for what seemed like an eternity. Eventually, she opened the door wide. "There will be no need for that. My husband is in his study."

Meyerstein followed her down a long carpeted hallway.

"If you must know, my husband began to feel unwell and had to return home. The doctor has just left."

"I'm sorry, I didn't realize."

"No, I don't suppose you did."

Mrs. Black escorted Meyerstein to the study at the far end of the house. She knocked on the door.

"Come in, Esther."

Esther Black opened the door. "Darling, sorry to trouble you again. Assistant Director Meyerstein has come by to see you."

Lieutenant General Black looked up from a pile of papers on his huge teak desk, and stared at Meyerstein. He was wearing a button-down shirt, chinos, and dark-brown loafers. A desk phone and a cell phone sat neatly beside each other. Two lamps were on, the wooden blinds drawn. Black-and-white pictures of the general with various presidents over the years decorated the walls.

"I see. Well, you'd better show her in."

Meyerstein stepped into the room.

Mrs. Black looked at her husband. "Can I get you a coffee or tea, darling?"

He shook his head. "I'm fine, thank you."

"Assistant Director? Coffee or tea?"

Meyerstein smiled. "No, thanks. I'm good."

Mrs. Black shut the door behind her. Lieutenant General Black pointed at one of two leather sofas. "Take a load off."

Meyerstein sat down and cleared her throat. "I've been trying to contact you, General. Have you heard what happened to Sam Chisholm?"

Black's eyes were hooded. "Indeed I have. Appalling. In all my years—"

"I've got some questions for you, if you don't mind. They're starting to build up."

"I'm sorry, I don't follow. I thought this was about Chisholm."

Meyerstein felt his gaze on her and she instinctively shifted. "Sir, I have grave concerns. And I feel the need to ask you some questions, once again, face to face."

"Well, here we are."

"My first question, General, is why wasn't I told that you were ill? You're chairing this special access program, which I'm leading."

He sighed. "I apologize. I should have made you aware of that. My doctor advised me to get the hell out of my office." Black leaned back in his leather chair and sighed again. He was playing it cool.

Aloof. "Forget me. What about Chisholm? How the hell did that happen? I heard you found him. Meeting up with some source."

Meyerstein nodded, images of Chisholm's bloodied face seared into her mind.

"What was the meeting about?"

She wondered how much she should reveal. "I got a call from Chisholm saying a source of his wanted to speak face to face with me. A source that used to work at the Pentagon."

Black nodded. "I've listened to the call. And I know who the source was."

The news was a surprise to Meyerstein. She wondered who had passed on that information. Was it someone within her team? Outside the team?

"You've listened to the call?"

A thin smile cracked his face, as if he was enjoying toying with her. "Marcus Belling was in the car with Chisholm. We went back a long, long way. Hell of a nice guy, but he was . . . how can I put it . . . more cerebral than practical."

Meyerstein averted her gaze for a moment. "He had documents. Documents about you, General. Did you know that?"

Black said nothing.

"Do you have any idea why Marcus Belling would want to speak to Chisholm urgently about you? What sort of documents do you think he was talking about?"

Black's steely gaze fixed on her. "Marcus Belling was a good man. But he was naive."

"Naive? In what way?"

"He believed that this great country of ours always has to play by the rules."

"And you don't believe that?"

Black let out a long sigh. "Meyerstein, you should know better than anyone that, sometimes, you've got to break the rules to get results. You turned a blind eye to the rules when you tracked down that government scientist, Luntz, didn't you?"

Meyerstein felt her face flush. She was tempted to rise to the bait. But she focused on the questions at hand. "You seem to know a lot about me, General. I've been finding out some information about you. And it makes for interesting reading."

Black said nothing.

"Why didn't you tell me you worked for the CIA?"

"I didn't think it was relevant."

"Isn't it? We have the documents, General. The documents that Belling knew about for all these years. The plans you drew up. Top-secret plans. False flag operations across the US. Plans to kill Americans. Bombings. Shootings. Plans to galvanize public opinion against Iran. Plans that would have allowed the military to launch a full-scale war. The same kind of plans that were hatched in the sixties to try to start a war with Cuba. Back then it was called Operation Northwoods. But you had drawn up plans for Operation Dustbowl. And now we have the latest plans that we're seeing playing out in real time in New York. You wanna talk about that, General?"

Black smiled. "Do you know anything of military strategy? Do you understand the first thing about what it takes to protect the cherished freedoms we have at our disposal?"

"I know what this great country of ours stands for."

"Meyerstein, you're a very competent assistant director. But you've got a helluva lot to learn when it comes to knowing how to keep our country safe. We need to fight each and every day across all parts of the world, each and every goddamn day, just to make sure we can live as free people."

"According to whose rules, exactly, General?"

Black said nothing.

"Do you believe in democracy, General?"

His gaze wandered around the room for a few moments, as if considering the nuances of the argument. "Up to a point."

"And what point is that, General?"

"The point where the people lead us over a cliff. Politicians, for example. Sometimes, the average American doesn't realize what the hell is happening in Washington. We have to be aware of all threats that politicians are either too scared to confront or too afraid to reveal to the American people."

"What threats? Real or imagined?"

"Don't denigrate what people like me do, Meyerstein. We make tough calls, day in, day out. Every goddamn day, every goddamn night. Unseen. Unappreciated. We do the dirty work that is necessary so we can all sleep at night. You need men like me to do what's necessary."

"Sir, I'm going to ask you straight."

Black stared long and hard at her. "Fire away."

Meyerstein felt a knot of tension in her stomach. "And I expect a straight answer," she said.

Black nodded.

"Is a false flag operation underway? Is Ford spearheading this operation? Is that what this is all about?"

Black closed his eyes for a moment, and smiled as he allowed a silence to open up. "There are forces at work—both within the borders of this great country, and outside—whose job is to look after the interests of America."

Meyerstein felt her blood pressure rise up a notch. "*The interests of America?* And what exactly do you deem to be in the interests of America?"

"We need friendly governments who understand freedom. We need governments who make sure that the insidious presence of communism, in all its guises, is crushed. We need governments to understand the ever-present threat of radical Islam. They don't want to convert us. They want to crush us. That threat has never been so real. It's never gone away."

It was clear he was on a roll.

"What do you think the Crusades were all about? It was pacifying them. That's what we're doing every day across the globe. We need to be strong. They want to wipe Christianity and America off the map."

"Who's *they*?"

"You know full well, Meyerstein. We also need to remind people, from time to time, that there are venal regimes that will stop at nothing to wipe us off this earth. It's an ongoing battle. And sometimes, things get messy."

"Is that right? Is that what this is, General, a false flag operation to galvanize a new wave of public support for this war against Islam?"

Black said nothing.

"You're not above the law, General."

"The law? Gimme a break. The law is an ass. We all know that. People like me ensure that our way of life is preserved. And along the way, there have to be casualties."

Meyerstein paused for a few moments. "Are American casualties OK, General?"

"You don't see the big picture, Meyerstein."

"I find your earlier reply to my original question interesting, General."

"In what way?"

"You didn't answer a straightforward question as to whether there was a false flag operation underway in the United States. What I got was a rationale for false flag operations."

Black leaned back in his seat and sighed. "Sometimes, Meyerstein, it's better not to see the full picture. If the public really knew what was done in their name, they would descend on Washington in their millions and burn it to the ground."

"Let's get back to what's going on right now. And I'm going to ask you a second and final time, General . . . is there a false flag operation, either authorized or unauthorized, underway in America?"

"Meyerstein, I don't see where this line of questioning is leading us."

"Could you answer the question?"

"What are you really wanting me to say?"

"Tell me the truth."

"Meyerstein, you have no idea what the truth is. No idea at all, hidden away in your ivory tower in the goddamn Hoover Building, not seeing what is really going on."

"Are there others involved? Because, if there are, we will find them, and they will be hunted down, no matter who they are."

"There is no false flag operation."

"You know what? I don't believe you." Meyerstein pulled out her phone and called Stamper, who was on her speed dial. "Roy, you at Liberty Crossing?"

"That's right."

"Send around a full team to the home of Lieutenant General Robert J. Black, including FBI forensics and computer specialists. How long before you can be here?"

"I'm sorry?"

"You heard me, Roy. How long?"

"Eh . . . A matter of minutes."

"Get to it."

Meyerstein ended the call and looked at Black. His face was ashen.

"This is not going to be pleasant for any of us, including your wife."

He leaned forward. "What the hell do you think you're doing?"

"We're taking you in, sir. You've got a lot of questions to answer."

"Are you serious?"

"Deadly."

His eyes were glassy. He opened his mouth for a moment, as if at a loss for words.

"Have you lost your mind?" he said finally. "I mean . . . we're on the same side, aren't we?"

"I don't know—are we?"

Black got to his feet. "You have no idea who you're dealing with."

He stood staring at her, his lined face beaded with sweat and his jawline set as if it was granite. His eyes bored into hers.

She didn't flinch. She stared right back at him. She had learned from her father the importance of eye contact. Not being afraid. The sound of an old grandfather clock was all she heard.

"Sir, you're going to be taken from here and interviewed at length."

"Can I pick up some things?" He was breathing harder.

"No. Nothing."

"What about Esther?"

"What about her?"

"What will I say?"

"Tell her whatever you like."

Black bowed his head for a moment, seemingly weighed down by events. Then he looked up. "I need to go to the bathroom. Do you mind if I freshen up?"

Meyerstein looked at her watch. "Five minutes. And leave the door ajar."

Black fixed his gaze on her before leaving the room.

The sound of running water. A long silence.

Then a single shot rang out.

Thirty-Nine

The shocking news of Lieutenant General Black's suicide, amid the real possibility that a false flag operation was underway, was still sinking in as Reznick, Gritz, and the Feds watched Ford from the FBI control hub within the Flushing Meadows suite. And what was crystal clear to everyone within the special access program was that their assumptions about an Islamic threat were groundless.

It was a worrying sequence of events, and intelligence was still being pieced together. They'd been blindsided.

Gritz was staring through the binoculars, cell phone pressed to his ear. "Fucker is still just sitting there."

Reznick was handed a phone by one of Gritz's men.

"Assistant Director Meyerstein wants a word," he said gruffly.

Reznick took the phone. "You OK?"

"What do you think?"

Reznick said nothing.

"Look, I'm just about to land at LaGuardia. I need to be on the ground." She sighed. "So, what do you make of this?"

Reznick could hear the anxiety in her voice. The doubt. The fear.

"You did the right thing by speaking to him. The whole thing has suddenly become clearer. Here's how it is—we were wrong.

Flat-out wrong. The Islamic threat is their cover. And the real and present threat comes from Ford and those who are behind this. Black was only the tip of the iceberg. And that's why we need to haul Ford's ass in right now. A false flag is underway."

Meyerstein went quiet for a few moments, her mind processing a mass of facts, analysis, and data. Her senses were switched on, knowing that something was going to go down. But no one knew what exactly. "Have you read Stamper's analysis about false flags?"

"I know the people that wrote the CIA manual on it."

"Which brings us back to General Black. He was CIA. No one told me."

"That's the way they operate. Need to know. If you're not one of them, you don't need to know shit."

"Jon, I need to be clear on this. This is an inside job, hidden within the veneer of an Islamist threat, right?"

"Meyerstein, firstly, you need to know that it will go deeper than Black. He can't be the only one. You need the military, Pentagon, CIA, and NSA axis to make this work. But it might be wider than that."

"Jesus . . . why would anyone want to make this work? I mean, killing Americans?"

"You don't know the half of it."

"Black's suicide is a game changer. The probability of an attack scenario from a false flag operation is now being described as highly likely, according to Counterterrorism. And they believe Adam Ford will deliver."

Reznick picked up the binoculars and stared through the glass at Ford eating another hot dog.

Meyerstein sighed. "I see that you flagged up the color of his eyes. What's that all about?"

"The colored contact lens is a very elaborate ruse. Sometimes used by high-end card sharks. They can read cards marked with ultraviolet pens, invisible to the naked eye. But in this case it may—I stress *may*—enable Ford to read hidden messages. The added attraction of that is that it helps them stay clear of electronic chatter."

Meyerstein was quiet.

"What are you thinking?" Reznick said.

"I'm thinking I want him out of there now, before the crowds all disappear at the same time. That'll make it tricky to keep an eye on him."

"Absolutely."

"But I don't want to draw attention to us taking him away. I'm thinking . . . I'm thinking we should wait till he next goes to the bathroom and take him then."

"Sounds good. I'll pass on to Gritz and his guys."

"Jon, I'm due to land in fifteen minutes. All you need to know is that Ford doesn't leave our sight."

Reznick stared through the binoculars as Ford dabbed the corner of his mouth with a napkin. The roar of the crowd outside the box made Reznick wince.

"Got it."

Meyerstein said, "There are a lot of questions. Caroline Lieber is still missing."

"Consider her dead."

A long silence. "We don't know that for sure, Jon."

"Trust me. She's out the way. What about Jamal's sister?"

"Chantelle McGovern? Still under surveillance. But we think she was radicalized by her brother. And Akhtar is part of the same East Village grouping . . . The question is, were these guys planning a terrorist campaign? No evidence as yet."

"And we return to my point. They're brilliant cover for the main event. Ford leaves this trace, and we pick up the morsels they're feeding us. It's real cute. Someone wanted us to get the Islamic connection if we latched on to Ford. But we're being played. Have been since day one."

"Ford I still do not get, despite the Chechen link."

"The Chechens and the East Village Islamists are the cover. They're the backdrop. Ford is the key. Has been since the get-go."

"Stamper's still working on piecing together Ford's past."

"He needs to pull his finger out. Why is this taking so long?"

"Jon, I've got another two calls. I need to take these."

"Speak again soon."

Reznick ended the call and relayed the message to Gritz, who in turn fed the information to the rest of his team.

A few minutes later, Ford got up from his courtside seat and headed up the stairs.

Reznick spoke into his lapel microphone. "Stick to him like glue, you hear?"

Gritz pressed the binoculars almost up to the glass. "That's affirmative. Tail him. We don't lose this guy."

A few moments later, an FBI agent's voice. "Joined a line for the bathroom."

Reznick was handed a bottle of water by a young Fed, and he chugged it back in one go. He stared at the monitors in the suite, showing the line for the bathroom and the half-dozen agents milling around on the periphery. Scores of people in and out of the washrooms every couple of minutes.

He looked across at Gritz. "Who's going to take him and when?"

"Special Agents Atkins and McKiernan. Both ex-college wrestling champs. Trust me, he ain't goin' nowhere."

The seconds became minutes.

Reznick adjusted his headset. "The match has just ended. That's nearly five fucking minutes he's been in there. Get in there and pull him out."

Gritz nodded. "Yeah, that's a go. Repeat, get him out of there. Don't care if he's goin' for a dump. Get him out, right now."

The two Feds barged through the line. A few beers spilled and there was shouting and pushing until three other Feds flashed badges and the boozed-up tennis clowns backed off.

A few moments later, the radio crackled into life with the voice of Special Agent McKiernan. "We got a problem."

Gritz clenched his teeth. "What do you mean?"

"He's gone. He must've slipped out."

Gritz pointed to his right-hand man. "Run the surveillance cameras again from the moment he went in. Shit! Shit! Bullshit! You believe this?"

Reznick headed for the door of the suite, earpiece in. "Get the facial recognition guys to scan everyone leaving the bathroom. He's changed his outfit and given us the slip. I think he left before the match finished."

"Fuck!"

Reznick negotiated a series of teeming corridors, full of people mingling and chatting, before he was swept along by a crowd of people. He emerged from the stadium into the sticky night air with dozens of Feds.

Gritz's voice sounded in his earpiece. "We need to seal off the perimeter. He's not in his seat. There's no one there. The fucker is on the move!"

Reznick stared off into the distance. Hundreds of people were streaming away and heading for the train back downtown "He'll have gone. Check the cameras in and around the stadium. We need to pick up the scent quick, before it's too late."

"What a mess," Gritz said.

Reznick's blood was boiling. "Let's quit whining and find the bastard."

He barged past the crowds and headed instinctively in the direction of a ramp that led to the adjacent subway stop.

Gritz's voice in his earpiece. "Jon, there's a seven train about to leave! Get yourself onto the northside platform. The Citi Field side."

Reznick was there in seconds, but saw the magenta circle with the number 7 moving away as he got onto the platform. "Fuck."

"We're checking the cameras on board."

"You've ID'd him?"

"Not sure."

"Fuck. What's he wearing?"

"We have footage of him heading up the ramp . . . Yup, three minutes ago, wearing glasses, khaki trousers, sneakers, and a black T-shirt. A backpack. You're right, Jon, the fucker has changed."

Reznick said, "The 7 train. That heads directly to Manhattan?"

"Goddamn super express."

"How long till Manhattan?"

"Stops at a couple of shitholes in Queens. Twenty-five minutes. Times Square, end of the line."

"You need to stop the train."

"We're already trying to do that. No one seems to have the fucking authority."

"What about boarding at one of the Queens stations?"

"Hold on, Jon, I got something. There are cameras on the train and we're scanning all the passengers. Hold on . . ." The waiting seemed to take forever. "Shit. He didn't get on the train. Target is not on the train. I repeat, target is not on the train."

"So where the hell is he?"

Reznick looked over and saw the huge silhouette of the Mets' stadium, Citi Field, in the distance.

"The fucker's out there somewhere. He's still in Queens."

Forty

Meyerstein's plane was just about to land when the phone on her armrest rang.

"Martha, it's Roy."

"What've you got?"

"We've been negotiating through a back channel with the Russians, and they've opened up their own secret files on Americans in Chechnya."

"So how does Ford fit into this?"

"The CIA was, in effect, the operational commander for operations in Chechnya. The Chechens were our proxies. Special Forces including SEALs were involved. And I was given the name of a former SEAL in Chechnya who knew Ford very well indeed."

"You're kidding me, right?"

"Nope. Apparently Ford saved this SEAL's life."

"What?"

"Dr. Adam Ford was Captain Adam Ford, assigned to Special Forces operations as a lead medic. But he was funded through college by the CIA."

"You're kidding me?"

"No, Martha. But there's no record of it at all in official files. Incredibly high IQ—148. Fast-tracked. Took a shake-and-bake, month-long army course. Operated in a support capacity. But that's not all. He's a crack shot, a sniper, and super fit. Classic SEAL material."

Her mind was struggling to take it all in. "Slow down, are you saying—"

"The guy I spoke to said his fitness levels were remarkable and he fit their profile. He didn't shoot his mouth off. He blended in. Analytical thinker. Problem solver. Very value-oriented, patriotic— so much so that he put service above self. But he was as cold as they come."

"Ford is CIA?"

"Yes, he is. The guy said that Ford was afforded great cover when he entered war zones as an NGO medic. But he was feed- ing back information all the time from field hospitals, contacts he established, enabling the CIA to build up a picture of things on the ground, without any fingerprints."

"Shit."

"There's more. The man in charge of recruiting Ford was . . ."

"Black."

"Got it in one. General Robert Black."

"Christ . . . how didn't we know about this?"

"Who the hell knows? One final thing. And this is where it gets really, really unsettling."

"Oh, great."

"Firstly, Ford was adopted by a childless couple in DC."

"Yeah, I think I read that. So?"

"Just bear with me. His natural parents died when he was a baby. Car crash. He was adopted by an older couple in DC. They died when he was at college. His adopted mother was called Alice Ford. His adopted father was Peter Ford."

"Roy, I read that. So?"

"We started digging further back. There were incomplete records, and that's what's taken us so long. It's been a nightmare trying to piece it together. But we've got it, and we've connected the dots. It hasn't been easy, let me tell you. Do you know who Peter Ford's second cousin was?"

"Roy, you wanna quit playing games and tell me?"

"The second cousin was a woman named . . . Esther Beveridge."

"And?"

"When she married, she became Esther Black."

Meyerstein's blood ran cold. "The general's wife."

"We've triple- and quadruple-checked this, and gone over and cross-checked the records, both paper and computer—incomplete records held by the Children's Bureau and numerous other agencies. Robert Black saw the boy had a high IQ. But he also saw the kid was manipulative, superficial, charming, and unable to relate to others. And he referred him to a CIA psychologist. The boy was deemed to be a highly intelligent psychopath. But this has all been hidden away, out of sight.

"The records show that the boy was a bed-wetter until well into his teens and was often setting off fires in the community where they lived. Esther Black asked her husband to see if he could help with the boy. And it was from there the connection between Black and Ford was formed, unseen all these years."

Meyerstein was struggling to take it all in. "You think Ford's primed to carry out an attack?"

"He's the one. I'm sure of it."

Forty-One

Half an hour later, Reznick's mood was darkening. He was sat buckled up in the back of a speeding SUV, as he and four Feds headed across the 59th Street Bridge into Manhattan. Through the steel struts and beams, he saw the Midtown skyline, the smokestacks, the Empire State, the city lights.

Gritz was sitting in the passenger seat. He turned and looked at Reznick. "How the fuck did we allow this to happen? He might still be in Queens, for all we know."

Reznick said nothing, not wanting to engage in conversation. His mind was still racing, thinking about the information contained within Stamper's report on Black.

Gritz scanned his iPad to read the latest update. He shook his head. "We don't even know if he's in Manhattan."

Reznick's nerves were twitching. "That's where he'll be headed. Manhattan is the epicenter of all things New York. To the rest of the world, Manhattan *is* New York."

"This false flag is bullshit. Are we seriously to believe that Black would have authorized such actions? Are you kidding me? This is goddamn treason."

J. B. Turner

"You need to read Roy Stamper's report. It's all there about Black. He's CIA. He was responsible for drawing up a false flag plan based on Operation Northwoods, and Ford is the triggerman for this operation."

"He's a goddamn doctor."

"Yeah, a CIA doctor and a trained sniper."

"It doesn't make sense."

"That's the whole point. You need to keep up, Gritz."

Gritz shook his head. "The whole thing is a crock of shit."

"It makes sense in their world. The end justifies the means. Doesn't matter who gets hurt."

"O'Grady, Froch, Chisholm. How do they fit into this?"

"It's all about shutting down those who pose a threat to the operation. The attempt on Meyerstein's life. And let's not forget Caroline Lieber is still missing. Almost certainly dead."

Gritz shook his head. "I've been with the FBI for the best part of twenty years, and I've never seen anything like this."

Just then, Gritz's cell rang. He answered on the first ring. He nodded. "Get this information out to the other teams now. I want the remaining teams in Queens to head into Manhattan." He ended the call. "Ford popped into the East 81st Street hostel ten minutes ago, and CCTV images show him leaving three minutes ago, backpack still slung over his shoulder. Step on it, Jimmy."

Reznick said, "We staked him out there before."

Gritz screwed up his face. "What?"

"Yeah, we staked him out. He also worked a homeless shelter in the East Village, and a soup kitchen."

"So why the hell is he going back there now?"

Reznick stared out of the window. Yellow cabs crawling by, neon-lit delis, and pedestrians and tourists shuffling around on the sidewalks. Skyscrapers nearly blocking out the inky-black sky. "I think we're reaching the endgame."

256

"Tonight? No one is saying anything is going to go down tonight."

"I'm saying it."

"You gotta be kidding me."

"It's tonight."

"Let's focus on what we do know. He's on the move. He's on foot. Let's assume he's within twenty blocks of the hostel by the time we arrive."

Reznick's mind was racing. "Why is he returning to that hostel? Unless . . . unless he's returning for a pickup."

"A pickup? Of what?"

"Final instructions? A weapons stash, perhaps? The hostel must have cameras—"

Gritz's phone rang again, and he held up his hand as if to silence Reznick. "You're in the hostel? Good, we need to know where he went, who he talked with, and if he picked up anything. You know the drill. ETA's maybe three minutes for us." He ended the call. "FBI SWAT is all over it."

"First thought that comes to mind is: what crowded, enclosed areas are within walking distance?" Reznick said.

"Hundreds. Bars, restaurants, outdoor cafés. And then there's Central Park. Fuck."

"Are there any VIP functions around this area tonight?"

"Are you kidding? There are functions and openings and new bars and restaurants and A-listers all over the Upper East Side, three hundred and sixty-five nights a year."

"OK, that narrows it down."

"Jon, we're working on an assessment—which is really an assumption—that Ford is going to carry out an attack. We just don't know that."

"It's gonna be around here. Very close."

"We're flooding the place. We're combing every street on the Upper East Side."

"What if he goes to ground?"

"Where?"

"What about the Lenox Hill doctor he stayed with? He's within the radius."

"Outer edges. But I can't see him heading back there."

"Worth getting a team there, just in case."

"Jon, we haven't got enough information to storm in there . . . It doesn't work like that."

"So how does it work?"

"Well, you need legal authorization for a search."

"Then get it. Ford is the number one suspect in the city, he's a terrorist risk, he's on the loose, and he's stayed there before. You want me to go on?"

Gritz flushed red as he picked up his cell and made a call. "I want the go-ahead to get into the townhouse of William Rhodes, medical director of Lenox Hill Hospital. Lives on East 63rd Street." He nodded. "Let me know when it comes through." He turned to face Reznick. "Would he be dumb enough to go there?"

A few minutes later, a member of the FBI SWAT team at the hostel called to say Ford had arrived earlier to say he had to pick up some belongings from a locker, then he'd left in a hurry with a backpack. But after a SWAT search of the hostel, they found ceiling tiles in a bathroom had been removed.

Gritz shook his head. "What the fuck?"

Reznick's pulse quickened. "He's picked up his cache. He's going for his target."

Gritz's cell rang. "Yup." He nodded and began to frown. "Yeah, but I thought he was at The Plaza tonight? So what changed? We have him as staying at the goddamn Plaza." He let out a long sigh. "OK, OK, relax, I hear you. That's real close to us. But the hotel will be on lockdown. Staff vetted. Let me know if you need us." He ended the call.

"Who were you talking about?"

Gritz said nothing for a few moments.

"Gritz, talk to me. Who were you talking about?"

Gritz cleared his throat. "The President and his family are staying two blocks from here tonight. The Surrey. Secret Service has the hotel secured. It's on lockdown."

Reznick's mind was racing. "What was all that about The Plaza?"

"Secret Service is a law unto itself. Short-notice change from The Plaza to The Surrey. No questions asked."

Reznick ran his hand through his hair, matted in sweat. His mind flashed back to Ford taking photographs in the park. "Shit."

"What is it?"

"When I was tailing Ford, he took pictures of The Plaza. I think he was intelligence gathering. Perhaps checking the line of sight. What if it's the President who's the target? And Ford is here now to take out the President at The Surrey?"

Gritz went quiet for a few moments before he looked at his watch. "Two blocks from here."

"Gritz, listen to me. This shit is gonna go down. And it's gonna go down tonight at The Surrey. So what exactly is on his schedule tonight at The Surrey?"

"Only one thing. A private meeting with a handpicked group of 9/11 families, survivors, and first responders. There will be no press or media of any sort. No advance notice. A White House photographer will take some pictures and footage, which will be released to the media tomorrow morning. Trust me, the whole street will be shut off so no one can get near when he arrives or leaves. There is no chance of anyone, let alone Ford, getting close to him."

"Let's assume that's correct. Then it just leaves one option, doesn't it?"

"Sniper?"

Reznick nodded.

"This is Manhattan. Towers and skyscrapers everywhere."

"Let's get over there, see for ourselves."

"Reznick, it'll be crawling with Secret Service. They don't like people stepping on their toes."

"Yeah, well, that's just too bad."

Forty-Two

Reznick and Gritz were reluctantly allowed through the cordon on Madison, and stood outside The Surrey on East 76th Street. Secret Service guys in dark suits were checking through last-minute schedules. Meyerstein was already there, talking to the head of operations.

They walked over to her as she ended the conversation. "We need to talk."

The Secret Service guy took that as his cue and moved away to join the rest of his team.

"Goddamn," Meyerstein said.

"What is it?"

"FBI's computer team is saying that for ninety seconds, a thirty-five-yard radius of surveillance cameras on the Upper East Side went down. It's like a corridor from 81st Street."

Reznick shook his head. "Jamming. Shit, this is what I was worried about. Does the Secret Service know about this?"

"They do now. You wanna know where they've pinpointed as the fulcrum of the last signal?"

Reznick turned and looked toward Madison Avenue. Towering over the intersection was a monolithic building with an art gallery at street level. "The Carlyle?"

Meyerstein nodded.

"You see what I see?"

"Line of sight?" she said.

"Precisely."

"Yeah, but that would be a red flag. Secret Service would spot anything moving within a block of here. They've got people on roofs and inside that very building. Sniper teams watching everything. Besides, the place will have been swept room by room."

"If it were me, that would be my top choice."

Meyerstein turned again and looked across at the windows of The Carlyle.

Gritz intervened. "Reznick . . . the hotel's been swept."

Reznick stared up at the huge windows looking down on one of the busiest intersections on the Upper East Side, and the AC units outside each room. "When people tell me a building has been swept, you know what I think?"

Meyerstein looked at him as Gritz shrugged.

"You can never be certain. And that means you check again. I say we go in."

Meyerstein cocked her head, and they strode across Madison and along East 77th. A black canopy showed the entrance to the apartment complex.

"Carlyle House. Apartment complex adjacent to the hotel, but there's access between them," said Meyerstein.

Reznick shook his head. "No Secret Service presence. Nothing."

Gritz's gaze wandered around the scene. "That ain't good."

"Jon, I'm giving you authorization to get in there," Meyerstein said. "So how do we work this? Do we evacuate first?"

Reznick felt the adrenaline begin to pump around his body. "No. Low-key, room to room. I know this stuff."

"What about SWAT?"

"Definitely not. That's not what you need in these circumstances. We don't want to alert him that we're in the apartment complex or hotel."

Meyerstein said nothing.

"Let's start with hotel rooms and residences with line of sight to The Surrey."

Gritz began to shake his head. "This is nuts. I can't believe what I'm hearing. None of this makes sense. Besides, you need Secret Service authorization."

Meyerstein stared at him, stone-faced, a haunted look in her eyes. "Leave that to me."

She turned to Reznick. "So, what are you waiting for? You're on."

Reznick turned and headed for the side entrance.

Forty-Three

Meyerstein pulled out her cell and found the secure direct office number of FBI Director Bill O'Donoghue. He picked up after the third ring.

"Martha, what the hell is going on? How did we let Ford slip? The last update I saw was that Ford was watching goddamn tennis. I've just gotten out of a meeting, and I hear Ford has dropped off our radar and General Black has shot himself."

"I know. It's a mess," she said. "Sir, we've accessed the building adjacent to the Carlyle Hotel. But I need Secret Service authorization to get full access."

"But the Secret Service . . ."

Meyerstein updated him on the surveillance cameras going down around The Carlyle. "Bottom line? I don't believe the area is secure."

O'Donoghue let out a long sigh. "We lost Ford. And now you're saying you don't trust the Secret Service to secure an area?"

"Yes, sir." Sirens blared in the distance. She raised her voice. "Sir, the analysis my team has is that a false flag operation is underway. CIA fingerprints."

"The Secret Service leads on this, Martha, you know that. They don't like people encroaching on their turf."

"I don't doubt that, sir. But I'm requesting that you use your influence. We need to get in there and do a fuller sweep. I need you to cover for me, sir."

O'Donoghue said nothing, as if contemplating his options.

"Sir, I need you to make this happen. Jon Reznick is already in. But I need authorization for a full sweep. We're running out of time."

A long pause. "I've heard enough. Leave this to me."

Five minutes later, O'Donoghue was back on the line.

Meyerstein looked across Madison and saw the throng of Secret Service men, police manning the cordon tape. Her gaze was drawn to a black canopy—almost certainly bulletproof—being pulled out, securing the entrance to The Surrey.

"Any news?"

"Martha, I've just spoken to Director Steel. I explained our concerns in depth . . ."

"And?"

"He has agreed that the FBI can lead on a fresh sweep of the whole hotel, just as soon as the President is safely inside his hotel."

"But, sir . . ."

"That's the best I can do, Martha."

Forty-Four

Reznick's heart was racing as he swiped the master room-card he'd stole from the concierge and cracked the door. Suite 3103. Thirty-first floor. No sign of life.

He shut the door and pulled a penlight from his back pocket. He pointed it around the room. It was a plush tower suite with views of Manhattan through the huge windows. The penlight strafed the room. Grand piano in the corner. Monogrammed cushions with the letter *C* in a fancy typeface. He crouched down and pressed his ear to the carpeted floor. Muffled chatter in a downstairs room.

He scoured the rest of the suite: bathroom and bedroom, closets, under beds. Nothing. Just a fresh scent of pine and cleaning polish in the air. He headed back into the living room, switched off the penlight, and crawled across the carpet toward the windows.

The terrace was empty.

He got up and headed toward the door, pressing his ear against the wood. No sounds in the corridor, only the vibration from someone walking in suite 3203 above. Low humming, as if from a nearby air-conditioning unit.

Reznick quietly opened the door and gently pulled it shut after him. He looked straight ahead and headed down the hallway, then up the stairwell to the thirty-second floor. He stopped at the doors, cameras tracking his movements.

"I'm about to enter the thirty-second floor," he whispered into his lapel mike. "Are we clear?"

A long pause. "Hold on." The voice of Gritz.

Reznick stood and waited for a reply. He needed to move. What was taking so long?

A long sigh. "Finally clear, Jon. Go on."

Reznick headed through the doors and saw suite 3203. He swiped the card and opened the door.

The suite was cloaked in semidarkness, with only the glow of the moon from the Manhattan sky giving any light. Sofas, ornate antique tables, the smell of beeswax polish. He took out his penlight and flashed it around the room. He headed down the hallway to a small bedroom.

Creaking from above, the sound of voices. Loud TV—a game show playing.

Reznick checked the bathroom, which had monogrammed towels and a hint of eucalyptus in the air. He looked in drawers, under the bed, in closets, but found nothing.

He went back into the living room, and opened the doors that led to the terrace. A warm breeze blew in, billowing the lace curtains, the lights of the city as far as the eye could see.

Reznick carefully shut and locked the terrace doors and headed out of the suite. He pressed his ear to the door. Just the vibrations from the nearby elevator. He opened the door.

Then he felt cold metal pressing against his neck.

Forty-Five

Meyerstein was pacing outside the side entrance to The Carlyle as the area went into full lockdown ahead of the motorcade. She thought of the threat they were facing, and wondered if she had made the right call. Even amid the din of distant sirens and agents talking loudly into cell phones, her doubts and lingering fears returned.

She moved her team into a nearby high-tech mobile command vehicle—which had just arrived—containing those involved in the forthcoming full sweep once the President was safely ensconced at The Surrey.

Meyerstein made a beeline for an FBI techie with headphones on, who was monitoring The Carlyle's security cameras. She tapped him on the shoulder and the young agent pulled off the headset.

"What's the latest?" she said.

"Don't know. We seem to have lost his connection."

"Goddamn. Gimme a break."

"Reznick asked for a list of empty suites on the Madison Avenue side of The Carlyle, from the eighteenth floor up."

Meyerstein saw Reznick's logic. It made sense for Ford to hide out in an empty room with line of sight. He wouldn't be heard if he was in radio communication with a handler.

"I want his connection back up and running. Fast! Do you hear me?"

The techie nodded. "I'm on it."

Meyerstein turned to face the assembled, heavily armed Feds. She thought of Reznick alone, perhaps prowling the corridors of the upper floors, going from empty room to empty room. The not knowing what was going on and why the connection had been broken was unbearable.

She glanced at her watch, radios crackling in the background, monitors switched on to the same feed as the surveillance cameras inside the hotel and the residences they were about to search.

"I make it that we have a minute until the President arrives and is escorted inside The Surrey. Special Agent Gritz is in charge of search operations on the ground, and I'll be coordinating with the technical and computer agents here in the mobile command vehicle."

Matthew Suarez, director of security at The Carlyle, said, "Ma'am, I've got to say we have no indication that there has been any breach of security. Our cameras have detected no one who shouldn't be here. Every guest and resident we know very well. Besides, we've been in lockdown for hours."

"Mr. Suarez—firstly, I appreciate your cooperation. The surveillance cameras within The Carlyle and within a thirty-five-yard radius of where we believe Ford was situated blacked out, probably because of jamming. It lasted no more than ninety seconds. But we have to assume the worst."

Suarez flushed a deep crimson. "I can assure you that—"

Meyerstein put up her hand to silence him. "Look, we're going in. We have the authority."

Suarez nodded his head, suitably chastised.

"OK, while we believe he will be higher up, we can't take anything for granted. Therefore, first floor to seventeen, what are we talking?"

Suarez said, "It's mixed. Some hotel rooms, some residences owned by the hotel."

"What about above seventeen?"

"That's the tower."

"OK, what about access to each and every residence and room?"

"Each agent has a Carlyle uniform and a master card."

Meyerstein turned to the search team and held up a glossy printout of Ford. "We're behind the curve on this and have been from the get-go. I want to make this clear. He is very dangerous. He's Special Forces-trained. A crack shot. Ferociously fit."

Then Meyerstein's attention switched to the surveillance footage outside The Surrey, as the first outrider appeared and the Secret Service crowded around the entrance like a protective shield. Her throat felt dry and her stomach knotted. A few moments later, the Beast, as the President's limousine was called within Secret Service circles, swept into view. A huge Secret Service agent got out and opened the rear door of the presidential Cadillac. A female agent did the same on the opposite side of the vehicle, and a cordon of agents formed around the car.

A few moments' delay, and the President got out and headed toward the canopy as his wife and kids were ushered inside, out of sight. They were visible for barely five seconds as the huge entourage followed them into the hotel. Time seemed to stop.

Forty-Six

Reznick's hands were raised and the gun was pressed to the side of his neck. He felt the man's warm breath on his face.

"Are you lost, Mr. Simpson? This isn't your room, is it?"

Reznick said nothing.

"Who are you, sir?"

Reznick counted down in his head. *Three, two, one.*

He swiped his arm back as if swatting a fly and grabbed the gun, redirecting the weapon away from his body. Then he elbowed the guy with a ferocious jolt to the side of the neck. The man collapsed in a heap as if hit by a sniper.

He tucked the gun into his waistband, swiped the keycard to open the door to the empty suite, and dragged the unconscious man inside and into the bathroom.

Reznick tore up the bedroom's Egyptian cotton sheets and tied the man to the toilet, his mouth gagged and his hands bound behind his back. He rifled through the man's inside pockets and pulled out an ID. He scanned it. *Jeff Renoz.* Secret Service.

Shit.

He tapped his earpiece and whispered, "Why no heads-up?"

"Cameras have all gone down, Jon."

"Shit."

"The search is focusing on occupied residences. You're checking the handful of empty ones."

"Got that." He then relayed what had happened.

A long sigh. "OK, got that, Jon."

"I'm heading to the next floor."

"You gotta be careful. The Secret Service guy you bumped into must've been part of their presidential protection detail. They've got a suite on the thirty-third."

"Which one?"

"Thirty-three zero five, which has perfect line of sight, apparently."

"I've still got thirty-three zero one and thirty-three zero three to go."

"Both empty. And both leased by a Hong Kong guy for when he's in New York on business."

"Ford must be in one of them."

"Take care, Jon."

A few moments later, just as he was about to leave the suite, his earpiece buzzed again.

"Jon." The voice of Meyerstein was soft, almost a whisper. "Where are you?"

"Thirty-second. Nothing so far. What about the others?"

"Negative. Look, the red and blue teams are going room to room. There's only the floor above the one you're on. Those are duplexes, on two levels. So they reach the top, the thirty-fourth, although entry is only from the thirty-third."

Reznick said, "Copy that."

"If he's anywhere, he'll be there."

"What about the stairwells and elevators?"

"Cameras are down. Still trying to get them up again . . . Hang on."

A long silence opened up.

Reznick said, "You still there?"

"Hold on, Jon. Just been messaged by Agent Bryan Simon."

"I'm listening."

"Jon, hold on, we're just checking this. Something about the President's itinerary." The silence lasted for nearly a minute. Eventually, she came on the line again. "I don't believe this."

"What is it?"

"Jon, we've got a problem."

"Yeah, no kidding."

"No. Another problem. In exactly seventeen minutes, the President is meeting the families of nine eleven victims."

"How's that a problem? He's out of sight."

"Negative. The reception is on the rooftop terrace at The Surrey."

"No fucking way."

"It's all been arranged. There's going to be a string quartet playing . . . No one knows about it. The details aren't out there."

"Well, someone knows about it. And I'll bet that someone is Adam Ford, and the people directing this operation."

Meyerstein said nothing.

"Look, while we have Ford on the loose, surely it would be safest for the President to be kept away from prying eyes? It's a no-brainer."

"I know, Jon, but this is out of my hands. I spoke with Steel but he brushed aside my concerns. Jon, I feel sick. I think this is when it's going to happen."

"No question—this operation is a green light. I bet Ford has been hunkered down up there since he got in, right under the noses of the Secret Service snipers."

"Jon, there are seven rooms on the thirty-third. We've got to find this guy. No ifs, ands, or buts. You must get this guy, at any cost."

"On it."

Reznick headed up the stairwell to the thirty-third floor. The final floor to sweep. There were only a few more suites to check. He whispered into his lapel mike, "I'm about to enter the thirty-third. Contact the counter-sniper team and let them know I'm on their floor."

"Gimme a minute."

Less than sixty seconds later, Meyerstein's voice was back in the earpiece. "The message has been passed on."

"I'm going in."

He crouched down and cracked open the door to the thirty-third floor. No sign of life in the narrow corridor.

Reznick pushed open the door and got to his feet. He headed down the hallway, got to the first empty suite, and pressed his ear to the door. A faint sound of water in an old lead pipe, maybe underneath the floor. He swiped the card and peered into the darkness of the huge suite. Then he edged inside and shut the door quietly behind him.

He didn't move as he got his bearings.

Slow is smooth, smooth is fast. The military mantra he still used.

Reznick took his penlight from his jacket and searched the room. Piano in the corner, antique walnut furnishings, just like the other empty suites. But his senses were cranked to the max.

He felt something. He just didn't know what.

He reached for his Beretta, and took it from the belt strapped to his chest. He felt his finger on the cold trigger. His heart was beating hard as he began to scour the three-bedroom suite. He headed up the duplex's stairs, the lights of the city below, partially illuminating the room. The glass doors to the balcony were open, and the curtains were billowing in the breeze.

Reznick slowly approached the open door. As the curtain blew in, he noticed black boots sticking out from below. He crouched down and inched forward. The curtains billowed again, and he saw the crumpled bodies of two counter-snipers with a bullet to the forehead each.

Suddenly, a figure emerged from the shadows to Reznick's right. He dived to the floor and shot twice at the figure's head. A flash of light from the gun, and a muffled *phut* from the silenced 9mm. The figure crashed to the floor, face first through a glass coffee table. He wasn't moving.

Reznick edged closer. He was in the kill zone. He turned the body over and stared at the bloody face. It wasn't Ford.

His earpiece crackled into life. "What the hell is going on?" Meyerstein shouted.

"I've just taken out a trigger man. It means Ford isn't alone. It also means Ford is still on the loose."

A few seconds later, he heard Meyerstein's voice again. "Jon, we've lost radio contact with the counter-sniper team. The line of sight from terraces and balconies on that floor to the President is wide open. You have to act now!"

Reznick said, "I'm heading straight there."

"Jon, the President is on the roof terrace. I can see him on our monitor. There are scores of people around him. There's a Plexiglas shield that's been erected all around the terrace . . ."

"That won't stop Ford!" Reznick hissed.

He knew that someone like Ford would have access to military-grade bullets that could tear through the best Plexiglas.

Reznick bounded down the stairs of the darkened duplex, opened the door, and crouched down as he headed along the corridor to suite 3304.

He pressed himself against the wall as he moved closer. He swiped the card and pushed open the door, knowing he was a sitting duck. He ducked through and shut the door as quietly as he could with a soft, metallic clicking sound. He thought of the suite layout he'd just seen a few moments earlier.

The smell of cordite. Sweat. The faint sound of traffic seeping into the room.

His eyes adjusted. Too slowly.

It was happening. Here and now.

Reznick kept low and crawled through the living room, past a table. Breathing hard, the sound of his heartbeat the only noise. He knew he couldn't afford one false move. He had to get this right. His gut reaction was to storm through the suite. But that wasn't the smart way.

Slow is smooth, smooth is fast.

He stayed in a crouch as he headed for the duplex's stairs. He took the first step. A second. And the rest in a matter of seconds.

Reznick got down lower and crawled through the upper living area, past a table.

From his right, the sound of traffic. The French windows to the balcony were open, the same as in the last suite. Drapes billowed from the open windows at the far side of the room.

He was within six yards.

Then he saw something crouched at the far end of the huge terrace. A spectral figure in black. A rifle on a tripod. The figure seemed oblivious to Reznick closing in. He was peering through the night-vision scope and adjusting the eyepiece. Reznick saw the green LED indicating that the scope was on.

Then the man's head turned, and he stared at Reznick.

Reznick was already in the zone. He didn't hesitate for one second. He pointed the handgun and pulled the trigger. Nothing. He pulled it again. An empty click.

His 9mm had jammed.

Fuck.

The world seemed to slow down.

Reznick's brain switched gears. He lay down so he was flat on his stomach. The man stood up, but Reznick had already pulled the Secret Service agent's Belgian-made FN Five-seven pistol out of the back of his waistband. He aimed the gun and squeezed twice.

Two shots rang out.

A flash of light exploded, temporarily illuminating the room; a sharp recoil and a deafening noise.

The masked figure stumbled back as if in slow motion before collapsing in a heap on the balcony. Writhing in agony, he knocked over the rifle and tripod.

Reznick scrambled to his feet and jumped on the man's chest, ripping off his mask. Staring back at him, eyes blazing, was Adam Ford. Fine-boned, a strong jawline. Reznick gripped his face and squeezed tight on his jaw. "Who else?"

Ford's eyes were open wide as he grinned up at Reznick.

Reznick smashed his fist into Ford's nose. The sound of a bone cracking, and blood spurted onto his face. "Who sent you?"

Ford stared up, bleeding, face impassive. His eyes began to roll around in his head. Then he slipped away.

Forty-Seven

The moments that followed were a blizzard of activity. Secret Service agents sporting semiautomatic weapons, and a fully armed SWAT team stormed in, tied the unconscious man's hands behind his back with zip ties, and dragged him out to the waiting paramedics. The rest of the Feds conducted a thorough sweep of the suite and the one opposite. They found the two dead counter-snipers—bound, gagged, and shot in the head. They were already cold.

Reznick relayed the information to Meyerstein.

"Goddamn."

Reznick felt numb as he was hustled out and crammed into the elevator with three Secret Service guys. No words were spoken as they descended to the lobby.

When the doors opened, Meyerstein was waiting, cell phone pressed to her ear. She held up a finger to indicate she didn't want to be disturbed. "Yeah, it's over, we got him. Being transferred as we speak to a safe facility. Speak to you later."

Meyerstein was expressionless. She cocked her head in the direction of the mobile command center. "Very well done." Then she smiled.

Reznick said nothing.

"You OK?"

"I'm OK."

Meyerstein sighed. Tears were welling up in her eyes, but she managed to maintain her composure. "We lost some . . . We lost some good men along the way."

Reznick had never seen her like that before. "It would have been a helluva lot more if you hadn't had faith in me. The same way you did when you made the right call in Key West, remember that?"

Meyerstein dabbed at her eyes. He could see how empty she was. He knew that empty feeling better than anyone. Despite taking down the bad guys, the crushing loss of the good men whose families would have to live without them was too much to bear.

When Reznick got back to the command center, there were a few pats on the back and "Good work, big guy" from some of the tech guys. But the overriding mood among the Feds was down.

Reznick looked across at the monitors, most showing the upper floors of The Carlyle where he'd just been. "Who's on the top floors right now?"

Meyerstein sat down beside him. "Gritz and his guys have got it covered. Forensics, too. Jon, I think you might just have saved the President's life."

"Where is he now?"

"Secret Service are handling things. He's just been discreetly taken inside. No one is any the wiser. At least for now."

"What about the media?"

"What about them?"

"They must have got wind of something with all the SWAT guys around?"

"There's a media blackout. So that will work in our favor."

"Or the people behind this . . . maybe it will work in their favor, too."

Meyerstein gave a wry smile. "Indeed."

"So, where they taking him?"

"Military facility. He'll be flown to Andrews Air Force Base."

Reznick nodded.

"Roy Stamper is monitoring—"

Her cell rang, interrupting her, and she rolled her eyes. "Never a goddamn break."

She pressed the green button to receive the call. "Yeah, Meyerstein." She frowned. "What the hell are you talking about?"

Reznick looked her way.

"SWAT has him. Andy's in charge, right?" A long silence. She closed her eyes for a moment. "That doesn't make any kind of sense, Roy. I watched them go in myself. Shit! I'm going to switch to radio." She ended the call, and one of the techs wearing headphones handed her a two-way radio. "Talk to me, Roy."

The voice of Roy Stamper, working from the special access program's offices in McLean, could be heard. "Martha, the SWAT guys were diverted to Midtown with authorized FBI codes."

Meyerstein stepped out of the command center and paced up and down the sidewalk, sirens in the distance. Unmasked SWAT guys were milling about looking wired. She had the radio pressed tight to her ear when Reznick joined her. He could see and hear something was wrong. "I'm standing right beside them. So, who's got him?"

Stamper said, "They took him away in a dark blue SUV."

Reznick interrupted, feeling his anger rise. "There's been a switch, hasn't there?"

Meyerstein stared at him and nodded. "Roy, which direction?"

"I'm pulling up the footage. OK, they're heading down East 76th Street."

Meyerstein ended the radio link and looked at Reznick. "You're right, there's been a switch. We need to track them down before this crew disappears with Ford."

She turned to the SWAT guys near her. "I need four of you to go with Reznick."

"We don't have time for this," Reznick said.

He ran out onto the street and saw a passing motorcyclist slow down at the lights. He pulled his gun and jumped in front of the guy, who braked hard.

The guy flicked up his visor. "What the fuck?" he screamed.

Reznick hauled the poor guy off the Ducati, climbed on, and adjusted his earpiece before giving the engine a few revs and speeding away.

Stamper's voice on his earpiece said, "Reznick, got a sighting of vehicle. Clarification, it is in fact a black Nissan SUV and is heading down Park Avenue."

Reznick's body was flowing with adrenaline as he began the pursuit through the Manhattan night. He hung a right and headed down Park Avenue, weaving in and out of the traffic, past red lights, narrowly avoiding being flattened by a couple of trucks. The smell of car fumes and the sound of blaring horns, and the sight of neon lights as he took a left.

"Jon, we're tracking your signal." He sped past a Capital One Bank on his right.

"Where the hell are they?" he shouted.

"Jon, you're heading down East 59th Street. We think they might be heading back to Queens."

"Copy that."

Reznick caught sight of the car as it sped toward the lower level of the Queensboro Bridge. "Fifty yards behind! I got this."

The getaway car was doing eighty at least, the other drivers pulling over before they were rammed.

"They're on a rampage!" Reznick shouted. "We need support."

The sound of a chopper approaching above the bridge.

Reznick revved hard and raced across the bridge, the East River below.

"NYPD is on this, too, Reznick. Heading onto Queens Boulevard. Ease up."

Were they serious? *Ease up?*

Bullshit.

Reznick kept his head down as they headed deeper into Queens. Speeding down the Long Island Expressway at ninety plus, keeping the SUV in his sights. The wind buffeting his face and body, he held on tight as the high-powered bike threatened to send him crashing off the road.

He accelerated and glimpsed Ford's face silhouetted in the back seat, two huge guys on either side of him.

Reznick reached for his gun with his left hand as he steered the bike with his right. Suddenly, a rear passenger window came down and a handgun appeared.

He braked hard and the SUV tore ahead of him, leaving him in its wake.

"You OK, Reznick?" Stamper shouted.

"I'm on it."

Reznick felt the endorphins kick in. He screwed up his eyes as he went through the gears. He was catching up with them again as he saw a sign for Grand Central Parkway.

Then the Nissan took a hard right, and a Buick cut in front of him. The bike screeched to a near halt as the SUV with Ford disappeared into the distance.

"What the fuck are you doing?" Reznick shouted at the wide-eyed driver of the Buick as he sped away, tires screeching as the rubber tried to get traction.

The lights of the chopper were on the SUV. Reznick's mind was racing. Where were they headed?

The rushing wind was nearly taking his breath away. There was grit in his eyes.

"Goddamn!"

He saw a sign for JFK. Farther and farther away from Manhattan, the lights of the chopper guiding him.

Suddenly, from the getaway car up ahead, the sound of a rifle shot. Above him, the helicopter veered out of control.

Reznick felt his focus sharpen, blocking out everything that wasn't in his sights. He was in the zone again.

It wasn't long before he was on the Van Wyck Expressway heading south. He spotted the black Nissan veering wildly across the road. "He's in my sights again," he said. "I'm gaining."

"Jon, the NYPD and the FBI aren't far behind."

Reznick couldn't see shit, apart from the Nissan and the glare of oncoming headlights. It was a bleak stretch of road. He felt his stomach knotting tight.

"Jon, you're now on the Nassau Expressway and you're heading for Rockaway Boulevard."

Up ahead, Reznick could see the Nissan weaving around the slower cars as if on a slalom course.

Reznick checked his speedometer, which was showing 108 miles per hour. "They're doing a hundred and ten, easy!" he shouted, unable to know if his voice would be heard in the wind.

"We hear you, Jon. Be careful. I repeat, be careful. This is a dangerous stretch of road. Brookville Boulevard. It's known as Snake Road. Hang back if need be."

Reznick smelled salt water on his face as he stormed onto Rockaway Boulevard. He was starting to make a mental calculation. He was now within yards of the Nissan, which was careening wildly around a narrow bend, and then another. He was aware they were close to water. The salt marshes.

Suddenly, the barrel of a rifle was smashed through the rear window of the Nissan and pointed straight at him. He swerved as a shot rang out. The bullet ricocheted off the chrome on the bike.

It had to be now.

He pulled out his gun, and with his right hand controlled the bike at full speed. A quick switch to his firing hand. He took aim and fired three shots at the Nissan's left rear tire. The tire exploded, sparks flying as the rubber was chewed up at high speed.

He crouched down low over the bike's gas tank, fearing another bullet.

The Nissan flipped violently through the air and off the road, disappearing into the darkness and crashing into the water.

Reznick screeched to a halt and ditched the bike. He sprinted across the road toward the water, gun in hand. The smell of gasoline wafted across the dark salt marshes. The light from the moon showed that the car was maybe thirty yards out, on its side and nearly totally submerged. He waded into the dark water, chest deep. The car was still maybe ten yards away from him.

A vehicle pulled up behind him and three Feds ran toward him.

"They're in the water!"

A split second later, he heard police sirens and saw the lights from the chopper swooping in low.

He turned. "They're all in the car. No one got out. We need to get them out."

The cop waded in and pulled Reznick back to shore. "Stay back, sir."

Reznick watched as the cops formed themselves into a chain and, using the lights of their cars for illumination, waded into the water to search.

The minutes ticked by. Fire crews pulled up. Slowly, they began to drag out the bodies, which had been trapped underwater in the locked car.

Three bodies were taken from the water and laid out, side by side. Three men, and Ford wasn't one of them.

"There's one more," Reznick said. "There's one missing."

One of the cops turned around, shaking his head. "There's no one else, buddy."

"I'm telling you, there is one more. I saw three in the back, one driving. There's four!"

"He ain't here."

"Goddamn, there's one more guy."

But as the minutes passed by, no other body was found.

Slowly, it began to dawn on Reznick.

Ford had escaped.

Epilogue

Reznick and Meyerstein were in an FBI mobile command center on the periphery of JFK. She stared out of the window and sighed. "How the hell could he have gotten away? The only goddamned one . . ."

Reznick shook his head. "The others were his cover. He had the training to survive virtually anything, even with gunshot wounds. We know that."

"Shit."

Reznick felt the exhaustion wash over him. "Means he's still out there. You reckon the airport was where they were headed?"

Meyerstein nodded. "The FBI has impounded a private jet registered in the Caymans to—get this—a Chechen warlord."

Reznick shook his head. "Classic false flag. How convenient."

Meyerstein was silent.

"This was a false flag from the get-go."

She sighed. "I've said enough."

Reznick stared at her and saw the anger in her eyes. "So, what now?"

"People need to know what really happened. I don't believe for a minute that General Black and Ford were the only ones involved. This goes way deeper."

A silence opened up between them for a few moments. Reznick spoke first. "What a mess."

Meyerstein nodded. "There's going to be a Senate intelligence hearing. It'll be a closed session. You'll be asked to appear."

"We were played. From the outset."

"The talk on Fox is of an Islamist plot. Same with CNN."

"Like I said, this is more than Black and Ford."

Meyerstein stared at him, eyes tired. "Let's go for a walk."

They headed outside and walked along the Jamaica Bay shoreline, the Manhattan skyline in the distance. They heard planes landing nearby at JFK, saw birds in flight.

Reznick said, "You know what's really going to happen, don't you? Are you prepared for what awaits you?"

"What are you talking about?"

"Here's how it's going to work. If you put your head above the parapet, you're going to be made out to be a loose cannon. An oddball. They're going to isolate you. And then the media will be fed stories about you."

Meyerstein ran a hand through her hair. "Listen—"

"Meyerstein, I'm going to spell this out for you. There are two ways to destroy a person."

"What do you mean?"

"You can either put a bullet through their head, or there's something more elegant. You neutralize that person by dredging up their private life. They'll make you out to be an unfit mother. They'll leak stories about you having a recent breakdown. Having affairs. Being unpatriotic. That's always the killer."

"Jon, that's not going to happen . . ."

"Isn't it? Listen to me—that's what awaits you if you speak out. That's what awaits me if I speak out. This goes way beyond General Black. This is worse than Operation Northwoods. This made it off the drawing boards at the CIA. Soon, in a matter of days, there will be foreign intelligence agencies friendly to the US pointing the finger at whatever regime we don't like. That's how it works. That's how it's always worked."

Meyerstein knew he was right. "My father was a lawyer. A very good lawyer. And he always stressed to me that there were two kinds of people in the world. Those that bent with the wind, and those that stood firm."

"And where do you stand?"

She smiled. "I've spent a lifetime in people's faces. I'm not about to turn the other cheek now, Jon."

Reznick nodded. "We understand what went on. It's important America learns from this. We need to root out this cancer. But bear in mind they're going to try to bury you first."

Meyerstein's throat tightened. "Well, they better bring a mighty big shovel. Because I'm ready for them." For a few moments, her gaze lingered on the sparkling waters, before she looked up at the vapor trail of a huge plane leaving JFK. "What about you?"

Reznick looked at her. She seemed vulnerable and alone. "What about me?"

"How are you going to deal with this?"

"The way I always have. I tell them straight. They don't like it, that's their business. I'm going to stand beside you and tell it like it is. Like I said before, I don't do walking away."

Meyerstein looked at him, long and hard. Then she smiled and her face softened. "You saw this earlier than anyone. You didn't yield."

"Never."

"Why is that, Jon?"

"It's in the blood, it's the way I am. It's the way my mother was. It's the way my father was. We do not yield."

"Amen to that."

They stood together, and stared out over the water as a new day dawned.

Acknowledgments

I would like to thank the following people:

Many thanks to my editor, Jane Snelgrove, and everyone at Thomas and Mercer for all their hard work, enthusiasm, and belief in the Jon Reznick books.

Special mention has to go to the FBI's Angela D. Bell and Jonathan B. Zeitlin in the Bureau's Washington DC headquarters, who assisted my numerous queries with impeccable professionalism.

I would also like to thank my family and friends for all their support and encouragement. But most of all to my wife, Susan, who read an early draft of *Hard Kill*, offering terrific advice with good grace and infinite patience.

About the Author

Photo: © John Need, 2013

J. B. Turner is the author of the Jon Reznick trilogy of conspiracy action thrillers (*Hard Road*, *Hard Kill*, and *Hard Wired*), as well as the Deborah Jones political thrillers (*Miami Requiem* and *Dark Waters*). He loves music, from Beethoven to the Beatles, and watching good films, from *Manhattan* to *The Deer Hunter*. He has a keen interest in geopolitics. He lives in Scotland with his wife and two children.